PRAISE FOR

Amelia Westlake Was Never Here

"A love story steeped in social justice that feels **fresh, funny, fierce, and full of hope**."
—*Entertainment Weekly*

"**Quirky, original, and completely charming**....
I loved everything about this book."
—Sarah Watson, creator of *The Bold Type*
and author of *Most Likely*

"**Come for patriarchy-smashing pranks; stay for the sweet love story**."
—NPR Books

"Pulses with **hilarious, defiant** heart.... **Gratifying and genuine**."
—Adrienne Kisner, author of *Dear Rachel Maddow*

"**Empowering and insightful**.... This book is **a feminist, romantic delight**."
—Ashley Herring Blake, author of *Girl Made of Stars*

"**Sharp-witted** and **unapologetically queer**, with an opposites-attract romance I absolutely adored."
—Malinda Lo, author of *Ash* and *A Line in the Dark*

"Filled with surprises and twists.... **Clever and effortless**."
—Katrina Leno, author of *Summer of Salt*

★ "Quick-witted, **fiercely intelligent storytelling at its finest**—a testament to the power of women, LGBTQ strong, socially conscious, **enormously fun**, and **utterly irresistible**."
—*VOYA*, starred review

★ "The perfect balance between **heartwarming queer romance** and **essential social criticism**."
—*Shelf Awareness*, starred review

★ "**Refreshing, timely, and downright delightful**."
—*School Library Connection*, starred review

"Well-paced and satisfying.... **Empowering**."
—*Kirkus Reviews*

"Plenty of high-stakes drama. **A vigilante justice story with a moral compass and a tender heart**."
—*Booklist*

"**Creative, funny, and satisfying**."
—*The Horn Book*

"[For] readers who like their **feminist empowerment** and **gay-positive** romances with a healthy dose of fun."
—*The Bulletin*

AMELIA WESTLAKE WAS NEVER HERE

AMELIA WESTLAKE WAS NEVER HERE

ERIN GOUGH

POPPY

Little, Brown and Company

New York Boston

Copyright © 2018 by Erin Gough

Cover art and design by Karina Granda
Cover copyright © 2019 by Hachette Book Group, Inc.

Poppy
Hachette Book Group
1290 Avenue of the Americas, New York, NY 10104
Visit us at LBYR.com

Originally published in 2018 by Hardie Grant Egmont in Australia
First U.S. Hardcover Edition: May 2019
First U.S. Trade Paperback Edition: May 2020

Poppy is an imprint of Little, Brown and Company.
The Poppy name and logo are trademarks of Hachette Book Group, Inc.

The Library of Congress has cataloged the hardcover edition as follows:
Names: Gough, Erin, author.
Title: Amelia Westlake was never here / Erin Gough.
Description: First U.S. edition. | New York ; Boston : Little, Brown and Company, 2019. | "Poppy." | Originally published: Australia : Hardie Grant Egmont, 2018. | Summary: Harriet Price, a prefect at elite Rosemead Grammar, risks her perfect life by joining forces with bad-girl Will Everhart in a hoax to expose the school's many problems.
Identifiers: LCCN 2018024913| ISBN 9780316450669 (hardcover) | ISBN 9780316450652 (ebook) | ISBN 9780316450676 (library edition ebook)
Subjects: | CYAC: Sexism—Fiction. | High schools—Fiction. | Schools—Fiction. | Feminism—Fiction. | Hoaxes—Fiction. | Lesbians—Fiction. | Australia—Fiction.
Classification: LCC PZ7.1.G686 Ame 2019 | DDC [Fic]—dc23
LC record available at https://lccn.loc.gov/2018024913

ISBNs: 978-0-316-45068-3 (pbk.), 978-0-316-45065-2 (ebook)

Printed in the United States of America

LSC-C

10 9 8 7 6 5 4 3 2 1

FOR EMMA AND RORY

PART ONE

chapter 1

WILL

I've been thinking a lot lately about hoaxes. My life, for instance. Lately it feels less like a life and more like a joke. Somebody's practical joke.

Don't get me wrong. It's nothing I can't handle. Terrible stuff has been happening to me since I was born. Mum and Dad named me Wilhelmina for a start. I've had three pets hit by cars. Last winter I was mildly electrocuted by a faulty hair dryer. Then there are the elements that make up my daily slog: Having separated parents on different sides of Australia. Living in a shoebox beneath a flight path. Going to a school full of rich, selfish brats.

But lately things have been particularly vile. Case in point: phys ed this morning. Coach Hadley held me back to swim extra laps along with Ruby Lasko and Harriet Price.

Hadley has always been a jerk, especially to me, although

it's true he likes to pick on most of his students a few times each term. It's his idea of equal opportunity. Today, though, he reached a special category of loathsome. When Harriet and I finished swimming, Hadley wouldn't let us go until Ruby completed her laps. It was probably the pressure of us watching that made Ruby trip on a ladder rung on her way out of the pool and crash back into the water.

"Too many muffins for breakfast, hey, Ruby?" said Hadley, grinning.

Now, you don't need a psychology degree to know Ruby is sensitive about her weight. She forced out a laugh, but I could tell she was working hard not to cry. This time, Hadley had gone too far. "What Ruby eats is none of your business," I said.

"Come on, Will," he replied, a twinkle in his eye. He tried to poke me in the ribs, but I stepped out of reach. "I was kidding. Ruby knows it was a joke, don't you, Ruby?"

Ruby, who was struggling up the ladder again, smiled bravely.

"See?" Hadley threw up his arms. "Why should you mind if Ruby doesn't?"

What a creep. I shot him a look of disgust. He met it for a second before turning away.

"Prick," I muttered under my breath.

Hadley whipped around, his expression dark.

I heard the sound of footsteps.

"Will Everhart. What did you just say?" Miss Watson, head of the Sports Department, was standing behind us with an armful of floating aids.

Just my luck. Watson has hated me since I skipped this

year's athletics carnival. Not to mention the ones before that. "Answer me," she said coolly.

"Fine. I called Coach Hadley a prick," I said, equally coolly.

Watson's whole face twitched.

"Well, he *is* one," I said, and turned to Harriet Price for backup.

For the record, it's not that I couldn't manage Watson on my own. I've got experience in Crappy Life Moments, as I've said. But I knew that having Harriet's support would help. She's a prefect. She's won debating competitions. Plus, Watson worships her because she plays for the tennis squad. She's also on some fancy sports committee Hadley set up. She heard what Hadley said to Ruby. She could have called him on it.

The problem with Harriet Price is that she's also a prime suck-up.

You know those ads for vacuum cleaners so powerful that they can pick up furniture? When I see those ads, I think of Harriet Price: groveling to the principal, or ass-kissing one of the teachers, or giving a speech at assembly about how Rosemead is educating "Australia's future leaders."

I shouldn't have been surprised when, instead of backing me up, Harriet stood there with her mouth hanging open like one of those clown heads waiting for a Ping-Pong ball at the Sydney Easter Fair.

I wish I'd had a Ping-Pong ball.

"I'm sick and tired of these performances, Will," said Watson, once her twitching face had settled down. "This is not the first time I've had to speak to you about inappropriate language, but you'd better hope it's the last. I am quite frankly disgusted...."

On and on she went. As she was ranting, I let the sound of her voice wash over me, and my mind wandered to an old movie Dad and I watched a few years ago. It's called *The Truman Show*, and it's about a guy whose whole world is the set of a reality TV show in which he's the unwitting star.

"You'll hate it," Dad told me, by which he meant "you'll love it." He and I have been playing a game of opposites since he was feeding me with an airplane spoon. He's progressed from "you'll love these mushy beans" to "you'll love washing the car for me, Monster Child." In true opposite game spirit I always reply, "You are the best father in the whole wide world," before giving him the finger.

I was skeptical about *The Truman Show*. "What makes you so sure I'll think it's the worst film ever?"

"Because you *love* reality television, and the film critiques that whole genre."

Dad adores the word "genre." He also likes "hegemony" and "oeuvre." This is what I've had to put up with as the daughter of a fine-arts journalist. But he was right about the movie. It was great. At the end, Truman figures out the whole living-in-a-reality-TV-show thing. He gets in a boat and travels to the domed edge of his bogus world. The boat's bow pierces the dome's painted sky, revealing what he's long suspected: He's been trapped in a farce.

Watson's rant went on for so long that I missed half of biology. After that, there didn't seem much point in showing up for the rest. So I headed to the year-twelve common room for twenty minutes of peace.

I'm sitting there now, eating someone else's cookies from the fridge and thinking about the final scene from that movie. It's exactly what I'm waiting for, I realize. I'm hanging out for the day I get to launch a boat off the wrecked shore of my own existence to discover my true unblemished destiny beyond the EXIT sign.

What will I find there? A world in which people like Hadley get what they deserve. A world where my classmates care about sticking up for each other more than they care about whose parents have the most expensive car. A world where there are no teachers, no swimming coaches, no prefects.

And no bloody Rosemead.

chapter 2

HARRIET

I adore my history class. It is one of the absolute highlights of my week. Today's class is especially wonderful because we are discussing Defining Moments.

"History is about turning points," Ms. Bracken explains. "I want each of you to share with us one big event that has influenced your life."

We go around the room.

"When I learned to read," says Eileen Sarmiento.

"When I got my platinum credit card," says Millie.

"My first ski trip to Aspen," says Beth.

Then it is my turn. "In all honesty? My Defining Moment was when I first set foot on the grounds of Rosemead."

A few loud groans and sick noises come from predictable corners. Apparently it is "in vogue" to be critical of this school and the opportunities we have as students here. I think this is basically a very ungrateful attitude given the fees our parents pay, especially since not everyone's parents are lucky enough to be oral surgeons as both of mine are.

The truth is, I owe a heck of a lot to Rosemead. If you said, "Harriet Price, please name three reasons why your life is great," I would answer first that it is difficult to isolate just three reasons because there are so many reasons why my life is great! Then I would tell you the top three excellent aspects of my life, all of which are Rosemead related:

1. My excellent marks.
2. Being on the brink of winning the Tawney Shield for senior girls' tennis doubles, something I have been working toward for almost six years (as in one-third of my life).
3. Having Edie Marshall, future prime minister of Australia, as my girlfriend.

People think I'm exaggerating when I say Edie will be prime minister one day, but I am definitely not. Not only is she the captain of Blessingwood Girls, our sister school, but she is also a talented sportsperson and the best school-age public speaker in New South Wales. This has been formally recognized by three statewide competitions in which she won first place last year: SpeakOut (topic: "democracy is the best form of government"), SpeakEasy (topic: "fashion victims I have known"), and SaySomething (topic: "discipline is not a dirty word"). After she blitzes the exams this year, she is going to go to university and get a Rhodes Scholarship. And when she comes back from Oxford, she will enter politics, and everyone will vote her in because she is incredible.

I would have never met Edie if it weren't for the Tawney Shield. We have both been playing in the competition since year nine. This year, Edie and I are competing as a team in the doubles competition against different school groups. This is perfect for us since we (a) are ranked in the top players at Blessingwood and Rosemead, respectively, which are in the same school group, and (b) happen to be going out.

Interesting fact: My mother won the shield when she was at Rosemead, as did my grandmother. They like to tease that if I don't win this year, I'll be excommunicated from the family!

After history, I find myself at a bit of a loose end. While Edie and I usually train on Tuesday afternoons, today Edie is hosting an afternoon tea at Blessingwood to raise funds for refugees. I would ordinarily make my way home, but Arthur, my little brother, jams with his band at home on Tuesdays, and although they are nice guys, the music gives me a headache. So when the final bell rings, I collect my things from my locker and head across to the staff building to find Ms. Bracken.

Ms. Bracken relies on me a lot because she knows how diligent and responsible I am. She suffers from arthritis and a few other degenerative diseases, so I like to assist her with odd jobs when I can. When I reach her office, I find her struggling with a PowerPoint presentation. (Ms. Bracken is far from technologically savvy.) I offer to lend a hand.

"It's perfectly fine, Harriet," she says, bent over a paper-strewn desk that I am tempted to help her tidy: That level of mess can bring on one of my migraines. "Thank you, but I don't need your assistance."

This is exactly the response I anticipated. Ms. Bracken always feels so guilty about taking up my time. "Don't give it a second thought, Ms. B. I happen to have a free window this afternoon."

"But I don't. I'm on detention duty." She gathers her books.

"Oh. Well, I'm sure we can do the presentation and monitor the detention students at the same time."

"I don't know about that." She hurries down the hallway. "There's only one student in detention, and she's in your year. I think that would be awkward."

"That's kind of you, Ms. Bracken," I pant. For someone with arthritis she is walking at a startling pace. "But I'm used to this kind of thing." It's true. As a prefect, I constantly have to monitor the behavior of other students, including those in year twelve. I can't exactly tell off a year-seven girl for failing to wear a regulation Rosemead hair ribbon and not do the same to someone in my own year.

"Awkward for her, I mean," Ms. Bracken says.

"The presentation will be done twice as quickly with me helping." I follow her into the detention room.

I hear Ms. Bracken sigh quietly. "Good afternoon, Will," she says.

That is when I see Will Everhart sitting at the very back of the room, slouched over a notebook.

Oh dear. After what happened at the pool this morning, I really could have done without encountering her again today.

She seemed terribly put out when I didn't defend her to Miss Watson.

I was not comfortable with what Coach said to Ruby. Ruby was clearly upset, and understandably so. But I am sure he was only trying to make a joke, albeit one in poor taste. Anyway, how could I possibly have taken Will's side? I am Coach's chosen representative on the school's Sports Committee. An incredible honor. And as a prefect, I am duty bound to uphold the authority of Rosemead's staff.

Will Everhart's problem is that insolence is her trademark. She is one of those girls who thinks asymmetrical haircuts are the definition of "edgy" and who takes every opportunity to show her disrespect for teachers. I personally will never forget our food technology class in year ten when Mrs. Lavender taught us how to cook pad thai with prawns. After everyone agreed it was the most delicious meal of their lives (it was important to be nice to Mrs. Lavender that year; her husband had just left her for a hand model), Will Everhart launched into a story about how prawn trawling kills kilos of unwanted fish that are accidentally scooped up by the nets. She finished by saying we were all morally obliged to be vegetarian, before scraping the contents of her plate into the trash.

That is just the type of impertinent person Will Everhart is.

Now I wish I hadn't come to detention with Ms. Bracken after all. But it is too late to walk out. Instead, I make a point of greeting Will with a cheery wave.

She does not wave back.

Ms. Bracken puts her laptop on the teacher's desk and

walks up to collect Will's detention slip. "What have you done this time?" she asks.

"Why don't you ask Harriet?" Will says, eyeing me with contempt. "She was there."

I feel a throbbing in my forehead. I hold my mouth in a firm smile and open Ms. Bracken's laptop.

"Gone quiet again, Harriet—just like this morning?" Will calls.

Really. Why does she have to bring up this morning? She is the most provocative person I have ever met.

Ms. Bracken examines the detention slip. "Swearing at Coach Hadley. Why did you do that?" she asks Will, and not in the weary, slightly cross way she usually asks questions, but more like she is genuinely interested. Her prescription pain-killers must have just kicked in.

"Because he's a sexist creep," says Will, chin in hand.

I genuinely cannot believe the things that come out of that girl's mouth. Yes, I can see how some of Coach's remarks might come across as sexist, but I am fairly certain he does not mean them in that way. He is probably just trying to relate to us. He knows how important it is to hold up Rosemead's core value of respect regardless of a person's identity, background, and abilities. Besides, he deserves veneration as our teacher, not to mention in his capacity as a former Olympian. There are photos of him wearing his silver medal in all the Rosemead brochures.

I wait for Ms. Bracken to tell off Will. But instead Ms. Bracken does something I have never seen her do in my entire Rosemead career: She smiles.

"Give me your pen," she says.

Will hands over a black felt-tip. Ms. Bracken signs her detention slip with it and looks at the wall clock. "Half an hour will suffice, I should think. Feel free to leave at four."

She marches up to the front again, swipes the laptop from beneath my poised fingers, and walks out of the room.

chapter 3

WILL

The look on Harriet Price's face when Ms. Bracken exits is worth five detentions. For a whole minute she stares at the door, as if expecting her to return. She glances at me. Then back at the door. Then at me again.

I watch her grapple to reinstall meaning and purpose in her life without a teacher to impress. She purses her lips. She readjusts her Butterscotch Blonde™ ponytail. "I suppose Ms. Bracken wants me to stay and supervise," she says.

"Ah, no."

Harriet makes a weird huffing sound. "I've got a lot to do here anyway. Those chairs at the side need to be put back behind their tables, and the whiteboard needs cleaning, so I'm very happy to keep you company."

I begin to collect my stuff.

"Where are you going?"

You know what astounds me most? How this school manages to brainwash allegedly smart people. They say Harriet Price is topping the year in math. How can she understand quadratic equations but not the simple fact that Rosemead is a crackpot institution that entrenches blind obedience? Not even Ms. Bracken expects me to stick around. "I won't tell if you don't," I say.

Harriet looks pained. Of course she'll tell. Not telling would conflict with her screwed-up moral universe. I think again about the scene by the pool this morning, and anger burns my throat.

I try to calm myself. What should I expect? Harriet Price is a lemming who does everything by the book. All she cares about is being a disciple of Rosemead and clogging up her résumé with useless committee memberships. She probably has a private-school boyfriend and a ten-year plan involving the usual marriage-mortgage-kids trifecta as well. Why would she risk a blot on her perfect school record for me?

More trouble is the last thing I need, and four o'clock is only half an hour away, so I resign myself to thirty more minutes in Harriet's company. At least I can get some drawing done.

Before Harriet and Bracken showed up, I was doodling ideas for my major work, the project that will make up 50 percent of my final-year art mark. I'm massively behind. Everyone else has started their pieces, but I keep changing my mind. I considered doing something about world poverty or global warming, but Mrs. Degarno says that the best type of art does two things at once: It speaks to current events and tells a story about the artist. That's why my latest idea is to explore the dangers of air travel.

Every time I turn on the news these days I hear about another crash in which hundreds of people have died. It's been four years since I flew on a plane, and after what happened that last time, I've vowed never to fly on another one.

I take up my pen.

I've just finished drawing three commercial jets of varying sizes—one exploding, one tearing in half midflight, and one spiraling nose first into a mountain—when I look up to see Harriet staring at me from behind a row of chairs she's been straightening.

"What?"

"Excuse me?"

"You're staring at me."

"No, I'm not."

I put down my pen. "Feeling guilty, are we?"

Her eyes widen. "I don't know what you're talking about." She probably doesn't even remember what happened at the pool. Why would she care about what Hadley said to Ruby Lasko? Harriet Price wouldn't have a clue what it's like to be picked on.

She begins dragging the chairs to the side of the room and stacking them loudly. I go back to drawing planes.

A minute later she says, "What good would it have done? Me saying anything? Miss Watson would still have put you in detention."

So she *does* remember. Interesting. "I guess we'll never know, will we?" I say.

Red blotches appear on her neck and I smile. She marches off to toss around a few more chairs.

I've just finished drawing my fourth plane when she pipes up again. "For the record, I don't entirely disagree with what you said about Coach Hadley."

I raise an eyebrow. "That he's a prick?"

Harriet gasps. "I wasn't referring to *that*," she whispers. "I mean what you said to Ms. Bracken. About him being... sexist. He doesn't mean to be, but it's definitely true that very occasionally he can be."

"Very occasionally?"

"Yes. Not at all often. Hardly ever, really."

It's a record-breaking backtrack. I rock forward on my chair. "You don't remember last term when he referred to the 'nonsupportive' bra Nakita Wallis was wearing?" I ask.

Harriet looks uncomfortable. "Well, yes. But he was only kidding around...."

"What about the time he told Anna Yemelin that she was too 'top heavy' to be a competitive swimmer?"

She bites her lip. "Swimmers have to have a certain body shape. That's the reality."

"Or how he once tried to get us to stretch before class by saying how guys appreciate flexibility?"

Harriet pauses. "I'm pretty sure that was a joke. Admittedly one in poor taste..."

"Then what's your explanation for how he slapped Trish Burger on the—"

"Okay, you've made your point," Harriet snaps.

I let the back legs of my chair hit the floor. The sound makes Harriet jump. I pretend not to notice. "I've got loads more examples," I say. "It's a common story. Given how much time you spend at the gym, I'm surprised you don't have a few stories about Hadley yourself."

The red blotches on Harriet's neck darken. I wonder if I've hit the mark.

"Even if it's true that he can be somewhat sexist, girls know he doesn't mean anything by it," she says at last. "People love him!"

If that's her attitude, what's the point of pressing further? Clearly if Harriet does have stories, she's not about to share them with me. You can tell just by looking at her how carefully ordered she is. Everything's so neat and fitted. It's like her whole being is guarding against the presence of a single loose thread that, if pulled, would unravel Harriet herself.

I leave the thread alone. Instead I say, "*Some* people love him. Of course, the other possibility is that they're afraid of being told they can't take a joke."

"In any case," Harriet says, ignoring my theory, "I don't see what the point is of going on about his behavior, frankly, unless you're prepared to do something about it." She must see the disbelief on my face because she adds quickly, "Something apart from calling him a you-know-what to his face, I mean."

I laugh. Harriet Price is really something—standing like a statue beside a tower of chairs, lecturing *me* about taking action. "What did you have in mind?" I ask, loading on the sarcasm. "A petition? A meeting with Principal Croon? I tried both of those things last year to break the monopoly the school's uniform shop has. I got nowhere. I doubt she's going to sack Hadley on my say-so. Or were you thinking we should have one of Rosemead's famous charity bake sales? Perhaps we could use a picture of Hadley's face with the word 'misogynist' in red icing beneath it."

"Bake sales can be very effective," Harriet says, clasping her hands together like an earnest Maria von Trapp. "When I organized our homeless persons' bake sale—"

"I was being sarcastic."

"I know that," she says crossly. She strides across the room in an attempt to look purposeful. I'm unconvinced.

"How about you write an article for the school paper, then?" she calls over her shoulder. "You're friends with Natasha Nguyen, aren't you?"

I'm surprised Harriet knows this. Still. What a crappy idea. Nat's the editor of the school paper, but that doesn't automatically mean she'd publish something written by me. She'd bang on about her editorial integrity first. "What would be the point of a stupid article?"

"To draw attention to the issue, if that's what you're so keen on doing."

I snort. Doesn't Harriet know that drawing attention to issues is what I've been trying to do since I arrived at this school over two years ago? I've pushed for a fund-raiser for Indigenous Literacy Day. I've campaigned for energy-efficient lighting. Fat lot of good that was ever going to do, given the chair of the school board is also the deputy CEO of its electricity supplier.

"Take it from me, Harriet. If it's good for the world but bad for Rosemead, they won't change a thing," I say.

She hauls a table across the room, its legs screeching. "If you're not prepared to do anything, then please stop complaining," she says.

It takes me a moment to recover from such blatant hypocrisy. Another moment passes as I wait for her to finish maneuvering the table against the back wall. She can't be serious about calling out Hadley's sexism in the school paper. It doesn't exactly align with her blind allegiance to Rosemead.

I decide to call her bluff. "All right. You've convinced me. Let's write an article."

Harriet looks shocked. She sits down on the table with a thump. "I didn't mean I wanted to help. I can't be involved."

Just as I figured. "Why not?"

"I'm a *prefect*."

"That's exactly why you *should* be involved," I argue, twirling my pen.

"Oh my God. I can't write something like that about a teacher," she says, swinging her legs. "Like him or loathe him, Coach Hadley is a notable public ambassador for Rosemead. He has put this school on the map."

I study her. "Do you really believe that crap?"

Harriet blinks. "Excuse me?"

"Something tells me you know it's bullshit. If you don't, fine. But if you do . . ."

"Then what?"

"Then you're a fucking coward, Harriet Price." My pen

twirls off my fingers. It crashes to the floor and rolls across the room, landing right beneath her swinging feet.

Harriet bends over and snatches it up.

It's worth eleven bucks, that pen, and I nicked it from Mrs. Degarno's art supply cupboard only an hour ago. I scrape back my chair.

When I reach her, she slips back onto the table and holds the pen away from me.

Talk about high maintenance. If she wants me to grovel, fine. "I shouldn't have said that." I put out my hand for the pen.

Harriet grips it tighter.

I sigh. "Calling you a coward was going too far."

Looking me square in the eye, Harriet holds the pen high above her head.

I can't lose that pen, dammit. There's no way I can steal another one without Mrs. Degarno noticing, and she's already on my back about some missing sheets of pressed metal. I could tackle Harriet for it, of course, but I don't need an assault complaint on my record. "Look," I say. "How can I write the article if you won't return my pen?"

This works. Harriet lowers it. I grab it and go back to my seat. With my pen safe I'm free to walk out of here, and with Harriet refusing to help, she has no grounds to stop me. But an angle for an article about Hadley has just occurred to me. And it's not like there's any need to rush home. I may as well write it down.

I turn over a fresh page in my notebook. As soon as I find my rhythm, I've filled it with a lucid argument in no time. I read it over, make a few changes, and read it again. It's good, possibly very good. I walk it over to Harriet, who is now attacking graffiti on various pieces of furniture with a shredded tissue.

"What?" she asks when I hold out my notebook to her.

"I need you to proofread it," I say. "You're in Advanced English, aren't you?"

Harriet hesitates, then takes it, as I knew she would. Control freaks can't help but stick their fingers in. I watch her skim the article.

"Way too ranty," she says, handing it back. "Hyperbole is never persuasive."

Condescending, infuriating little—"You do it, then." I thrust my pen at her.

Harriet folds her arms, this time refusing to take it. "I've already told you I'm not getting involved." She nods at the sketches on the facing page of my notebook. "I see you like to draw."

I bet nobody was ever this patronizing to Frida Kahlo. "It's for my major work, if you must know."

"Are you any good at cartoons?"

Some people just like bossing others around. It's what sets the prefects in this world apart from the nonprefects. As it happens, I *am* good at cartoons. "Why do you ask?"

"Maybe you could do a cartoon instead."

A cartoon about Coach Hadley and his sexist ways. It's not the worst idea I've ever heard. He would be easy enough to caricature. But what would the picture be? And the caption?

"I could give you an angle if that would help," Harriet says casually.

Now I see how it is. She wants the control without the responsibility. She's unbelievable.

On the other hand, it's not like I have any ideas of my own. "Fine," I say, making it clear I don't give a shit one way or the other.

She talks me through her idea.

I should say at this point that Harriet Price isn't known for her wit. Where some are ironic, she's earnest. While others smirk, she weeps into a lace-trimmed handkerchief. Okay, I've never seen her weep—she's always so upbeat—but I imagine that when she *does* succumb to her darker emotional side— if she has one at all—there's a lace-trimmed handkerchief involved. "That's quite funny," I concede.

I spend the next ten minutes in deep concentration, drawing up her idea.

When I've finished, I hand it to Harriet and watch for her reaction.

A smile spreads across her face. "This is really good."

Despite her condescending tone, I'm pleased. "You came up with it," I say generously.

"Hardly. It was your idea to do something, not mine."

"But the cartoon was your idea."

"But you executed it. You deserve the credit."

I look at it again and get an excited flutter in my chest. "Can you write the caption? I reckon your handwriting would be a lot neater than mine."

She takes the pen and writes carefully beneath the picture. "How's that?"

Her contribution is predictably orderly. "Good. Look,

I'd feel bad taking all the credit," I say. "Especially now that you've written the caption. I really think that both our names should go on it."

Harriet shakes her head decisively. "There is no way you are using my name."

"Believe me. I know Nat," I say. "She won't publish anything without a name. Anonymous pieces are against the school rules, and anyway she has this whole journalistic principles thing going on when it comes to anonymous contributions."

"You are not using my name," Harriet says again.

"We can't use mine. Not with my reputation. They'd put me in detention until I'm eighty."

It's a dilemma. We've created something that other people really should see. But how can we get it out there without incriminating ourselves?

"How about using a pseudonym?" Harriet suggests.

I shake my head. "They're not allowed, either."

She frowns. "What if Natasha doesn't *know* it's a pseudonym? You could use something that sounds like the name of a real student."

Harriet's idea could actually work. Then again, a plot to deceive my friend isn't without its problems. If Nat ever found out I'd done it—well, to say she'd have me kneecapped is putting it mildly.

But how else will the cartoon get published?

I look again at what I've drawn, and the hairs on my arms stand on end. "Okay," I say. "What name should we use?"

Harriet points to the whiteboard where a list of student

names from a previous class is scrawled. "What about that as a first name?"

I follow her finger. "Too unusual. It would sound suspicious."

"That one, then?"

"As good as any, I suppose. And a last name?"

"You need something that sounds credible," says Harriet.

"*We* do, you mean." I have a thought. "Have you ever played that game where you work out your porn-star name?"

Harriet stares at me. "My what?"

Of course she hasn't. "What's the first street you ever lived on?"

"McGill Street. Why?"

"What's the name of your first pet?"

She thinks about it. "Budgie."

"Then Budgie McGill is your porn-star name."

"What's yours?" Harriet asks.

"Dottie Mulvaney. Pretty good, hey?"

She folds her arms. "Okay, let's try a variation on your game," she says. "What suburb do you live in?"

"Marrickville."

Harriet's eyes grow wide. "Isn't that miles away?"

"Not really, but it's on the wrong side of the bridge, so you've probably never been there. Where are you?"

"Mosman."

"How about we combine them? Mossville? Marrickman?" I shake my head. "What about streets? I'm on East Street. How about you?"

"Bay Street," says Harriet. "Not that this needs to have anything to do with me at all," she adds quickly.

I think about it. "Eastbay" could work. It's better than the other options. Although...

I remember the opposite game my father and I play. I grab the pen and work on a few variations. "How about this?"

The name is innocuous. It's not too fake sounding. And there's nothing to link it to either of us.

"Amelia Westlake," Harriet reads aloud. "I like it."

chapter 4

HARRIET

I am still running the name over in my head as I shuck off my school shoes inside our front door. *Amelia Westlake*. It has a fabulous ring to it.

"Hello?" I call out. Nobody answers, which is completely fine. I can hear Arthur's band practicing in the central atrium, and I doubt anyone else is home. When your parents' oral surgery skills are in high demand, you cannot expect to have dinner with them every night or even most nights, and I totally understand and appreciate that.

The music coming from the central atrium is even more disharmonious than usual, and as I smooth smoked trout pâté on a water cracker in the empty kitchen I wonder about my brother's emotional well-being. Last week a girl called Candice dumped him on the grounds that he will never amount to anything. It sounds as if he isn't taking it very well at all.

Finally the music stops, and there are footsteps in the hall. I hear the front door close, and Arthur appears. He drags himself onto a kitchen stool. "Everything okay?" I venture.

He shrugs miserably. Since this morning he has done something horrible to his hair. It is cropped close to his scalp everywhere except for a narrow wad along his crown. The poor thing has clearly gone mad with grief.

"Candice still?"

He groans like a dying polar bear.

I love my brother, but sometimes I can see this girl Candice's point. Arthur has an artistic temperament. While it is possible he will one day become a world-renowned musician, it is just as likely, if not more, that he will fail his exams, have to get a job selling flat-pack furniture, and live in a one-bedroom apartment on a main road. What he needs is cheering up. "I'm making your favorite snack," I tell him.

"Thanks, but I'm not hungry."

He is just being polite; Arthur is always hungry. "Nonsense. I've already got the nacho chips in the oven." I open a can of refried beans. "It is time to move on," I say. "Forget Candice. You need to find someone else. Or focus your energy on something completely different, like schoolwork."

"But she's perfect." He has his head on the quartz counter, as if it is too heavy to hold up. "How can I move on from perfect?"

"Sometimes we have to compromise."

He sits up. "You mean like you have with Edie?"

"Excuse me?" I stir the beans vigorously in the saucepan. "Edie is probably *beyond* perfect. Most people have to settle for something less."

"People like me?" grumbles Arthur, scratching the newly shorn part of his scalp.

I put down my wooden spoon. "Oh, Arthur."

He sniffs.

"There's no need to cry."

"I'm not crying. I smell smoke."

"Oh! The corn chips." I open the oven door and a plume of thick smoke curls out.

Arthur crumples back onto the counter. "I suppose Edie's coming around tonight?"

"It *is* Tuesday." Somehow the beans have stuck to the bottom of the saucepan. I lever them off with a spatula. "Would you like to join us for dinner? I'm thinking of making my famous salmon quiche."

"No thanks. Your nachos will be more than enough for me."

It makes sense that Arthur would find it hard being around the two of us when he has just had his heart broken, but I do not want him to feel unwelcome. "The invitation is open if you change your mind."

"Thanks, Harri."

Just then my phone lights up. I pluck it off the counter.

> Darling Bubble, I am exhausted from a long
> albeit successful afternoon tea and need to lay
> low tonight. Rain check? X

One of the many things I love about Edie is her text-messaging technique. She never abbreviates words or employs emojis. However, I am a little disappointed by the message's content.

> Poor Edie, you work so hard, my love. Can I tempt you with my salmon quiche? Or you could cook something for us if you prefer? Would LOVE to see you. X

My capitalization in the final sentence is somewhat crass, and I regret it as soon as I press SEND. I hold my phone and wait for her reply. Although it makes sense that she is tired after running an event, I have been really looking forward to seeing her. I am very keen to talk to her about Will Everhart's cartoon.

Will Everhart. When I think about her, my heart does a strange little flip. What a peculiar afternoon it has been, helping her out with a piece of artistic commentary. This would be bizarre enough had it been with one of my friends—Beth, say, or even Millie. But Will Everhart? This is the girl who, for a history assignment on "The Effects of War," presented a twenty-minute video, spliced together from old movies, of people getting stabbed, macheted, or shot. I wonder if it was wise to light a further flame beneath a person who courts controversy so keenly.

The more I think about it, the more I realize it was probably a very bad idea indeed.

If Will did as we agreed and dropped the cartoon into the *Messenger*'s office on her way home, by Monday it will be published for everyone at Rosemead to see. The possibility makes my jaw ache. Coach can be insensitive, and I certainly have personal experience of that, which is partly why I suggested Will draw the cartoon. But there have also been times when he has been very kind to me, complimenting me on my hair, posture, and even eye color ("as green as the Coral Sea" he has said more than once). And if it weren't for Coach persuading Miss Watson to give me a chance at tennis in the early years, I would never be playing for Tawney and fulfilling my lifelong dream.

Although lately he has not been quite so friendly.

He certainly never used to hold me back to swim extra laps like he did this morning.

What will Coach say when he sees the cartoon? What about Principal Croon? Thank God I convinced Will she should use a pseudonym.

"Why are you staring at your phone?" Arthur asks.

"Waiting for a text from Edie." I hope she isn't judging me for capitalizing "love"!

"She always makes you wait," Arthur says. "It's mean."

Maybe Edie does delay her replies. But her teasing ways are part of her charm. I put the chips and beans together on a plate and place it in front of Arthur. He pulls a chip away from the cheesy brown mound, takes a small bite, and puts it back. "Taste okay?" I ask.

"Delicious," Arthur says, and coughs, which is a common reaction to spicy food. "I think I'll eat it in my room if that's all right with you."

"Of course."

When he is gone, I start my quiche preparations, checking my phone every couple of minutes. Beth texts to confirm that our music excursion to *The Mikado* is leaving at eight tomorrow and to express a firm hope for a good-looking bus driver. ("A hottie" are her exact words. She is so hilarious.) Millie sends through a venue suggestion for the year-twelve formal, and I text back confirming I will consider it in my capacity as Formal Committee chair. My mother texts to say she and my father will eat at the office, and to give a "big hug" to Edie (she and Mum adore one another). I've just popped the quiche in the oven when a text finally comes through from my girlfriend.

> My darling Bubble, my dove, my destiny. I am so
> sorry to have kept you waiting for a reply. I fell
> asleep right after pressing send! Let's meet on
> Saturday, and you can help me with my public
> speaking topic for SpeakOut—they just sent
> it through a few minutes ago. You have such a
> talent for putting words together. What would
> I do without you, Bubble? You are my lucky
> charm. XXXX

Edie never uses more than three Xs. She considers it over the top. That she has done it now is her way of saying she forgives me for capitalizing "love," I am certain. I read the message again. I am her darling Bubble, her dove, her destiny. I hold the bright screen to my face.

chapter 5

WILL

"I spoke to your father last night."

Mum is at the sink with her coffee mug, face to the window, watching a bird on the lawn. Birds on the lawn are about as exciting as it gets at our place. Apart from the occasional wildlife—if a magpie can be described as wildlife—our yard is a square patch of grass dotted with bindi-eye weeds. Stooping around the edge like retirees at a bowling green are one limp acacia, one diseased lemon tree, and one anemic tomato vine. In the middle of the grass are two epic rotary clotheslines.

Since moving to our ground-floor flat, playing guess whose washing is Mum's favorite new pastime. "That must be Julie's load," she'll say, nose to the window. "I can tell from the crocheted bedspread. And are those Emilio's overalls? I should duck round and let them know it's about to rain."

We've been in the unit since Christmas—that's when Mum and Dad finally sold our North Shore house and split the difference. Mum and I hauled our stuff to the Inner West, which is closer to her sister and has cheaper real estate. Dad kept going west until he couldn't go any farther without falling off the continent.

"Did you hear what I said, Will?"

"What did you speak to him for? You guys are divorced, remember? That means you no longer have to sleep together, go to each other's work dinners, or engage in conversation."

Mum rinses her mug. "He's disappointed you didn't go over last week. He says you would have loved it. It was a celebration of Western Australia's emerging light and space movement, you know."

I know. Dad sent me an invitation to the launch of his new art magazine a month ago. Like it never occurred to him that short of a spare five days to drive across the desert, I'd have to spend four-and-a-half hours on a plane to get there. He knows I don't do planes anymore. "He should have thought more about how much I'd have loved it before having his launch party ON THE OTHER SIDE OF THE COUNTRY," I say.

"Come on, Will," says Mum. "Perth is where the magazine is based. And where he lives. Would you have preferred it if he didn't invite you at all?"

From my chair, I throw the dish towel I've been using as a napkin onto the kitchen countertop. Just one of the advantages of living in a shoebox. Honestly, if you asked me which living arrangement, old or new, wins the overall Sucks Most award, I'd be hard-pressed to decide. In our old suburb, the streets were too quiet, and everyone looked like they'd just stepped out of a fifties catalog of British knitting patterns. At least here the streets are loud with traffic, and the smells of fish sauce, oil, and tamarind spill from the Vietnamese restaurants. All sorts of people live around here—immigrants from Tonga, refugees from Somalia, Portuguese who have been here for generations. A group of Lebanese oldies holds court every day outside the local pizza joint, where they eat oregano pizza and drink cup after cup of black coffee. Down the road, hipsters pour single-origin coffees while stroking their beards. Posters and political slogans decorate building walls.

I love all of this: Walking around the suburb, I feel its heartbeat. The only part I can't stand is the noise from above. Living under a flight path is the worst. I wake in the mornings to the rumble of plane engines and fall asleep to it at night, when it enters my dreams. With my eyes closed, my ears pop, and suddenly I'm in a cabin with shaking walls and flickering lights. I haven't slept properly since we got here.

The toaster pops. Morning sun arcs across the kitchen floor.

"We've talked about this," Mum says.

"Then there's no need to repeat ourselves."

"You could at least give him a call, Will."

"Those phone companies have higher profit margins than the GDPs of some small island nations, you know."

"He's your father."

"There are legal avenues to change that."

The bird on the grass buries its beak in its feathers.

"Don't be late for school."

* * *

First period on Mondays is Miss Fowler's English class. Nat and I always sit together and catch up on the weekend. Today, Kimberley Kitchener has plonked herself in my usual chair. Nat looks ready to kill her, but Kimberley is too busy WhatsApping to notice.

The only other spots are in the back of the room. I sit down, turn my phone to silent, and get cracking on my overdue creative writing homework. This week's challenge: an obituary.

> WILL EVERHART of Sydney, Australia, had a keen wit and a sharp mind. Greatly admired by her peers for her principled approach to life, she was also deeply artistic. Renowned critics considered her to be nothing less than the future of Australian art.
>
> The quality of the work she produced during her heartbreakingly short life only compounds the tragedy of her passing. After a drawn-out period of suffering, Everhart died during first period on Monday, of boredom.
>
> She is survived by her philandering parents.

There's something too elegant about the word "philandering," so I change it to "cheating." But "cheating" is too mild, so I change it to "double-crossing."

"Will Everhart," Miss Fowler calls out from the front. "I asked you a question. What on earth are you doing?"

My classmates turn in their chairs to stare at me. I don't blame them. Today's lesson on the poetry of Robert Browning is about as fascinating as a water cracker.

"Practicing my synonyms," I say in an injured tone, glancing at my notebook. I like "charlatan," but is "charlatan" the adjectival form or does it need a suffix?

She is survived by her charlatanous *parents.*

She is survived by her charlatanizing *parents.*

How about "swindling"? No. None of them is right. I draw a line through "double-crossing" and write "crazy" instead.

"Crazy" encapsulates it. How my father philandered/cheated/double-crossed my mother by sleeping with an installation artist named Naomi and then moving with her to the other side of the country. How Mum philandered/cheated/double-crossed him back by having an affair with an actuary named Graham. How they've chosen to handle their breakup: with calm conversation when there should be shouting, tears, and hospitalization.

Since splitting, my parents get along better than before. They expect me to be happy about it and happy about the airborne commute.

"Crazy," "stupid," "senseless," "cracked." Any of them will do.

"We're not looking at synonyms today, Will," Miss Fowler says, her expression fixed. "Now tell us, please, in what year did Browning publish 'My Last Duchess'?"

From the corner of my eye I see Nat reach under her desk.

I rack my brain for the answer. "I know it was sometime in the mid-nineteenth century."

"I asked you for the year," says Miss Fowler.

"1860?"

"I've just gone through this."

I can't believe she's pressing me. "Why does the exact year matter? Surely it would be more relevant to talk about the broader social context of the poem?"

"Will…" Miss Fowler warns.

"For example, the nature of the patriarchy at that time, and what 'My Last Duchess' implies about violence against women?"

Miss Fowler is not fond of discussion points that deviate from her lesson plan. This is why at the end of class I am forced to endure a lecture from her about my recent academic performance.

"You pay no attention to anything I say, and your consistently abysmal marks reflect that," she says. Her eyes bore into me. "What's more, your marks are showing no signs of improvement. I'm sorry, but I'm going to have to talk about your progress with Principal Croon."

My stomach cramps. "What about my Virginia Woolf essay? Surely that will bring up my average mark."

"To the contrary," says Miss Fowler, drawing it out of a manila folder.

I look at the mark. "Seventy-two? What complete balls!"

Miss Fowler gasps. "Language, Wilhelmina!"

"I worked really hard on this one." I'm not lying. I even footnoted my sources.

"I'm afraid your hard work doesn't show."

"Are you serious? This is one of the best essays I've ever written."

Miss Fowler looks flustered. "Then you can tell that to Principal Croon."

✻ ✻ ✻

When I finally get out of class, Nat is waiting for me on the landing. She's shouting at a year-nine kid who accidentally spilled juice on her uniform. Silly girl: Everyone knows better than to cross Nat Nguyen.

Nat's fierceness is one of the reasons we hit it off immediately when I started at Rosemead in year ten. It's also part of what makes her such a great editor. The articles she publishes in the *Messenger* are passionate and well argued. And nothing motivates contributors like threats and intimidation. There are girls at Rosemead who audibly whimper when she walks past.

The juice girl scampers. Nat watches her with a flicker of amusement before turning to me. "I was texting you during class."

"What about?"

"Only one way to find out."

I dig into my pocket.

> Well THIS sucks. What is KK thinking? We
> have business to discuss.

> You free at lunch? 12:30 at the newsroom?
> Text me.

WORLD 2 WILL. What are you even doing
back there???

Robert Browning who gives a shit I don't.

Look at your phone. I'll be at newsroom at
12:30 if you want to come.

FYI: the business to discuss—you'll like it.
Re: something in our latest edition.
Also you & me business, naturally ;-)

1842

"1842," I say out loud. "Of course. Thanks." But the publi-
cation date of 'My Last Duchess' isn't what's grabbed my attention. Something in our latest edition. Does Nat mean the latest
edition of the *Messenger*? Is she referring to our cartoon?

The paper always comes out on Mondays, but I haven't
seen a copy yet. I think again about the cartoon. I've been
thinking about it on and off since I drew it, but with every
passing day it has seemed less real.

Did I really collaborate on a protest art project with Harriet Price in detention last week? The girl, it is rumored, who
sends her teachers a Christmas basket each year with a card
quoting Seneca on gratitude? What caused this horrible lapse
in judgment? A microsleep? Hypnosis? A covert alien mind
probe?

It also strikes me for the first time how truly risky it is that the cartoon is about Hadley. As Rosemead's Olympian poster boy, he is untouchable. It's risky enough to mouth off at him as I did last week at the pool, but another level of riskiness entirely to publish something in print. If the cartoon has made it into the *Messenger*, there's no telling how the administration of this totalitarian regime masquerading as an educational institution will react.

I can't let Nat suspect that I know anything about the cartoon. "You want to talk about some *Messenger* article? Sounds intriguing," I say.

Nat's eyes glimmer like black ice on asphalt. She riffles through her book bag and pulls out a copy of the paper. "Duncan's delivering it to all the drop-off points now." She opens it to page three. "And it's not an article. Here." Nat jabs the middle of the page. "Take a look at this."

chapter 6

HARRIET

When Beth starts wailing loudly in the change room after netball, I barely bat an eyelid. She is a regular star of Rosemead's theatrical productions and prides herself on her dramatic edge. "Ohmygod, ohmygod!" Her cries hit the tiles and bounce back along the taps.

I peer over her shoulder. Page three of the *Messenger* is spread across on her lap. Oh my God indeed.

Cooling my cheek with the back of my hand, I lean in closer and feel something unexpected: a burst of pride. It is an excellent reproduction. Every detail of the cartoon is crystal clear: the row of girls in their Rosemead swimwear, lined up along the side of the pool; the cartoon's caption, "uniform inspection," underneath; the man with the whistle standing before them, his neck craned forward, ogling their breasts.

From the way Will has captured his chin dimple, stubble, and bald patch, there can be no doubt whom it depicts.

"Who is this Amelia Westlake?" Liz Newcomb says, calmly undoing her netball skirt. "Does anyone know her?"

Millie squeezes into our huddle. "I don't get it. What's Coach Hadley supposed to be doing?"

"Isn't it obvious?" says Liz.

"This is seriously controversial." Beth grins, ignoring them both. "Hasn't Ning Nong heard of defamation? My dad would never let something like this go to print in *his* paper. Coach is going to hit the roof." She looks up as the rest of our phys ed class spills into the change room. "Hey, guys, check this out," she calls.

A dull pounding, rather like being hit repeatedly with a brick, starts up behind my left temple. Beth is absolutely right. Of course Coach will be livid. What if the school somehow finds out it was my idea? What if Coach guesses? And how can I trust Will Everhart, of all people, not to tell anybody? What on earth have I done?

This could basically end my school career, I realize. With one impulsive act I've potentially waved good-bye to the Tawney Shield, to the school formal, to finishing year twelve.

All the oxygen leaves my throat. *In for six, out for eight,* I silently recite. I press my back to the wall and slide slowly down it.

"You okay, Harriet?" asks Millie, looking over, the freckles on her forehead crowding.

Thank God for Millie. I don't know how I would survive

without her and Beth. Happily, I rarely have to think about it because they have been there for me since I began at Rosemead in grade four.

Well, except for the first few months. I was No Friends Harriet to begin with. That's what happens when you start at a new school after the cliques have already formed.

Young girls can be quite horrible, especially with wet crepe paper and safety scissors at their disposal.

Not that I like to think about that time very much.

All I will say is that if Beth hadn't been going through a spa bath phase and discovered we have two at my house, who knows how my life would have turned out?

Beth glances up from the *Messenger*. "God, Harriet. Not another one of your migraines. Hey, do you know this girl? Amelia Eastlake?"

"*Westlake*," I correct her impulsively, and silently curse myself.

"The name does sound familiar," says one of the girls who has just come in. "I think she might be in Ms. Pile's hockey squad."

"Hang on. Isn't she the one who sings alto in the choir?" Beth asks. "A boat person of some sort?"

"That's Amelia al-Assad," Millie answers promptly.

"Oh. What about the girl who sits next to her? Who never says anything? Muppet eyes."

One of the others shakes her head. "Nobody knows *her* name."

"Whoever Amelia Westlake is, she deserves a medal,"

says Liz Newcomb, grabbing her stockings from a pile of clothes on a bench and putting them on. "I think the cartoon's fantastic."

"It's pretty mean about Coach Hadley, though, don't you think?" says Millie, frowning. "He's not that bad. He just likes to muck around sometimes."

Liz Newcomb snorts.

There is a loud crackle from the wall speaker, signaling the start of prelunch announcements.

"A reminder that the computer labs will be closed on Friday so the new computers can be installed," booms Deputy Davids's voice. "All of Friday's classes will be held in the Lower Hall instead. And a reminder to Kimberley Kitchener. Kimberley, if you don't collect your trombone from lost property by four o'clock this afternoon, it will be sequestered by the Music Department. Thank you."

After a final crackle, the speaker goes silent.

"What's taking you girls so long?" says a voice from the door of the change room.

My chest grows tight.

Around me there is a flurry of hoisted towels and half-dressed girls shuffling into cubicles. Liz holds up her netball skirt to cover her lower half. In a swift one-two Beth drops the school paper and slides it under the bench so that by the time Coach Hadley pops his head around the doorway it is out of sight.

I feel my jaw tense. He must know I came up with the cartoon. That is why he is here. I press my fingers into my palms so hard that my knuckles go white.

Coach Hadley peers inside, his expression as smooth as the surface of an empty pool. His eyes twinkle. He smiles. "Chop, chop. The junior squad will be in here soon."

A sort of squeak escapes Millie's mouth.

Scratching his cheek stubble leisurely, Coach Hadley looks at her. "Something the matter, the divine Miss Levine?"

Girls giggle nervously. Millie shakes her head, her freckles disappearing in a sea of red.

He gazes at each of us: Beth, Millie, Liz, and, finally, me. He looks at me the longest. Does he know about the cartoon? Oh dear God in heaven, is he reading my mind?

"Move along, girls," he says cheerily, and disappears from the doorway.

In for six, out for eight. I breathe.

I run a finger along the metal badges pinned to my lapel. There are five of them: my house badge, my prefect badge, my Sports Committee badge, my Tawney team badge, and, of course, my Rosemead badge. Feeling them there, freshly polished and pinned in perfect symmetry, is a comfort.

With the immediate danger past, I look around for Liz Newcomb. She has put on her uniform and is doing up her shoelaces nearby. Privately I have always considered Liz to be overrated. She runs the annual spelling bee for the lower-school kids, which is obviously very commendable, but there is certainly nothing outstanding enough about her to merit, for example, her being elected as prefect or, to take another random example, her being chosen as Rosemead's Tawney Shield tennis captain over other highly qualified candidates. It is not *Liz Newcomb* who is poised to bring home the shield in the doubles competition this year.

However, I am willing to put all this aside for a moment to hear more about what she thinks of the cartoon.

"Do you think Beth is right?" I murmur. "Will Coach Hadley sue?"

Liz glances at the door before meeting my eye. "How can he? Did you see what he did just now? He shouldn't be loitering around the change room at all. He gets away with it because of how friendly he pretends to be, but really he's just a perv. Heaps of us know it, but nobody's brave enough to say anything about it. Maybe now, thanks to what's been published, they'll have to do something about him."

"Really?" A flight of butterflies fills my stomach.

"I don't see how they can't."

"But what will happen to the girl who drew the cartoon? It's a pretty serious accusation," I venture.

Liz Newcomb shrugs. "They can hardly get her in trouble for pointing out what's in plain view."

I hope that for all her faults, Liz Newcomb is right for once.

I stand up. My head feels slightly better. "Are you going back up to the main building?" I ask Liz.

"Yeah, to the cafeteria. I think it's about to rain, though. Should have brought my umbrella down."

I am about to offer to share mine with her when she speaks again.

"I saw you and Edie training on the courts the other week. Looking good."

"Oh! Thanks."

"Although your backhand volley still needs a bit of work, doesn't it?"

That's when I remember my umbrella has a broken spoke. It will be no good to share with anyone. I had best return to the main building by myself.

Besides, I am in a bit of a hurry: I need to find Will Everhart before the end of lunch.

chapter 7

WILL

I get to the newsroom just after twelve thirty. I knock on the door, and Nat hauls it open. She kicks aside a stack of empty boxes and ushers me in.

I survey the familiar chaos: Nat's desk covered in piles of paper. Her beat-up computer with Post-it notes fluttering along its side. The stereo, with Nat's awful garage punk blaring. The corkboard, set lopsided against the peeling wall, where draft *Messenger* pages jostle for space. The rusted filing cabinet. The moth-eaten couch.

Duncan Aboud, Nat's unofficial editorial assistant, is sorting papers on the floor. No one barring Nat herself knows how Duncan manages to spend so much time in the *Messenger* newsroom when he's supposed to be in class at Edwin Street Boys' Academy across the road. When questioned on the subject, he tends to mumble the phrase "cross-institutional learning" a lot.

"Duncan, out," Nat commands.

Duncan pushes his glasses up his nose, gets to his feet, and rushes for the door.

As soon as it closes behind him, Nat's demeanor shifts. She steps toward me. With a coy smile she leans in and kisses me on the lips.

It's new, this thing between us. It started last Monday night. I was helping her with a *Messenger* article on refugee policy. We'd drunk a tank load of Red Bull. Then Nat found a bunch of cat videos online that had us both in hysterics. I was crouched against the filing cabinet wheezing with laughter, saying, "That is *so* funny," and Nat was saying, "*You* are," and I was saying, "No, *you* are," and then in a different voice, a low-down voice like she was telling me a secret, she said, "You're seriously great. You know that, right?"

That's when things heated up.

But that was a week ago, and now it's Monday again, and lunchtime. Daylight is streaming onto the crumb-caked carpet, lighting up the floating dust whorls and catching the scratches on the desktop. The voices of our classmates echo in the corridor. As I kiss Nat back, it occurs to me that what was exciting a week ago on Red Bull in a dark room now seems weirdly sordid.

I hear the boom of Deputy Davids's voice outside. "Inez Jurich, get down from that balcony rail at once."

I pull away from Nat, indicating the door.

She nods in agreement. "Another time." Wiping her mouth with her sleeve, she falls into her desk chair. I flop onto the couch.

We look at each other.

"So. About this cartoon," says Nat, turning businesslike.

My stomach turns. Here it comes: the moment I've been dreading. Nat's worked out that I drew it and is going to blast me for it.

Her eyes light up. "How great is it?"

I release the wall of breath inside my chest. "Incredible," I say.

"Hadley deserves it," Nat says. "More than deserves it. What a creep." She grins. "Do you know this Amelia Westlake person, by any chance? The name sounded familiar to me, but I can't put my finger on it."

She hasn't a clue it's me, then. Better still, she thinks it's someone real. This is exactly what we were aiming for.

I furrow my brow. "There's a girl in year ten who's in the Rhythmic Roses who's called Amelia," I say. The Rhythmic Roses is Rosemead's prize-winning modern dance troupe. "Mousey hair, I think. Actually, I have a feeling she's related to Duncan," I throw in.

Nat shakes her head. "He has a cousin Emily at Rosemead, but her hair isn't mousey, and she doesn't dance," she says matter-of-factly. "She's into horses," she adds, as if being into horses completely excludes either of those things. "Which means the Rhythmic Roses girl *could* be Amelia Westlake, which would be a relief"—she is saying all of this incredibly quickly—"because I had this awful feeling that it might have been a pseudonym, and you know the school rules about publishing anonymous contributions. And after the investigative piece I ran on the cafeteria's supply chain, Croon's already looking for an excuse to ditch me as editor."

"Of course." A wave of guilt sweeps over me. How could I have forgotten about the shit Nat copped for that supply chain piece? It exposed a link to an egg farm known for animal cruelty—a farm that also happens to be run by a prominent Rosemead family.

Croon wanted Nat's head on a plate. She would have kicked her off the *Messenger* in an instant if she'd been able to find a flaw in her research.

This is the tightrope Nat's always walking: breaking meaningful stories without getting offside of Principal Croon. Or if she does get offside, making sure it's in a way that's beyond criticism. Publishing a cartoon under a pseudonym is definitely not in the "beyond criticism" category.

"I've done a bit of searching already," Nat says. "There are no references to Amelia Westlake in any recent Rosemead publications. They keep the student rolls on the staff intranet behind a firewall, so I haven't been able to check those yet, but I'll find a way. I really hope I can locate her," she says. "This cartoon is one of the best contributions I've received for a long time."

"I agree." I'm burning with guilt, but still pleased she feels this way.

"Usually all I get are excursion reports or rants about how there should be more gluten-free food options at the cafeteria." She sets her mouth in a line; when most people do that, it means they're furious, but when Nat does it, it means she's impressed. "I've been wanting to do something on Hadley for ages, but there's no way I'd get away with it in an editorial. A student's contribution is a different story. I'm at arm's length. It's perfect. It's about time Hadley faced the music." She laughs and looks at me. "Of course, when Croon finds out about the cartoon, and if Amelia Westlake doesn't exist, I'll be in deep shit. Luckily Croon's not back from her trip until later this month."

Principal Croon is currently on her annual junket to Rosemead's Japanese sister school in Osaka. Why she needs a whole month there each year is anybody's guess.

"It's the only reason I took the risk of publishing the cartoon," Nat says. "It's unlikely Deputy Davids will even see it. She never reads the *Messenger*. But if Croon were here..." She shakes her head. "And if someone shows Croon the cartoon when she gets back, before I can confirm that Amelia Westlake is legit..." Nat draws a finger across her throat. "Anyway, I thought you might be able to help me."

My stomach flips. "Why me?"

"I thought of you as soon as I saw the cartoon," Nat says. "There's something about it that's similar to your drawing style, don't you think?"

"I *wish* I could have drawn this," I bluff, chest thudding. "I can think of plenty of *other* people who could have, though."

Nat flips a paper clip in the air and catches it. "That's exactly why I thought you could help. This Amelia person is obviously artistic. Maybe you could have a word with Mrs. Degarno about whether she has anyone called Amelia in her art classes."

I nod, swallowing hard.

Nat looks thoughtful for a moment, then grins. "You know who'd know, of course."

"Who?"

"Harriet Price."

I stare at her. "Why the hell would she know?"

"Calm down. I'm just saying she knows everything about Rosemead. I'm sure she could tell us the names and terms of each of the principals back to 1835 if we were interested."

"Oh yeah." I laugh loudly.

Nat looks at me like I'm a weirdo.

It occurs to me that I could simply tell her the truth. *So, Harriet and I got stuck in detention together last week....*

But once she knew she'd been tricked I'd never hear the end of it, not when her position at the *Messenger* is at stake. Also, Nat hates Harriet Price almost as much as she hates her rich princess friends, Beth Tupman and Millie Levine. She likes to call her Harriet the Why?

"Look, Nat, I've got some equipment to return to Degarno's supply cupboard before the end of lunch...."

"Fine." She's riffling through a folder on her desk. "I'm going to get to the bottom of this."

"Let me know if you find anything out."

"You too." She waves me away.

⚹ ⚹ ⚹

Out on the covered walkway, a blustery wind is throwing around sticks the size of bullets. I jog back toward the main building, shielding my face with a hand. I hear footsteps coming toward me, and I look up just in time to avoid a head-on collision with Harriet Price.

"What are you doing here?" I whisper, glancing back toward the newsroom.

"Looking for you," she says, urgency in her voice. "I wanted to talk to you about something."

If Nat sees us together, there'll be no end to the questions. There's a study space ten meters down the walkway, so I herd Harriet toward it. When we're inside, I pull out a chair and sit down. Harriet perches on the sideboard beside it. I watch her pat her windswept hair like she's soothing a pet cat.

She looks around. "What's that table doing in here? It belongs in the debate room."

Does Harriet have interior design ambitions? Is that why she's so obsessed with furniture placement? I wouldn't be surprised. Interior design is just the kind of superficial career wealthy kids aspire to.

Without waiting for a reply, she asks keenly, "Did you see the cartoon?"

"Of course I saw it," I bark at her.

She looks wounded. "Everyone's talking about it, you know. Beth. Millie. Liz Newcomb..."

Is that all she's got? Two rich brats and a jock? "That's who constitutes 'everyone,' is it?"

"Not just them." Defensiveness has made her voice high-pitched. "Everyone in my phys ed class. And everyone in the cafeteria line."

This is interesting news. "That was what we wanted, wasn't it? To make a splash?" I laugh at my pool-related joke.

Harriet doesn't join in. "I guess so," she says. She looks worried.

I decide to cut her some slack. "The people who were talking about it. What were they saying?"

Harriet leans back on her sideboard. "Some didn't get it. But others thought it was a great comment on Coach Hadley's, you know, perverted ways." She looks a little shocked by her own statement. "There was also a view that when he finds out, he will sue." Drawing her hands behind her head, she divides her hair into three strands and begins to braid it.

I watch her work at her hair. The tip of her tongue sticks out of her mouth as she concentrates. I wonder if she knows she does that. "Nat thinks it's a brilliant cartoon," I tell her, feeling suddenly generous. "She said it's really important."

"She did?" Harriet smiles briefly before her worried look returns.

"We nailed it, Harriet. You should be proud. It was a great concept."

"It was a great *drawing*," she says, flustered. "The concept had nothing to do with it."

I laugh. "Okay, fine. Look, I've got some paintbrushes to return to the Art Department before my next class." I stand up.

"Will, wait." Harriet's hand shoots out and grabs me above the elbow. "We should talk about what happens next."

I look at her hand on my arm. Seeing my glance, she hurriedly removes it.

"I don't have time right now," I say. "I've got to get these paintbrushes back. If Mrs. Degarno finds out I've borrowed them, she'll report me, and I'm already in trouble today for losing it over an English mark." I flash my Virginia Woolf essay at her.

"I just wanted to, well, check," Harriet says. "We've agreed to keep the, ah, details about the cartoon's conception to ourselves, haven't we? Because people are going to start asking about Amelia Westlake. Maybe even some of the teachers. It could create quite an uproar."

So that's what this is about: her precious reputation. "I'm not going to tell anyone you had anything to do with it, if that's what you're asking," I say.

She pauses. "You promise?"

"It's fine, Harriet. I won't be jeopardizing your Rosemead career for the sake of a laugh."

This appears to satisfy her. She stands up and moves to one end of the table that so disgusted her a minute ago. "I need you to grab the other end."

Seriously, how did she get so demanding? She's probably grown up with a nanny and a cook, paid to meet her every need. Or maybe it has something to do with astrology. Star signs are a load of crap, but I'm willing to bet she's a Leo.

She looks at me impatiently. "The debate room is just around the corner. It will take a few minutes, maximum."

"Do we have to go past the newsroom?"

"No. It's in the other direction."

I sigh. "Fine."

I steer the table to follow Harriet as she backs out the door. Outside, fat drops of rain are splashing on the railing beside the covered walkway. Puddles are forming on the study lawn. Two girls carrying umbrellas hop over them.

"If I ever meet that Amelia girl, I'm going to pin a medal on her," says one to the other. "She definitely deserves one more than *he* does."

Harriet catches my eye. I wink at her, and her cheeks turn pink. If the temperature wasn't a factor, I would swear I just made her blush.

We reach the debate room. "Let's set it down toward the back," she says. "Can you grab two chairs from that pile in the front?"

I consider mouthing back at her, but at this point I just want to get out of here. I drag the chairs roughly across the carpet, at the same time trying to figure out how I can get to my locker, where I've stashed the brushes, and across campus to the art rooms—all in ten minutes. When I reach Harriet, she is flipping through my Virginia Woolf essay. She looks up. "She gave you seventy-two for this?"

Stickybeak. I snatch the essay back.

"That's ridiculous. It's worth at least a seventy-five," Harriet says. "Possibly an eighty. Did you hand it in late?"

I don't want to explain the whole story. Not to Harriet Price. But I feel strangely touched by her outrage. "Miss Fowler always gives me seventy-two. It's her standard mark for me."

Harriet wrinkles her nose. "That makes no sense."

"It's what she thinks I'm worth. I'm an average student. I argue with her in class. And my parents never kick up a stink about my marks."

"And is this something she does with other people, or just you?"

"She does it with everyone."

Harriet's eyes are wide. "How is that possible?"

Did Harriet blow in from Perfect Land yesterday? She needs a lesson in Real Life 101. "You get lower marks if you challenge her in class," I tell her with deliberate slowness. "You get higher marks if your parents are the type to march up to the school and threaten to withdraw you. Brown-nosing also works. That friend of yours, Beth? She's in Fowler's other class, and from what I hear, she's a complete sycophant. Gets better marks than she deserves, most of the time. It helps that Fowler's a fan of her father's newspaper, of course." I slot the chairs into place. "Look, are we done?"

"It just doesn't make sense," says Harriet. "The Rosemead way is about nurturing every student equally to fulfill her potential. . . ." She sees my incredulous expression and stops.

"Is it possible you missed handing in a page or something?" she asks next. "Or wrote about the wrong topic?"

"I've got to go." I head to the door.

"Will!" Harriet calls out.

There's a crease in her brow, an intensity in her gaze. It's just enough to halt me in my tracks.

"Do you really think something will happen with Coach Hadley as a result of the cartoon?" she says. "That they'll, you know, at least talk to him about his behavior?"

"In a fair and moral universe I don't see how they can ignore it," I say, and it's impossible to tell whether she is pleased or terrified by this answer. "Look, I've really got to—"

"Just one more thing, Will." She looks nervous. "You know how you've promised not to tell anybody about the cartoon?"

I sigh. "Yes, Harriet."

"Is that a promise that's, you know, extendable?"

"Like a dishwasher warranty?"

Harriet hesitates. "Possibly. I'm not exactly sure how dishwasher warranties work."

No surprises there.

"What I mean," says Harriet, her eyes shining, "is I think I have another idea for you."

I look at her again in the peculiar light. Outside, the clouds have a tint of green—hail is coming—and the approaching storm has given her, has given everything, an irregular glow.

She grabs my hand. This time, I let her. The hint of a smile plays on her lips. "An idea for another cartoon you can publish."

"That *I* can publish?" I say, feeling light-headed. "If it's your idea then you're a part of it, too. You know that, don't you?"

Harriet pauses. "Officially neither of us is involved, are we?" Her fingers are warm. Her sneaky tone makes the breath expand in my chest.

I let it out with a laugh. "So what you're saying…"

Harriet nods. She smiles shyly. "I think Amelia Westlake should publish another cartoon."

PART TWO

chapter 8

HARRIET

I am ridiculously late for our first Tawney training session after Easter break.

"It's four twenty," says Edie as I push open the court gate. "Where have you been?"

She is looking fabulous as usual: Chanel sunglasses on, hair drawn up high, the Tawney Shield sweatshirt over her tennis gear giving her an elite-athlete charm. I unzip my bag and draw out my racket: a Wilson Blade 104, the same one the Williams sisters use. "The library," I tell Edie. "You want this end or the other one?"

Edie bounces a ball on the court. "You never go to the library. What were you doing up there?"

I begin a quick warm-up stretch. "An assignment," I say, drawing one arm then the other across my chest. "I'm happy to go up the other end. I brought a visor, so the sun won't bother me."

"What assignment?" says Edie, smacking the ball methodically.

"Just a little class thing for Ms. Bracken, that's all. On Egypt under Hatshepsut. I had to wait until the librarian got the book I needed out of storage. Sorry."

This is not what I have in fact been doing at the library. What I have been doing is creating an Instagram account for Amelia Westlake on my tablet: entering some basic information, then uploading a picture for her—a silhouette of a schoolgirl sitting by a window.

Then feeling a sudden tightness in my throat.

Then looking over my shoulder to make sure no one's been watching.

Then calming myself down with a few breathing exercises.

Then looking back at the screen and noticing my new profile's zero follower count.

Then noticing my new profile's zero following count as well.

Then putting "Beth Tupman" into the search box and finding her feed and hovering the cursor over the FOLLOW button.

Then thinking: No. Beth will remember the cartoons from the school paper, and if Amelia Westlake follows Beth and Beth looks at Amelia's profile and sees she has no followers, she will know she isn't a real person. Real people have followers. Most real people, anyway. Certainly the real people Beth hangs out with. And if Beth gives anyone a hint that Amelia Westlake isn't a real person, people will start asking who

Amelia Westlake really is, and Natasha Nguyen will refuse to publish our next cartoon.

Then going to close the screen window.

Then not in fact closing the screen window.

Then typing "Will Everhart" into the search box.

Then wondering, Why on earth am I looking up Will's feed? What interest could it possibly hold? She probably isn't even on Instagram. She probably isn't on social media at all. She is probably one of those privacy crusaders who has taken herself completely offline and communicates with people via carrier pigeon instead.

Then pressing ENTER.

Then seeing four Will Everharts pop up: three of them male and one of them female with a bio that reads, "Bios are bullshit."

It was Will, all right.

I studied that awful uneven haircut of hers, her dark hair all short on one side and long on the other, like her hairdresser had been called away to a family emergency midjob, and her brown eyes, which were glazed over like she had never been so bored in all her life.

In all her photos she wore the same expression: Will Everhart looking bored in a park. Will Everhart looking bored in a canoe. Will Everhart looking bored on a beach. Will Everhart looking bored with a groovy-looking older man—probably her boyfriend. It would be just like Will to have a boyfriend who wore a leather jacket. Will Everhart looking bored with Natasha Nguyen, who had her arm tight around Will's shoulders and was leaning in very close.

My heart rate quickened. It was probably the sugary cookies I had eaten for lunch. I was taking some deep breaths to calm myself down when my phone buzzed.

What hole have you fallen into, Bubble?
I'm at the courts

I am not sure why, exactly, I don't tell Edie any of this. I am not sure why I have not told her anything at all about Amelia Westlake. I know she would be incredibly supportive of the project. Possibly she would be concerned I was putting my future at risk, but once I assured her there was no way anyone could find out I am involved, she would absolutely applaud it. She would understand that the aim is simply to provide some gentle commentary to remind people about Rosemead's genuine values.

Still. I've never mentioned the cartoon about Coach Hadley that Will and I published in the *Messenger*. Nor have I mentioned the two cartoons we have published since.

We published our second cartoon a week after the first one. It centered on the practices of Rosemead's uniform shop. The idea came to me after a remark Will made that day in detention about how unfair it is to require students to buy all aspects of their uniform there. The rule doesn't just apply to our dresses, but also to accessories like socks, gloves, and scarves. As Will pointed out, it gives the uniform shop a monopoly, meaning it can set its prices as high as it likes.

This was not something that had occurred to me before. I wondered if the school's administration had properly thought through the consequences of the rule. I knew that if we pointed it out to them, they would see the problems it caused. So I agreed to work up a few ideas with Will.

The cartoon pictures two Rosemead students in conversation. "I love your new regulation Rosemead hair ribbon," says the first girl. The second girl says, "Thanks! I got it from the uniform shop for just $200!"

The cartoon was wildly popular, and we followed it up with another in the week before Easter, one about how female authors are underrepresented on Rosemead's English syllabus. It depicts a Rosemead student reading a book by Jane Austen. Another student walking by remarks, "Jane? That's a funny name for a fella."

I have to say that the whole process of producing these little creative pieces has been remarkably satisfying.

Our fourth cartoon is due to be published on Monday, and I am particularly nervous about it.

It is the one about Miss Fowler's marking practices that I came up with on the day our first cartoon was published. Given how critical it is of Miss Fowler, I got cold feet about it, and convinced Will we should delay sending it in. In the cartoon, a woman with a notable likeness to Miss Fowler is holding up a piece of paper. On the paper it reads:

HOW TO BOOST YOUR ENGLISH MARKS

Tip 1: Express the same views as your
teacher (extra marks for quoting them
verbatim).

Tip 2: Suck up to your teacher in class.

Tip 3: Do not under any circumstances
express an original thought.

Will thinks its message is too important *not* to publish, and now that we are into a new school term, I agree it is time.

I have it in my bag right now. It occurs to me that I could show it to Edie and ask her what she thinks—it would be the perfect entrée for her to Amelia Westlake. But then I decide this really isn't the right moment. We haven't long until the Tawney Shield, and we are woefully behind in our training schedule.

Telling Edie about the cartoons would also mean mentioning Will, which would be tricky. Not that Edie knows anything about Will. But I feel somehow this fact in itself could make things awkward.

"We've got serious ground to make up," Edie says, shaking her head so that her high ponytail dances. Edie's hair is the most divine chestnut, with a hint of red that happens to coordinate perfectly with the Tawney Shield stripe on our uniform. "And today I heard some seriously bad news. St. Margaret's has a new player. Apparently she's incredible."

I gasp.

Edie gives her ball another bounce and catches it on the ascent. "Her name is Bianca Stein. She was the under-sixteen champion in Queensland last year." She leans against the net post like she does after hitting a particularly impressive volley. "Apparently St. Mag's shipped her in at the start of last term and has been training her in secret. Today they announced their team, and she's the captain. Anyway, Sophie, from our squad, recognized the name. She's seen Bianca on court in Brisbane. She says she's one of the best junior players she's ever watched."

"This is completely unfair." I resist slamming my racket on the net.

Our other competitors are a known quantity. Edie and I have a profile of each of the top New South Wales players up on a wall in Edie's bedroom. On this Bianca Stein person from Queensland, we have nothing.

"I guess the question is whether she'll be playing in the doubles," I say. "There is no one else of any caliber at St. Margaret's. If she's from Queensland, she may not have connections with any other players down here."

Edie flicks her ponytail. "That's wishful thinking, if you ask me. She'll find someone to play with, or someone will find her. There's no reason to assume she won't play in the doubles."

"So what do we do?"

I must sound overly panicked because Edie puts down her racket and comes over. She presses her forehead gently against mine, which is one of our pregame rituals. I drink in the smell of her floral perfume. "Train hard," she says. "Learn what we can about her. Find out about her strengths, her weaknesses," she murmurs, her lips very close to my lips.

I sigh. "You always know exactly what to say to calm me down."

She steps back and smiles. "Don't worry, Bubble. I'm not letting this go. I was born to win this competition."

"We both were," I correct her.

"Exactly."

We begin our warm-up hit, which I always enjoy. It is hard to deny how great Edie looks in a tennis skirt. She has very long, very slender legs and arms. They are also the most beautiful natural tan color, like she just spent the summer on a yacht, although without the horrible moles and freckles she'd have if she *actually* spent the summer on a yacht.

At five o'clock Gillian and Tania, our practice partners, arrive. G&T (as we call them) made the second round of the US Open Juniors three years ago. They tone their game down a bit for us, but not much.

Today, though, I'm not in my best form. I keep thinking about Bianca Stein. What rotten luck that St. Margaret's has drawn a trump card the year Edie and I are finally ranked first!

It isn't the only thought keeping me from driving home my backhands. I found out today that Coach Hadley has not returned from Easter break. The school must have suspended him to investigate the cartoon's allegations of harassment.

I keep going back and forth in my mind how I feel about it. On the one hand, I feel sick that I have potentially ruined the career of a well-loved teacher. Without Coach Hadley's encouragement and support, I would never have become one of the school's highest-profile athletes. On the other hand, considering his behavior at times, I feel it is right that Rosemead has suspended him. It is the proper course to take.

"You weren't playing your best tennis today," Edie says with a sour look when we come off the court.

"I'm sorry. This Bianca Stein news has really thrown me for a loop."

Edie begins toweling herself down. "The mind game is half the battle, Bubble. If you can't handle that, then she's already won."

I zip up my racket miserably.

"Hey," says Edie gently, drawing the towel around the back of her neck. "It's okay. You're in shock, that's all. How about you come round to my place tonight and we can...debrief?" Holding my gaze, she presses the towel down the front of her T-shirt and across.

"I'd love to," I say, fumbling with the lid of my ball canister. "But I can't. I know Tuesday is our night, but I promised Arthur I'd go with him to see a movie. His band members have canceled practice because of some concert they have tickets to, and he's still down about this girl who dumped him. Could we reschedule?"

"Oh," says Edie, scrunching her towel into a tight ball.

There is nothing I hate more than upsetting Edie. I obviously haven't given her a clear enough picture of the situation. "I really would love to, but Arthur is a mess. I've never seen him like this before."

"Really, that's fine." Edie shoves the towel into her bag. "I just thought. Given it's been a while since we've spent time together." The bag lands on her shoulder with a thud. She starts striding toward the gate.

"I thought you'd be preparing for your public speaking competition," I call out.

Edie turns around slowly.

"I thought tomorrow night, when it's over..."

"The thing is," Edie says, walking back again. "Now that you've mentioned it, I could use your help with my SpeakOut prep."

This is a surprise. "But what about the ideas I already gave you?"

"They were great, really great," says Edie, suddenly enthusiastic. "I just need a bit of help fleshing them out, that's all. You know, like you've done before."

I blink. "You mean the debate card thing?"

"Exactly!"

The "debate card thing" I do for Edie is to set out each of the speech points on separate numbered cards. Beneath each point I write a list of subpoints that she can use to expand upon her main point. It is a heck of a lot of work, but it helps her tremendously.

I think about Arthur. He really is grieving over this girl. Last night I found him watching *Beauty and the Beast*, and he is strictly a horror movie man. That's when I decided to take him to the Wes Craven retrospective at the Verona. I know how much he is looking forward to it.

Edie looks at me hopefully. She has put her hair up in a loose bun and strands are playing about her ears. "Come on," she urges. "You're my lucky charm, you know."

She is so sweet. I was late to practice and played so badly. I have to make it up to her. Besides, what kind of a person says no when her girlfriend needs her help?

"Let me see if I can catch Arthur before he leaves the house," I say, pulling out my phone.

"Thanks, Bubble, I knew you'd come through." She begins jogging backward to the gate. "Meet you at the Lexus."

※ ※ ※

Arthur answers on the second ring. "You're canceling, aren't you?"

His voice, sounding terribly far away, echoes down the line. "Where are you?" I ask.

"Where are *you*?"

"At the courts. I'm about to leave."

"To meet me at the movies?"

"Oh, Arthur, I'm sorry. No. Are you in the kitchen? Is that why the sound is so hollow?"

"The bathroom."

"What are you doing in there?"

There is a pause. "Having a bath?"

Arthur only ever showers. In a flash I see him lying there, his head lolling against the porcelain, a razor floating in the water, blood running from his arms. "Do I need to call an ambulance?"

"What? No!" He laughs. "I'm not actually in the bath."

"Then what are you doing?"

"You don't want to know, Harri, believe me. Why aren't we going to the movies?"

I pause guiltily. "Something's come up."

"I see." He sounds very unimpressed.

"We could always go tomorrow," I venture.

"You mean tomorrow as in I'm-getting-two-teeth-wrenched-out-of-my-head tomorrow?"

Oh dear. I had forgotten about Arthur's teeth. Our father has diagnosed a crowded mouth and is pulling them himself. Arthur will be spending the night on the couch with an ice-pack strapped to his head. "Then can I cheer you up sometime on Saturday?"

My brother grunts. "I don't know. Do you think you'll be able to slot me in?" he says sarcastically.

"Come off it, Arthur," I say, irritated. "I've never known you to be in such a mood. This Candice girl wasn't all *that*, you know."

"*Sorry.*" He is clearly far from it. "How could I forget? How could *anyone, ever,* be as perfect as Edie?"

"Oh, Arthur."

"You're not writing another speech for her, are you? One where you give her all the material and she takes all the credit? I knew it was a bad idea for you to give up debate."

"What's that got to do with anything?"

Arthur sighs. "You gave it up so you could focus on tennis. Whereas Edie gets to do well at tennis *and* her public speaking because she makes you do all the work."

I clear my throat. "Look, I know you're very miserable, but it's no reason to lash out at Edie or me. I'm just trying to help. Anyway, tennis isn't the only reason I gave up debate. I'm also chair of the Formal Committee. It's a big responsibility. There is a venue to organize, not to mention tables, music, catering…Arthur? Are you still there?"

At Arthur's end something has been draped across the receiver. I hear the muffled sound of flushing water. A second later my brother is back on the line.

"I think I missed most of that," he says.

"I was just saying—oh, never mind. Come on. Please say yes to Saturday."

"All right," he grumbles.

"Good, then." I recover my jovial voice. "If you see Mum or Dad, tell them I'll be home around eleven."

"Since when do they care whether we're home or not?"

"Just tell them anyway."

We hang up. I walk quickly toward the car park. I don't want to keep Edie waiting. She gets in such a bad mood when she has to wait.

chapter 9

WILL

It's Sunday night. Mum is on the couch watching the news, trying to pretend she doesn't have a date. I know she has a date because she has her bathrobe on, which she only wears for two reasons: when she's about to have an actual bath (which happens roughly three times a year; showers are more her thing) and when she's pretending she doesn't have a date.

Before a date, my mother swans about doing ordinary things like watching the news or picking dust off chair legs or repairing wall cavities with polyfiller. Sometimes she'll even make the two of us an early dinner and mime eating it in front of me, chopping things up with her knife and fork, prodding food around the plate, and making "mmm" noises. Then surprise, surprise, the doorbell will ring, and she'll drop the bathrobe to reveal a glamorous outfit while slipping into a pair of three-inch heels.

"I'm just off to a movie with Jen," she'll call from the hallway, blocking my view of the open door.

Jen is her sister. Who hates movies.

"Hi, Graham," I'll call out.

"Um. Hi, Will," Graham, on the doorstep, will call back.

The whole masquerade has become its own pathetic ritual. I flop onto the couch beside her. "Nice bathrobe."

"Don't you have homework to do?"

"I'm doing so well my teachers gave me the weekend off."

"So you've finished your major work as well, I take it? I'd love to see it."

"I'm just waiting for the paint to dry. It'll be ready in an hour. You'll be around then to look at it, won't you?"

Mum is silent.

I victory punch a cushion.

Don't think I'm blind to the fact that Mum's whole no-date masquerade is entirely for my benefit. I get that it's related to the first time Graham picked her up for dinner and I threw a frying pan in the vicinity of his leg. I wasn't aiming to hit him. I am not a monster. I was just a bit reckless in letting the frying pan slip out of my hand while pirouetting on the linoleum.

Mum slides a piece of paper off the side table. "Do you know anything about this? It came in the mail from the school." She holds it up.

I glance at it. "Looks like an invitation to another fund-raising night," I say. "What is it this time? A two-hundred-dollar-a-ticket karaoke night to raise money for another state-of-the-art science lab? Or a three-hundred-dollar-a-ticket medieval paintball weekend to buy Rosemead a fleet of racing yachts?"

"A cabaret-themed dinner," Mum says. "For another swimming pool, it says here. You know, I wouldn't mind going to at least one of these things before you leave school, if only to see what they're like." She sounds wistful.

I level a stare at her. "Except you'd need to sell a kidney to afford it. Seriously, Mum. You pay enough in fees as it is."

Mum sighs and folds up the flyer. We turn back to the news.

The evening bulletin is full of tragedy, as usual. New South Wales has lost the State of Origin in rugby again. A federal politician has been caught emerging from a sex club. A breakfast television host has worn a revealing dress to an awards ceremony.

After those headlines the real news starts. There's a report on the aftermath of a recent earthquake in Nepal, with shots of flattened villages and teeming hospitals. Apparently foreign aid has been slow to arrive. First world governments are such jerks.

If that wasn't cheery enough, the latest plane crash story comes on. This one's been running for over a week now. They show the footage of the crash scene again: a rescue worker picking up a cabin bag from the rubble and dusting it off to reveal a Disney character, a close-up of a dead passenger's passport open to the photo page.

It's the passport photo that brings home the human tragedy and makes my tongue turn as dry as chalk.

The head shot stares out grimly as if she knew all along what would happen. *You think your life is the worst? Think again,* says her face.

My heart starts up a crazy beat.

"You don't need to watch this." Mum looks worried.

"It's not as if it didn't happen just because I'm not watching," I say, swallowing.

"But maybe you'll think about it less."

"It's research. It's the topic of my major work."

"You mean the one you finished tonight and therefore no longer need to research?" She readjusts her robe with a small smile, like the one she gets when she beats me at canasta.

As the news story cuts to a scene of distressed relatives crying at an airport, the phone rings in the kitchen. "Why don't you answer that? It could be Nat." Mum prods my arm when I don't respond.

"Maybe it's Graham calling to say he'll be late."

"Late for what?"

You have to admire her commitment to the ruse. I stand up and walk to the phone.

"How are you, Will?" says my father down the line.

Damn. "Couldn't be better."

Dad laughs in an overly cheery way. "That bad, huh? It's horrible to hear your voice."

"It's fabulous to hear yours."

The worst thing about these calls is how upbeat Dad is. I prefer the way he was before he left us for Naomi: suavely dismissive with a misanthropic edge. Pre-Naomi, Dad loved nothing more than ripping to shreds the latest exhibition of some poor emerging artist over a bottle of Scotch.

"How are you doing at that school your mother insisted she spend all her life savings to send you to?"

Dad hates Rosemead almost as much as I do. It's been a long-standing theme in arguments between my parents, even before they split. Mum's position is that schools like Rosemead guarantee a good education and opportunities, whereas Dad has always said they're a waste of money and breed a "dangerous elitism."

Whenever they used to have this argument, I wholeheartedly agreed with him. I still do. But then Perth happened, and I fell out with Dad, and leaving my old school for Rosemead after year nine like Mum wanted suddenly seemed like a good option. It was a way of getting back at Dad, for starters. If I'm honest, it was a way of solving some other problems I was having, too.

"Oh, you know. Topping all the classes. Winning all the awards. Same old," I tell Dad.

He pauses. "And on the friend front?"

I clear my throat. "Couldn't be better. Just last week I won the Most Popular Kid in Class trophy. Matter of fact, I'm polishing it up right now." I make a noise like I'm hocking a ball of spit into a handkerchief.

"Look, I was thinking about something that would really suck," Dad says.

"Breastfeeding babies really suck. Was that what you were thinking about?"

"What would you say about a visit to Perth next month?"

"At what point between me being born and you moving to Perth did you forget everything about me?" I say, and hang up.

Okay, I don't hang up. I *want* to hang up. However, hearing Dad's breath on the line, with its echo of desperate cheeriness,

I can't quite bring myself to do it. But I don't say anything for a really long time, and it's a very uncomfortable silence.

Instead I wait for Dad to say something else. He doesn't say anything. He's still there, though. There, in Perth. Not here in our microscopic unit, where the shelf above the fridge holds his half-empty Johnnie Walker bottle even though he's never lived here and where his Woody Allen movies are lined up in their anniversary box set on the bookshelf.

The box set makes me think of something.

"Hey, Dad?"

"No, Will?"

"Remember that movie you made me watch the year before last, the one about the guy who finds out his whole life is a hoax?"

"I forget it in vivid detail."

"Do you know any movies that work the other way around?"

The doorbell rings. Mum squeezes past me to grab her purse from the kitchen counter. Her bathrobe is off, revealing a green dress I've never seen before, which she's matched with a pair of extremely high platforms. I put a hand to my mouth in a performance of acute surprise. She squeezes back, blowing silent kisses in my direction, then pulls the front door closed behind her.

"Movies that work the other way around? I'm not sure what you mean."

"A movie where it's not the world that's the hoax, it's the person who's the hoax."

"A movie about a person who isn't real?"

"That's it."

Dad breathes into the phone. "What about *Victor Victoria*? Julie Andrews pretends to be a man to land a gig as a female impersonator."

He isn't getting it. "I'm talking about films with characters that don't actually *exist*."

"I can't think of any films, but remember Mr. Snuffleupagus from *Sesame Street*?"

I snort. "Is that all you've got?"

Dad pauses. "Have I ever told you about Nat Tate?"

"I don't think so."

At the other end of the line I hear a fridge door open and the rattle of an ice tray. "Nat Tate was an American abstract expressionist who committed suicide by jumping off the Staten Island ferry," says Dad. "Only he wasn't. And he didn't."

"Huh?"

Ice hits the bottom of a glass. "He was pure fiction." The fake cheeriness is gone; he's genuinely happy now that he's managed to shift the conversation from film to visual art. "Nat Tate never actually existed. David Bowie—you know, who sang 'Space Oddity'?"

"The 'Ground Control to Major Tom' song that was on your fortieth birthday party playlist?"

"That's the one. Bowie and a British author called William Boyd made Tate up. They published his biography in the late nineties and fooled the New York art world into believing he was an actual artist. They had quotes from famous people who claimed to have met him, reproductions of his surviving paintings, even photographs of him and his family."

"Where did they get all that stuff?"

I hear the sound of a drink being poured. "Boyd did the paintings—they were pretty terrible—and he used anonymous photos he'd found in junk shops for the family photos. He and Bowie asked famous people they were friends with to make up quotes about him, too."

"Which meant telling them about the hoax, I suppose?"

"Exactly. It was their big mistake. They let a few too many people, including a journalist friend of theirs, in on the game. The journalist published a scoop about the truth behind Nat Tate just a week after the biography came out." Ice clinks against the glass again. "Game over." Dad's lips make a smacking sound. "Shame, really. They could have kept the hoax going for a lot longer if they'd kept it to themselves."

"The moral of the story, then," I say slowly, "is to never trust a fine-arts journalist. Got it."

"Ha, ha. So what do you say, kiddo?" says Dad. "You, me, the Swan River? I could book your flight right now."

"I'm busy that weekend."

"But we haven't even talked dates yet!"

"I'm busy every weekend this year. Mum's just made dinner. Gotta go."

❊ ❊ ❊

Walking into school on Monday, I discover, to my great misfortune, that Principal Croon is back from Japan. I'm tossing an apple core into the nearest trash can as she rounds a corner. Unfortunately, I miss.

She stops in front of me.

Here's the thing about our principal: You know she's the devil incarnate, but when you're taking in her silk shirt and sheer stockings and breathing in her French perfume, you get sucked into an alternate universe where all you want to do is please her.

"Wilhelmina Everhart."

"Oh! I didn't see you there. How's it going, Principal Croon?" I say, glancing between the apple core splattered on the floor and her impeccable teeth.

She flashes me a blinding smile. "The trash cans are strategically placed to ensure we can find one when we need one," she says, holding my gaze with the steel of a thousand girders. "We therefore have no excuse for tossing rubbish up and down the corridor, do we?"

I blink. Like the synchronized proclamations of a Greek chorus, Croon's words are always a kind of hypnosis.

She taps her foot.

"No, of course not." I pick up the apple core.

"I had a conversation with Miss Fowler about you recently."

"You did?"

"We need to talk about your recent English marks. Say Wednesday? Come to my office at lunchtime." She dazzles me with her smile again and moves away down the corridor.

* * *

The second lot of crap descends just before the prelunch announcements finish. That's when I become aware of a mad rush in the corridor outside our math class. I spot Duncan rushing past the door wearing a crazed expression. Judging by the number of girls running after him, could aggressive facial acne and extreme nearsightedness have been declared a lethal combination by *GQ* magazine? Has Duncan become the sexiest man alive?

Nat sets me straight at lunch. "I organized a few strategic leaks late last week to inform the public we were publishing another Amelia Westlake cartoon today," she murmurs as we walk out of the cafeteria. "People have been lining up in front of the newsstands all morning. As they should be. The new cartoon is fantastic."

"Really?" I say, careful to conceal my pleasure. "What's it about?"

"Fowler's unfair marking practices. Seriously, Will, you should see it." Nat's eyes give an almost invisible twinkle, like someone's dropped a teeny-tiny sequin onto her retina. Then the sequin slips out, the twinkle disappears, and her expression turns dark. "But you can't."

"Why not?" I ask. "Didn't you just say it's in the latest *Messenger*?"

"It *was*," Nat sighs. "We had to pull it at the last minute. When Duncan distributed the paper before lunch and people found out the cartoon wasn't in it, they went feral. Everyone's been rioting, basically, since noon."

My heart speeds up. "Why did you pull it? Has Croon come to see you?"

"Not yet," Nat says grimly. "Come to the newsroom and I'll show you why."

We have to push through a crowd to get to the door. Duncan stands on the other side of it, peering through the mottled glass. "Back off, everybody," shouts Nat, causing the crowd to scatter instantly. She barges through the door, jamming Duncan between it and the bookshelf. "Give us a minute, will you, Duncan?"

Duncan edges his way out. The door clicks shut.

"Fancy that," Nat says, one eyebrow raised. "You and me in a locked room. Whatever will we do with ourselves?"

I grin and reach for her.

"Mmm," she murmurs as our lips meet. "Easter in Hanoi with the relatives was fun, but not as fun as this."

From the other side of the door I hear a shriek. I try to ignore it and focus on kissing Nat. She sucks at my neck. I grab a handful of her hair.

There's another shriek.

"I think he's getting mauled out there," I murmur.

Nat takes her mouth off my neck. "Should we let him in again?"

I shrug. "Maybe we should."

"I mean, only if you're sure," she adds, looking at me carefully.

An uncomfortable feeling has crept into my chest, just like the last time we kissed. "It *is* kind of hard to concentrate with all that racket," I say uneasily.

"Agreed," Nat says quickly. She shoots me a grin and I relax.

Nat grabs the door handle and tries to turn it. "Goddamn door's jammed again. DUNCAN. YOU CAN COME INSIDE."

The door crashes open and Duncan reappears, his hair

pointing in multiple directions. He closes it, steps forward, and trips over a pile of old editions.

"You guys need to seriously consider going digital," I say.

Nat rattles the mouse beside her computer. The screen lights up. "Speaking of digital, this is what I wanted to show you, Will."

I peer over her shoulder. "What the fuck?" I cry.

On the screen is an Instagram feed. The profile picture is a silhouette of a girl, the creepy kind they use in current affairs programs when they're not allowed to show the person's face for legal reasons.

Amelia Westlake, says the name beneath the picture. Beneath that, *Sydney schoolgirl*.

"Duncan found it last night." Nat gives him an aggressive nudge. "It's pretty suspect, wouldn't you say? Just the one photo and that bio. She's not following anyone. And she has no followers, either. What kind of actual living, breathing human doesn't have a single follower? Doesn't this Amelia Westlake have any friends? Or, barring friends, any random acquaintances who would follow her just to improve their own follow count? Even Duncan has some of those, don't you, Duncan?"

Duncan's ears turn pink.

"Seriously. The picture screams 'fake person.' But"—and here Nat does her fingers-on-chin-investigative-journalist impression—"this isn't enough evidence on its own to prove Amelia Westlake isn't real."

Nat strolls over to her whiteboard, which is not so much white as a kind of moody grey marbled with flecks of green from all the times she's accidentally used permanent marker on it. She writes

Possibility #1
AW is a real person with an Instagram account but no friends.

Possibility #2
AW is a real person who has no Instagram account, and an entirely different person has created a fake account for AW for the sole purpose of screwing with my head.

Possibility #3
AW is a fake person who never existed and never had any friends and has created a fake account using a fake picture for her fake, fake self.

"My money's on number two," I say.

"That's what I love about you, Will. Your sense of humor."

"I'm serious. What kind of a pseudonym is Amelia Westlake?"

At the same time as these words are coming out of my mouth, I'm trying to work out who has done this. Given the interest Amelia Westlake has attracted, it could be anyone. The most likely candidate, though, is Harriet. I understand why she'd be tempted—only this morning I thought it would be fun to scrawl some Amelia Westlake–themed graffiti in one of the toilet stalls. I also, on a whim, signed Amelia up for the year-twelve tetherball club and the Formal Committee. But creating a social media page for her? That's like getting a billboard erected outside Nat's bedroom window that says, AMELIA WESTLAKE IS A PSEUDONYM, and then adding neon lights to make the word "pseudonym" flash against her closed eyelids all night, and then coming into her room and writing the word "pseudonym" all over the walls and on the carpet and backward across her forehead so that when she looks in the mirror in the morning the first thing she sees is the word "pseudonym."

"I wish you were right, Will. No one wants her to be a real person more than me. I want to publish her cartoons in every edition until the end of time. But if Amelia Westlake isn't real and Croon finds out that I knew she was a fake and kept publishing her, she'll have the perfect excuse to dump me as editor. Which means no journalism job for me once school is finished. And the simple fact is that Amelia Westlake doesn't exist." Nat wrenches opens her bottom drawer and pulls out a manila folder. The cover is blank, but the way she slaps it on the desk and flips it open with the lightest of touches means it might as well be labeled KEY EVIDENCE TO BLOW OPEN THE CASE. "Duncan did a bit of digging on the staff intranet, didn't you, Duncan?"

Duncan nods. His face, apart from the tips of his pimples, changes from pink to dark crimson.

"It took him a while to work out the password, but after trying RosemeadStaff1 and RosemeadStaff2, he cracked it with RosemeadStaff3. These pages"—she thumbs through them—"are the rolls for every single class in the school. There's an Amelia al-Assad and an Amelia Prior. There's even an Annabelle Eastman. But nowhere—and I've read each roll twice now—can I find an Amelia Westlake. Which means..."

"The rolls are out of date?" I offer, thinking fast. "Or incomplete? Someone's lied about their name to the school's administration? Amelia Westlake is in a witness protection program? There's been a spelling error? The system's broken? We've got to fix the system?"

"We've definitely got to fix the system," says Nat. "And I'm going to fix the hell out of whoever's behind these cartoons for trying to pull one over on me." Her words are sharp with fury. "Believe me, Will, it's way too risky for me to keep accepting these cartoons. Amelia Westlake's publishing days are over."

chapter 10

HARRIET

As a general rule, I enjoy the bathrooms at Rosemead. The toilet paper is always well stocked, as are the supplies of perfumed soaps and hand creams at the sinks. A small wall-mounted machine emits pleasant scents into the air—mountain breeze, baking bread, or new car. The whole aesthetic is so agreeable that I sometimes forget I'm in a school toilet and not in one of our en suites at home.

So you can imagine my surprise when on the very day our fourth cartoon is supposed to be published, I enter a bathroom cubicle and find *Amelia Westlake woz here—or woz she???* scrawled on the back of the bathroom door in what looks suspiciously like black art pen.

A sudden thrill goes down my spine, quickly overwhelmed by a firmer, more reliable sense of indignation. Who would be perverse enough to vandalize school property using that name?

It is a rhetorical question; given the precise brand of humor on display, I already know it was Will.

Taking out my nail-polish remover, I quickly scrub off the graffiti. I have five minutes until math, so I hurry to the year-twelve common room to check on the volunteer list for the Formal Committee. We already have a core membership, but a few extras wouldn't hurt. Then we can get started with the preparations, which I am incredibly excited about.

I was elected chair of the committee in February, but organizing our year-twelve formal, which takes place in September, is something I have basically been doing on a pro bono basis for years. Every time I see an innovative table setting in a magazine I cut it out to add to my collection. I have a list of top venues, which the committee recently narrowed down to one: a haute cuisine restaurant at Circular Quay, called Dish. I cannot wait to hit the dance floor with Edie—she has learned ballroom dancing and has some really terrific moves.

On my way to the common room I hear the sound of familiar heels behind me in the corridor.

"Hello, Harriet." Principal Croon is beaming. "How lovely to run into you."

"Principal Croon!" What a pleasure it is to see her! Is that shirt made from kimono silk? The woman's taste is flawless. "I didn't realize you had returned! How was Japan?"

"Simply wonderful," she says gravely. "The cherry blossoms at this time of year..." She sighs luxuriantly. "And how is the Tawney training coming along?"

Her mention of Tawney training makes me think of the Sports Department, which makes me think of Coach Hadley. I consider asking Principal Croon about his suspension, but decide not to. Now that she is back, she will announce it soon enough. "On track, I'm pleased to report," I tell her.

"Keep up the good work." She briefly places a hand on my shoulder before continuing down the corridor.

I am still basking in the warmth of this encounter when I reach the common room. Beth is at the kitchen counter, stirring chocolate powder into a full glass of milk. "Hey, lover," she greets me, bending over to take a sip without moving the glass from the counter.

"Hi, Beth."

She laughs and chokes on her drink and coughs, and a cloud of chocolate comes out of her mouth like a speech bubble.

"What's funny?"

"Oh, nothing," says Beth, wiping her lips. "I just realized I called you lover, that's all."

"You call everyone lover. It's your new thing."

"Ye-es," says Beth, stirring her drink, looking at me with low-level amusement, the way she might look at someone with food in their teeth or a grossly deformed nose. Beth is so good at deadpan humor. "But with you it's not as, you know, wacky."

"Why not?"

"Because you're a lesbian, stupid." Beth picks up her glass. "Hey, I wanted to ask you something. You know James, that friend of your brother's? The dreamy one with blue eyes who plays the keyboard in their band?"

"Of course."

"He's in year twelve at Edwin Street, isn't he?"

"I believe so."

"Does he have a girlfriend?"

I frown. "Not that I'm aware of. But then I wouldn't really know. Arthur and I don't talk all that much about his friends' romantic pursuits."

"Could you make some inquiries? I was thinking of inviting him to our formal."

"All right. I'll talk to Arthur." I walk past her to the noticeboard.

There are only two new names on the Formal Committee volunteer list. Liz Newcomb is one. Amelia Westlake is the other.

This isn't good at all.

✳ ✳ ✳

I find Will Everhart midway through lunch exactly where I expect to find her: coming out of the *Messenger* newsroom. When she sees me, her face sort of spasms, as if it is spinning through a giant carnival wheel of emotions and doesn't know where to land. Horror, doubt, anxiety, suspicion, and anger—all of them flicker past. Unless I'm mistaken, there is also briefly something in the neighborhood of pleased, but within seconds the carnival-wheel needle has caught on vitriolic outrage, and I find myself firmly attached to Will Everhart's hand, being towed down the hallway at a threatening speed.

"Are you *out of your mind?*"

"I'm not the person abducting someone in broad daylight," I say, breathless.

"We need to talk."

"We certainly do. I've just been to the bathroom!"

"You're telling me this because?"

"Because of what's written there!" I am not going to let her pretend she doesn't know. "Not to mention what's written on the list of Formal Committee volunteers! And you'll never guess who just signed up for tetherball."

I expect some remorse, a small shrug of acknowledgment at the very least, but instead Will Everhart's outrage seems to balloon. "What a coincidence," she says. "You'll never guess whose Instagram profile Nat Nguyen was just showing me."

I get a constricted feeling in my chest and regret eating boiled eggs for lunch; they may be high in protein and amino acids but they always give me indigestion.

Will's grip on my hand tightens. Is that a fresh love bite on her neck? Has she somehow smuggled her groovy older boyfriend onto campus? I wouldn't put it past her.

"At least tell me where you're taking me," I gasp.

"As far away from the newsroom as possible."

We are at the edge of the second oval, and in front of us the pathway forks. If we follow Cassowary Path to the left, we'll end up at the gymnasium. Bronte Path, to the right, takes us to the Performing Arts Center.

Will turns right.

When we reach the PAC, instead of heading up the ramp to the front entrance, Will swerves to the side and follows a path I've never noticed before, which takes us down some steps and between the pillars at the base of the building. We go around the side until we come upon a door. Will presses the keypad beside it. I hear a click. She leans against the door and it opens.

Inside is a narrow room, about the size of my walk-in wardrobe. One wall is lined with shelves. On the bottom shelf is a neatly folded pile of clothes—an embroidered cavalry jacket and vest, as well as pants and a shirt—presumably a costume left over from one of Rosemead's annual musicals. Otherwise, the shelves are empty. At the far end, beneath a row of windows and streaked with sunlight, is a stack of padded chairs, like the ones populating the PAC foyer.

How perfect for an illicit rendezvous. Is this where Will brings her boyfriend? She lifts two of the chairs off the stack and places them facing each other on the carpet.

Of course. This is probably what she does with him. They probably put the chairs together, lie down together, and...

But enough of these completely irrelevant thoughts. God, my collar feels tight all of a sudden. I undo the top button of my shirt.

"What is this place?" I ask.

"One of the PAC storerooms," says Will. "Not that they're using it to store anything right now. They shifted everything out about two weeks ago."

I gaze around. "How do you know the door code?"

"I watched Mr. Tipper plug it in one time." She sits down on one of the chairs. Her eyes become slits. "You don't know who Mr. Tipper is, do you?"

I rack my brain. Tipper, sounds like "clipper." An image comes to me of a sailing ship. I wonder if he is a boatswain of some sort?

"Of course you don't. He's the janitor." Will gives me a scathing look.

The intensity of her outrage sends a strange heat through my veins. It is vital that I change the topic at once. "You've heard about Coach Hadley's suspension, I expect."

Will's eyes widen. "They've suspended Hadley?"

I try, somewhat unsuccessfully, to tone down the triumph in my voice. "He hasn't been at school since Easter break."

Will looks thoughtful. "Of course, he could just be on extended holidays...." She meets my eye. "But if you're right about the suspension, it means Amelia Westlake really is getting the message across." She pauses to glower at me. "What a shame you've just sabotaged the whole project."

"What are you talking about?" I cry.

Will throws up a hand and slaps the air. "Nat is refusing to publish any more cartoons because she knows Amelia Westlake is a pseudonym because you posted that bloody Instagram profile." She is staring at me again like I committed armed robbery.

Her stare is making me deeply uncomfortable and short of breath, and undoing another button would be entirely inappropriate. So I attempt to appease her. "Okay. I made a mistake," I say. "But for God's sake. Your graffiti, Will? It practically announced Amelia Westlake is a hoax. *Amelia Westlake woz here—or woz she???* If Natasha had seen that before she saw the online profile, it would have taken her three seconds to work everything out. Might I also remind you that vandalism is against the school rules?"

She scoffs. "And publishing under a pseudonym isn't?"

I hesitate. "Fine. But signing up Amelia Westlake on those lists? Nominating her to play *tetherball*? Nobody wants to play tetherball!"

Will exhales a long sigh, which stretches out into silence.

"I'm sorry Natasha found the Instagram account. I really am," I say at last.

"I guess the whole Amelia Westlake project is over," says Will.

When I hear her declare this so casually, panic unexpectedly fills my throat. Amelia Westlake is potentially fraught and certainly extremely risky, but we are starting to see results. Hadley is possibly being pulled into line.

And then there is the unanticipated—indeed, surprising—success of our partnership. Will's and mine. Our *creative* partnership is what I mean, obviously. The breathless feeling returns. "Surely this is just a setback!"

Will shrugs in a defeatist manner. "It's a bastard, I agree. Just when everyone was starting to pay attention."

"We've got to be able to think of a way forward."

Will shrugs again.

"Think!" I cry.

"Okay, okay," she says irritably. She stares at the blank wall behind me and jiggles around on her chair. She pulls her legs to her chest. She stretches them out again. She picks at a stray thread. She slams the chair base with her heel. She sucks at her bottom lip, grabbing it with her teeth and pushing it out again slowly.

The room really is incredibly stuffy; are these storerooms even air-conditioned?

She is rocking to and fro now.

Clearly Will is getting nowhere fast. Luckily, an idea occurs to me. "Amelia Westlake doesn't have to publish cartoons, you know," I say.

"What are you talking about?"

I fold my hands in my lap. "She doesn't have to publish anything."

Her forehead creases. "I don't get it."

She really doesn't. She is looking at me as if I'm speaking in Swahili. "What I mean is, we can leave Natasha Nguyen out of it altogether," I explain. "It doesn't matter that people know Amelia Westlake isn't real. In fact, it will probably make them more interested."

"What are you suggesting we do instead of cartoons?"

"Amelia Westlake can make a point about Miss Fowler's marking practices in another way," I venture. "One that will hopefully have even more of an impact than a cartoon." I watch carefully for Will's reaction.

She studies me. "I'm listening."

I take a moment, remembering what got us into this trouble in the first place. "Before I tell you, I need to say something. If we're going to keep this Amelia Westlake project going, we need some ground rules."

Will groans and slides down in her chair. "Priceless, you are."

Like I haven't heard that one before. I forge on. "If we're doing this together, neither of us can engage in any Amelia-related activity without telling the other one first. That will stop both of us from going off on a frolic that inadvertently undermines the common goal."

She sits up again. "Fine. I can live with that. But if we're going to have rules, then I've got one, too. The enemy here is exposure. If anyone finds out we're behind Amelia Westlake, the project's dead. We're dead, too, probably. Croon is already on my case. And now that Nat's worked out Amelia's not a real person, she'll do everything she can to find out who's behind her. Which means you've got to stop approaching me outside the newsroom. We've got to pretend things between us are the same as they've always been."

"You mean, in public we need to continue to act toward each other with indifference verging on outright hostility?"

Will grins. "You should make jokes more often, Price."

I press a cool palm to my flaming cheek. Gosh, it is airless in here.

"No contact outside this room, okay?" Will says. "We meet here and nowhere else. I'll give you the room code. Other than to arrange a meeting, we don't talk, we don't text. We don't even look at each other. Got it?"

"Fine," I say, my heart pounding.

"Okay. So what's your great Fowler idea?"

chapter 11

WILL

Harriet may be a superior suck-up, but her idea is bloody brilliant. It makes me think of the time I saw one of Louise Bourgeois's massive bronze spider sculptures in person. I'd seen a picture of it in an art book, but the picture didn't do justice to the spider's awesome scale, its dizzying breadth and height.

It's the same with this: If our Fowler cartoon was the picture, Harriet's idea is the picture brought to spectacular life.

✳ ✳ ✳

After Duncan and Nat's discovery of Amelia Westlake's Instagram account, it takes less than a day for word to get out that Amelia Westlake isn't an actual person. When it does, interest in her explodes, just as Harriet predicted. I hear "Amelia

Westlake" mentioned in the corridors. She is a constant topic of conversation in the year-twelve common room. Amelia even makes her way into my art class the next morning when Mrs. Degarno is sick. When the substitute teacher asks our names so he can mark them off the roll, Janine Richter tells him that hers is Amelia Westlake, and the class cracks up.

Harriet checks Amelia Westlake's Instagram account on Wednesday and finds that she has more than a hundred followers. We arrange to meet in the PAC storeroom at lunchtime to work out what to do with our sudden popularity.

"Who are all these people?" I say, scrolling through their profile pics once we're settled in our chairs with the sunlight streaming in from the row of high windows.

"Most are from our year," Harriet says.

"If the page is getting this much interest, I think we need to make some changes," I tell her.

My first priority is to remove the creepy silhouette Harriet has used as a profile pic. I find an arty picture to replace it of a girl wearing an animal mask at a fancy dress ball. We post a bunch of other pictures of girls with their faces obscured—a girl with a paper bag over her head, a girl holding up a sign so that it blocks her features, a girl on a beach with her back to the camera.

Over the next few days, comments from Rosemead students pour in:

Nice paper bag, Amelia.

Is the animal mask a clue? Should we be looking for a cat person?

Does this mean Amelia has brown hair?
WHO ARE YOU???

∗ ∗ ∗

"Wilhelmina Everhart."

I'm sitting on a designer chair in Principal Croon's air-conditioned office for the chat about my marks that she insisted upon. Around me are the spoils of her reign: fancy furniture, framed photographs of pivotal moments in Rosemead history with Croon in the foreground, and on the sideboard a porcelain doll, presumably a gift from our Japanese sister school. Croon is behind her wide desk.

"With respect, Principal Croon, Miss Fowler undermarked my essay. I've brought it to show you...."

Croon waves the essay away. "I trust Miss Fowler's judgment in these matters. She is the literature expert, not me. Your marks are consistently poor, Wilhelmina, which is not what I was led to expect when we accepted your transfer two years ago."

"I don't know why my marks have dropped. I have honestly tried—"

Croon silences me with a shake of her head. "It's not just your marks I'm concerned about. They point to a broader malaise." She pauses. "There was that horrific history-of-war video project you produced that left your classmates traumatized."

"But war is by its very nature—"

"Not to mention the havoc you wreaked in poor Mrs. Lavender's food technology class," tuts Croon. "And need I remind you of the unauthorized refugee placard you erected on the Pacific Highway directly in front of campus?"

Of course I don't need reminding. It read BRING THEM HERE in meter-tall letters and took me a whole week to paint.

"Your enrollment was conditional on the cessation of this type of activity. It was the basis upon which we agreed to help you settle in. As I recall, your mother was adamant about your needing help with settling in. Wasn't she?"

I mumble incoherently.

"Sadly, the ways in which we can help you are limited if you are unwilling to help yourself," Croon says. "Given that you've clearly made no effort to change your behavior, it is frankly very difficult to see any advantage for you or Rosemead in keeping you enrolled."

I dig my fingernails into the underside of Croon's mahogany desk. *Advantage for Rosemead?* How about the hard-earned fortune in fees my mother is paying for starters?

"We have a very impressive year-twelve final average and marks like yours bring down the reputation of the school. The way I see it," Croon continues, massaging her fingers, "is you have two choices. One. You stop all this nonsense. You knuckle down, study hard, and improve your marks. Two." She thins her lips. "Rosemead bids you farewell."

I'm going through the motions of nodding numbly when I wake up to myself. This is an outrage. Croon is considering expelling me because I'm bad for Rosemead's bottom line. Never mind nurturing underperformers or encouraging independent thinking. If you can't rise to the top of the pile, and in a suitable manner, the school has no place for you.

I know she'd throw me out on the spot if I said any of this, so I grit my teeth and hold in the words. That's when something on the top of Croon's inbox catches my eye.

"Oh yes," says Croon, following my gaze. "I almost forgot the other matter I wanted to raise with you." Delicately, she lifts a copy of the *Messenger* out of the tray and hands it to me. "The cartoon on page three. I'm assuming it is your handiwork," she says. "Not to mention the others that have appeared since. I know from Miss Watson that you insulted Coach Hadley last term. And that you and Natasha Nguyen are close. Was this your idea of revenge, perhaps?" She fixes her gaze on me.

I gaze back just as steadily. Does Croon really think she can get a confession out of me that easily?

I shake my head. "Not mine."

"And what about the other cartoons?"

"Believe me, I'd love to claim responsibility," I say with fake disappointment. "Everyone knows Coach Hadley has a reputation."

Croon's nostrils flare ever so slightly. "I understand that Coach Hadley is very popular."

"With some girls, sure. But others find him to be somewhat of a, um, sleaze."

Something flickers behind the principal's eyes. "Well, I've had no complaints."

"Oh?" I swing one leg across the other. "I can think of three instances of inappropriate behavior off the top of my head."

Croon pushes back her chair and stands up. Clearly, this is my cue to leave.

"You know what I'd do if I were you, Principal Croon?" I

say, staying in my chair. "Get Nakita Wallis in to tell you what Hadley said to her. She'll tell you how last year he actually took her by the—"

Croon leans so far across the table that I can make out the impeccable condition of her nose cavities, and the smooth lines of her eyebrows. I wonder if she tints her eyelashes or whether they're naturally that color.

"As I said, Miss Everhart. You have two choices."

She holds the door open.

chapter 12

HARRIET

Will and I agree that the best time for me to execute our operation is during my free period on Thursday. I leave math as soon as the bell rings and duck into the bathroom for some quick affirmations, which I always find helpful during tremulous times.

"You are a winner!" I whisper to the mirror.

"You are a success!"

"You can do this, Harriet Gwendolyn Price!"

I am about to begin a couple of energizing breathing exercises when Kimberley Kitchener and Palmer Crichton walk in.

Kimberley skids to a stop in front of me. She has a notebook on a string around her neck. She flips the cover open. "Want to place a bet, Harriet?" she asks.

"What on earth are you talking about?"

Kimberley and Palmer exchange a sly glance. "Don't

worry," Palmer says. "It's all above board. We're just running a small gambling thing, that's all."

"On who's behind Amelia Westlake," Kimberley adds. "Odds are currently four dollars for Beth Tupman, eight dollars for Nakita Wallis, five dollars for Will Everhart...."

I press a shaky palm against a tile. "How many people have bet so far?"

"About half the year," says Palmer.

I am keenly aware that refusing might come across as suspicious. "Okay," I say. "I'll put my money on Nakita." I draw out a few dollars from my purse and hand them over.

Kimberley hands them to Palmer, who stuffs the money hastily into her bra.

"And what does Amelia Westlake get, when it's all over?" I ask.

Palmer laughs. "Whatever she wants. She's a total legend."

The two of them swing around and head out the bathroom door.

Fortified by this exchange, I walk swiftly to the east corridor, where the English classes are held.

When I arrive, Miss Fowler's advanced year-twelve students are making a very slow job of leaving the room. We have decided to target this class rather than Will's to reduce the chance of people connecting the activity to her. I am doubly pleased about this decision now that I know the odds Will currently holds in Kimberley and Palmer's sweep. This way she will also have an alibi, since I am carrying out the entire operation during the time she will be in legal studies with Natasha.

Will knows Miss Fowler's modus operandi, and I know

from Beth that her class has an essay due today. I pretend to be reading an educational poster as the class files past. I watch each student put her essay in a box by the door as they leave, just as Will said would happen. After the last girl files out, I walk casually past the doorway and glance inside.

Miss Fowler is tidying papers on her desk and thankfully doesn't see me. I wait half a minute more and walk past again. This time she is writing notes on the whiteboard.

Carpe diem, I think giddily. I reach an arm around, pick up the box full of essays, and walk calmly away with it down the corridor.

It is a five-minute walk from the east corridor to the PAC storeroom. I keep a steady pace even though my heart is racing. When I reach the storeroom, I enter the code Will gave me.

The room is empty. I shut the door, relief sweeping through me. So far, so good. I take the essays out of the box and divide them into two equal piles, consulting a list Will and I have worked on together using a class roll I managed to obtain from Ms. Bracken's office. In one pile are Miss Fowler's pets. In the other pile is everyone else.

On the front of each essay is a cover sheet. This is where students have written their student number to facilitate blind marking, a technique that requires each teacher to mark an essay before looking up which student correlates to which number. It is supposed to neutralize teacher bias.

"Blind marking my left foot," Will said when we talked about it. "You want to see the comments on my last essay? Here's one: 'Your arguments supporting Hamlet's misogyny are highly questionable, Wilhelmina. See me after class.'"

Although it makes me sick to think a teacher has failed to

respect the school's marking code, I hope Will is right. Our operation is premised on it.

I carefully remove the cover sheets from each essay, making sure I keep the ones from the first pile separate from the ones from the second pile. Then I staple the sheets that have come from the first pile to the front of the second pile of essays, and the sheets from the second pile of essays to the front of those in the first pile. I gather the essays into a single pile again, and go through the essays one by one writing *AW* in small print—so small you would never notice it unless you were looking for it—on the back of each cover sheet in the bottom right corner.

When I am finished, I put the essays in the box and walk back to the east corridor.

I peek through the open doorway into the classroom. Miss Fowler's next class is in progress. Her students are facing the front with their backs to the door. Like before, I wait for Miss Fowler to turn to write something on the whiteboard. Then I replace the box.

When I get back to the empty common room, I check that no one is watching before indulging in a tiny fist pump. The whole thing has taken a total of twenty minutes.

✳ ✳ ✳

Six days later, I overhear a conversation between Liz Newcomb and two of Miss Fowler's students, Inez Jurich and Daphne Chee. They are sitting on the couches in the common room, their legs up on the coffee table. This is a habit I find deeply unhygienic and would generally say something about, only I don't want to draw attention to my eavesdropping.

"So this morning Miss Fowler hands me back my essay, and I look at it and I'm like, this is so not my essay. It's got my student number on it but it's totally not mine," says Daphne.

"And I'm next to Daphne," says Inez, leaning toward Liz, "and it's the same for me! I wrote on traditional class distinctions in *Emma*, and the essay in front of me is on, I don't know, Mr. Knightley and understandings of manhood or something."

"That's crazy," says Liz. She is wearing her Tawney Shield uniform. Most people change out of their sports gear after lunchtime practice, but given the tennis captain badge emblazoned on the front of Liz's outfit, there are no prizes for guessing why she never does.

"Next thing we know," says Daphne, "everyone is calling out their essay topics and passing essays back and forth, and Miss Fowler is stalking around the room with no idea what's going on. And then Beth Tupman comes over to me because Miss Fowler's handed my essay back to her and hers back to me."

Liz rolls her eyes, and Inez grins. They seem to be implying they don't particularly like Beth, which is strange. Beth is one of the most popular girls in our year.

"So I get my essay back from Beth," says Daphne, "and it's got her student number on the front, but it's *my* essay. And I look through it and there are all these complimentary comments in the margins, like 'Bravo, Beth!' and 'Beautifully expressed, Beth!' and 'I love you like a daughter, Beth!' Okay, I made up that last one, but you get the picture. Anyway, I turn to the back page, and Miss Fowler's given the essay—*my* essay—eighty-five! I, like, *never* get eighty-five."

Liz whistles.

"And it's the same with me," says Inez excitedly. "I get my essay back from Eileen Sarmiento, who Miss Fowler is totally in love with because she's always regurgitating whatever comes out of Miss Fowler's mouth, and I have an eighty, which is at least twenty marks more than I've had for an essay all year."

"Wowsers," says Liz.

"And then there's a kind of wailing sound at the other end of the room where Beth is standing, and it turns out she got a seventy for *her* essay—the one that had my student number on it—which is actually a pretty good mark for me," Daphne says confidentially, "but for someone like Beth, who is used to high distinctions, it's like now she just wants to, you know, kill somebody."

"So who do you think did it?" Liz asks. "Who swapped the essays?"

Inez and Daphne look at each other.

"Oh, we know who did it," says Inez.

"You do?" Liz says.

"Uh-huh. Her initials are on the back of all the cover sheets."

"It was Amelia Westlake," says Daphne.

I resist another fist pump.

Liz smiles. "I'm starting to really like that girl."

⚹ ⚹ ⚹

The following day at the lockers I find Beth telling Millie the same story.

"It's a complete outrage! Eighty, okay. But seventy? I mean Binkie could get that mark, and he's a labradoodle. And dead."

"Have you heard about this, Harriet?" Millie asks.

I nod. I have no intention of lying to my friends. Not directly, anyway. "Inez and Daphne were talking about it yesterday."

"Isn't it appalling?" says Millie. "This could affect people's university entrance scores! It could mean the difference between getting into their first choice of degree or their second."

This is a horrifying thought. Just last week when we filled out the form, I put medicine down first and, on a whim, a bachelor of arts second. All I can say by way of explanation is that I am confident I'll get the marks I need for medicine, so my second option hardly seems relevant.

Millie looks at her watch and panic contorts her face. "Is it ten to two already? Coach Hadley will tear strips off me."

"He's back?" I ask, trying to conceal my shock.

Millie nods. "Since Tuesday. We spent half the lesson looking at his photos from Seoul. They had an Olympic reunion thing there. His wife and kids got to go, too. It sounded amazing."

I stand very still. I can hardly believe what I am hearing. There I was, imagining Coach Hadley was having some quiet time to reflect upon the thoughtlessness of his actions—alone in a room, perhaps, a dark room without any natural light—when in fact he has been living it up with his whole family in the sunshine overseas!

"World to Harriet," says Beth, waving a hand in front of my face.

"Sorry, were you saying something?"

"I was asking whether you've had a chance to talk to Arthur yet about You Know Who." She plays an imaginary keyboard with her fingers.

I am so distracted by the news about Coach that it takes me a second to work out what she is talking about. "James? Oh! No. Sorry, I forgot."

This isn't strictly true. It has occurred to me numerous times to ask Arthur about James and whether he might be available for an invitation to the formal from Beth, but something always stops me. "I'll ask tonight," I promise.

I open my locker, still thinking about Coach Hadley. So, he was never suspended. Quite the opposite, it appears.

"Seventy percent. It's unbelievable," I hear Beth mutter.

If he wasn't suspended, has Rosemead addressed the cartoon's concerns in any way at all?

I put a hand on my chest. *Breathe, Harriet.* Principal Croon is doubtless conducting an investigation behind the scenes. Innocent until proven guilty—isn't that the rule?

"The problem is teachers like Miss Fowler have so much power," Millie remarks. "It's like being in a concentration camp or something."

"Exactly," Beth says.

An idea occurs to me, something that—unlike our cartoon, apparently—is bound to result in an immediate response from the school. I draw my head out of my locker. "Why don't you get your parents to complain about what happened with your marks?"

At this suggestion, Millie grows enthusiastic. "You should

definitely do that. Or get your dad to write an article in his paper about it. Or I'll tell my dad to mention it in parliament."

Beth nods, thinking it through. "I should, shouldn't I? I can't just let this go. I'm one of Rosemead's top students!"

The two of them begin an intense discussion.

I gather my books.

chapter 13

WILL

You know how in crime shows the police pin up all the information they've collected about a murder victim and draw lines to connect them to possible suspects? On Thursday morning that's what Nat's whiteboard looks like, except the name that all the lines run from is not some murder victim's. It's Amelia Westlake.

"Everything I've heard suggests Fowler had no idea about the essay swap until it was too late," says Nat, pacing in front of the whiteboard. "Which means whoever Amelia Westlake is got her hands on the essays before Fowler marked them. But how?"

I haven't seen her this worked up since the *Messenger's* printing company raised its rates. "Maybe they broke into her office," I suggest.

Nat shakes her head. "Possible, but unlikely. She always keeps it locked."

Duncan comes in with a mug of coffee for Nat. She takes a sip. "Needs more milk." She hands it back. "Know what I was thinking?"

Duncan wrestles with the broken door latch and goes out again.

"What?"

"You know how whenever Fowler collects essays she gets us all to put them in a box by the door?"

"Yes."

"And how on Thursdays she's in that classroom with back-to-back classes the whole morning?"

I click my fingers as if something just occurred to me. "You think someone waited until class finished and then took off with the box?"

Nat nods. "Then swapped the essays, and replaced the box, all while she was in the room."

"Which means it probably happened in fourth period, when you and I were in legal studies," I say. "That was the only time between when the students handed in the essays and lunch, when Fowler would have collected the box."

"Exactly." Nat purses her mouth to indicate her high level of regard for my reasoning. "So anyone we can account for in fourth period I can cross off the list of potential suspects. And I'm pretty comfortable narrowing the focus to year-twelve students, given the whole thing was targeted at a year-twelve class. If we narrow it to Anglo students, we cut down the possibilities again."

"What makes you think Amelia Westlake is Anglo?" I say, surprised.

"It's obvious," says Nat. "Someone wanted to come up with a generic name that wouldn't be picked as fake. For Anglos, an Anglo name will always be what they consider generic."

I realize she's right. I never thought of using anything but. I doubt Harriet did, either.

"Unless..." Nat looks thoughtful. "Our year group is what? Seventy percent white? Seventy-five?"

"Around that. Why?"

"I'm just thinking. If it was *me* behind this hoax, I'd want to maximize the number of suspects." Nat nods to herself. "We need to keep the search broad."

I breathe a silent sigh of relief.

"Then again..."

Nat certainly knows how to keep me on my toes. "What is it?" I ask.

"Think about it," she says. "Fowler's marking practices are shocking, but you know what's worse about Rosemead's English Department than Fowler's marking practices, in my opinion?"

She doesn't wait for me to guess. "Its perverse obsession with the narrow and elitist Western literary canon," she says.

"I could be wrong, but didn't Amelia Westlake have a cartoon about that already?" I say, making an effort to sound uncertain.

Nat shakes her head. "The cartoon was about the under-representation of women writers on the syllabus," she says. "But that's only part of the problem. Would it hurt them to include some Walker or Adichie on our reading lists? Or, God forbid, some indigenous or Asian literature? Why didn't Amelia Westlake target Rosemead for its lack of cultural diversity? Ask Daphne, say, or Zara or Prisha, and they'll tell you how outrageous it is." She bites her lip. "No. The more I think about it, the more convinced I am that Amelia Westlake is white."

Damn her flawless logic.

"Names and identities—it's an interesting question, isn't it?" Nat muses. "I might even explore it in my sign-off this week."

By "sign-off" Nat means her editorial. Magazines usually print editorials at the front, and newspapers usually have them somewhere in the middle. Nat likes to print hers on the very back page of the *Messenger*—that way, she can end with a pithy conclusion that will stick in people's minds. "Think global, eat local," for example. Or, "Let's kill off live exports."

Nat jots down a few notes. She drops her pen. Her fingers flit across my back. "God, investigative journalism is such a turn-on," she says, a hand on my waist. I lean into her, but she stops and pulls back. "Actually, before we do this, there's something I need to talk to you about."

"Okay."

"Croon called me up to her office yesterday."

My stomach squeezes. "The cartoons?"

"Yep."

"I guess it was inevitable," I say carefully. "What did she say?"

Nat holds up her thumb and index finger so there's barely a gap between them. "That I am this close to losing my editing job for publishing a series of pseudonymous contributions. That unless I help her work out who was behind them, she'll take me off the paper." She grits her teeth. "And that she thinks it was you."

I focus on projecting a calmness I don't feel. "She told me the same thing. What did you say?"

"That I had no idea who Amelia Westlake was. And that if you were behind it, I'd know." She looks at me steadily. "I wasn't lying, was I, Will?"

"Of course not!" The false anger comes surprisingly easily. "She's looking for an excuse to get rid of me. Last time I saw her she basically threatened me with expulsion because my marks weren't up to scratch."

"I can't believe that woman," Nat growls. "Then again, maybe I can. That's exactly the kind of trick she'd pull. I'm sorry, Will." She looks embarrassed. "Of course you'd tell me if you were Amelia Westlake. Anyway, we were in legal studies together when the last prank happened. But you understand I needed to check. A lot is riding on this for me."

"Of course."

I breathe in. Croon is going to take Nat off the *Messenger* if she doesn't help her find Amelia Westlake. Knowing this, how can I keep our secret from Nat any longer? We've been such good friends for ages and now we're...

Actually, the truth is that I'm not exactly sure what we are to each other right now. I haven't told anyone about our kissing in the newsroom, and I don't think Nat has, either.

I'm definitely into girls. That's not the issue. I know that Nat is, too, as well as boys. Even so, I'm not sure how I feel about kissing her. Not that the precise nature of our relationship is relevant to the problem at hand. One thing is certain: Keeping Amelia Westlake a secret from Nat is unfair to her and could put her in the firing line with Croon.

I breathe out.

Then again, I can't admit anything yet. At least, not until I've discussed it with Harriet. I owe Harriet that much after promising I wouldn't say a word.

If only there was a way to confess to Nat and keep Harriet out of it. But how would I explain the essay swap happening at the same time I was in legal studies?

Even if I could work out a way not to implicate Harriet, confessing to Nat would mean the end of Amelia Westlake. Nat would make me promise to cease and desist. I know she would. She'd consider any further activity a further risk of exposure, and once Croon knew I was involved, she'd find a way to bring Nat down with me.

Thinking this through makes me realize that I'm not ready to give up on Amelia. Harriet and I are just getting started, and I know how invested Harriet is in this project. Even though my loyalty should be with Nat, the thought of disappointing Harriet kind of kills me. I don't know why. Honestly? Harriet could benefit from some exposure to disappointment. But it's a strong enough feeling to keep me quiet.

"Were you going to say something?" Nat asks.

"Oh. Just that I heard Hadley's back," I improvise. "Liz Newcomb mentioned it in math. Apparently he was on some Olympic reunion trip with his wife and kids."

"Barf," Nat says. She looks thoughtful. "You know what

really gets me? That Croon's so keen on finding out who drew that cartoon but not whether there's any truth behind the cartoon's claim. What she should really be doing is interviewing students about Hadley's behavior."

I agree, and reel off my usual list of gripes about the fascist state of Rosemead. Then Nat repeats her usual list, adding a few extras, so I come up with a couple of new ones to even the score.

"Now. Where were we?" She leans in to kiss me and I freeze.

Nat looks at me sideways. "Are you okay?"

"I think so. I just..."

"What is it?" Nat takes a step back. "Will, are you into this?" she asks. Her voice has changed.

"Of course!" I lean in again but she backs away.

"It's okay if you're not," she says. "I'd be fine about it. Really."

"But this is great," I say, mustering my enthusiasm.

Nat tilts her head. "Are you sure?"

I look at her. "Are *you* sure?" I ask.

She hesitates. "Of course," she says at last.

I wish I knew if she really was, but her face is a mask.

Is it my guilt about Amelia Westlake that's getting in the way of this thing between us? Or maybe the problem is the newsroom. It's where we always hook up, and it stinks of moldy sandwiches and dust. Not exactly the sexiest of venues. "Perhaps we should try doing this off campus some time?" I suggest on a whim.

Nat shrugs, smiling. "We could try that."

"Then I'll call you," I say in my most seductive voice, wiggling my eyebrows.

She cracks up and gives me a friendly shove. "Get out of here, Everhart."

chapter 14

HARRIET

At assembly on Tuesday I sit with Beth and Millie, as usual. In our prefect spots in the front row, Beth fills us in on the latest news about Miss Fowler.

"Making a complaint was a great idea, Harriet," she says. "When I texted Richard what happened"—Richard is her father—"he was so riled he marched up to the school on the spot." Her eyes are gleaming. "He demanded a meeting with Principal Croon, but apparently she was at some interschool principal love-fest, so he was stuck with Deputy Davids. Anyway, the Dep hauled Miss Fowler in while he was there and quizzed her about the whole thing."

"She did?" I feel a flutter of excitement. I have played Beth like a fiddle, which is somewhat disloyal, but it appears to have reaped worthwhile rewards.

Our conversation is interrupted by the start of assembly,

which always begins with a guest speaker. This week it is Tania Janice, an alumna of the school. She used to be a Covergirl model before marrying a Hollywood director whom she met at a bar. Tania is widely considered one of Rosemead's most successful graduates.

"So what's going to happen to Miss Fowler?" I ask Beth in a whisper when Tania has finished recounting her regular celebrity dinner guests.

"They're making her review her marking practices," Beth whispers back. "And she has to apologize to the class."

Success at last!

My feeling of well-being is cut short when I look up. Coach Hadley has come onstage. An image flashes on the screen above his head—the Olympic rings.

Beth groans. "Not this again."

"Has it been a year already?" Millie whispers.

Every year on Coach's birthday, the whole school watches a recording of his silver medal win. Principal Croon considers it motivational. Afterward, one of the teachers always gives a speech about the value of "hard work," "determination," and "putting your all" into things.

It is as though Will and I never published that cartoon. I wonder why Principal Croon's investigation is taking so long.

If, indeed, there is one.

What am I thinking? There must be. I suppose it takes a while to do a thorough job. Which is no doubt the reason we haven't yet heard anything.

After Miss Fowler gives the motivational part of the presentation, everyone immediately starts talking until we are interrupted by the sound of Deputy Davids coughing into the microphone. "Your attention again, girls, please." She clasps her hands across her chest. "Mouths closed and eyes to the front."

Slowly the room settles down.

"First, I have some wonderful, wonderful news," Deputy Davids says. She clears her throat loudly. "This morning, our senior science girls won the highly competitive National Schools Robotics Competition. A truly tremendous achievement. Mr. Buddy, the robot they built, will be on display in the library foyer this afternoon." Deputy Davids starts clapping vigorously into the microphone. A handful of students momentarily join in. "My second news item is far less positive, I'm afraid." Deputy Davids lowers her head. "It has been brought to my attention that there have been certain, shall we say, *goings-on* recently that have sought to undermine the authority of the staff." She gazes down from the stage, squinting. "Certain, shall we say, presumptuous, shall we say, *activities*, that have wreaked no small measure of chaos on the learning operations of our classrooms."

A murmur starts up across the hall. A throbbing begins to resonate behind my right eyeball.

Deputy Davids hacks into her sleeve. "To the person responsible for these goings-on, I have two things to say. One. If you have an issue with a teacher"—here she glances across at Coach Hadley and Miss Fowler, who are sitting together to the far right of the stage—"the proper thing is to raise it with that teacher or with the school directly. Two. Principal Croon and I have discussed this matter, and we will be watching the student body very closely for further inappropriate behavior. Very closely. You stand warned."

My eyeball feels like a balloon that's being squeezed.

"What was that all about, do you think?" Beth asks as we file out of assembly. Or at least I think it is Beth—it is difficult to tell because I have my hand across my pounding eye and am concentrating very hard on keeping my lunch down.

"Amelia Westlake, of course," Liz Newcomb says.

"The Dep was just making the point that it's better to raise things directly with the school. Like you did, Beth, through your father," says Millie.

"How good am I?" says Beth.

"The best," Millie tells her.

✳ ✳ ✳

That evening Edie has to cancel our planned date for the second week in a row, which is absolutely fine. I want to see her, of course. It seems like ages since I've spent quality time with my Number One Gal. But Edie has an essay due the following day, and I couldn't bear to be the reason for her underperformance. At any rate, I could use the time. Deputy Davids's speech has left me with a growing knot of panic in my gut.

I go home and get changed, unpinning my badges from the lapel of my blazer. I take out a cloth and the bottle of tarnish remover I keep in my bottom desk drawer. Carefully, I polish each one. When I have finished, I line up the badges on the desk and reattach them to my uniform.

There is something soothing about this ritual—feeling the weight of them, seeing the polished shine, pinning them back on the fabric so that they sit just right. I think of Bianca Stein from St. Margaret's beating Edie and me at Tawney. I thread my Tawney badge through my lapel, and it is like I've put a skewer through the thought. I pin on my house badge, thinking of Coach Hadley. Its symmetry and shine keep him at bay. I imagine Principal Croon discovering that Will and I are behind Amelia Westlake and press my school badge into my palm until it leaves an outline.

It is clear that if we are going to keep Amelia Westlake safe from discovery, we need to be especially careful about covering our tracks.

It begs the question, How *does* one cover one's tracks? Given I am basically a very honest, open person who has never had to conceal anything from anyone, I have no idea. I conduct an online search for clues and up pops an article about how to evade tracking dogs, which I initially dismiss as being off the point. But when I read on, I am fascinated to learn that dogs track humans by following the scent of the dead body cells that continuously fall from our skin. The only way to truly evade them is to enclose one's entire person in a hermetically sealed suit.

I sit back from the computer. After everything Will and I have done with Amelia, it is definitely too late for a hermetically sealed suit. With the cartoons, the online profile, the graffiti, the sign-up lists, and the initialed essay cover sheets, we've left our trace everywhere.

But what if there is another way?

Of course, I have promised Will I won't do anything Amelia-related without her agreement.

Then again, after that speech from Deputy Davids, we

need to act fast. And I can hardly check with Will before taking action when she has forbidden any contact. She has left me no choice but to continue without her okay.

This is why, in lieu of catching up with Edie over a Moroccan tagine and Persian love cake, I spend our date night littering Amelia Westlake's tracks with the dead body cells of as many other people as I can think of.

From: Ameli3.Westlake@gmail.com
To: Deedee.Chee@gmail.com

> Dear Daphne,
> Thank you for your kind invitation to your
> eighteenth birthday party at Catalina's. I accept with
> delight.
> Love, Amelia

(To the untrained eye this is a perfectly innocuous response. Therein lies its subtle beauty. Millie is renowned at Rosemead for "accepting with delight." I know therefore that Daphne will instantly suspect the email came from her.)

From: Ameli3.Westlake@gmail.com
To: Liz.Newcomb.0968@gmail.com

> Hi Liz,
> Today I saw your looking for sugestions about a
> theme for this years Junior School spelling bee.
> I really think it should be Outer Space, with an
> emphasis on human colinization.
> Cheers, Amelia

(This one suggests authorship by Janine Richter, known for recently entering the international lottery to be a part of the first human colony on Mars, and for being the worst speller on planet Earth.)

From: Ameli3.Westlake@gmail.com
To: Eileen.Sarmiento@optusnet.com
Dear Eileen,
Thanks for helping me stand up to Miss Fowler. I hope we can work together again, and be friends. My friends are my estate. Forgive me then the avarice to hoard them.
AW

(The quote from Emily Dickinson embedded in this email points the finger at Rosemead's star English student, Nakita Wallis, a well-known Dickinson diehard.)

☀ ☀ ☀

When I have sent off the emails, I text Edie to say I hope she's done well with her essay. Edie sends me a text back saying I am her lucky charm, and I respond with her favorite Shakespearean love sonnet. I wait ten minutes for a reply before texting her second-favorite Shakespearean love sonnet. After waiting another hour for a response I realize Edie is probably exhausted from all that hard thinking and has gone to bed, so I go to bed myself.

☀ ☀ ☀

At school the next day, I am shocked to hear from Beth that she saw Edie at Cafe Belladonna last night.

"Are you sure it was her?"

"I swear on Binkie's grave," Beth says, spooning the chunky bits of a Cup-a-Soup into her mouth. "No one else I've ever seen wears her ponytail that high. Plus, she was in tennis gear. Plus, the girl she was with was in tennis gear. According to Millie, it was that new girl from St. Mag's, Bianca Rind."

My heart goes cold. "You mean Bianca Stein?"

"That's her."

"You and Millie went to Belladonna without me?"

She shrugs. "We thought Tuesday was your date night with Edie."

I suppose she is right. I try very hard not to take their oversight personally.

My next class is history, and during the lesson I do something entirely in breach of school rules: I use my iPad to get online for a non-class-related purpose. An image search for St. Margaret's star player brings up a disturbing number of pictures of a girl in a tennis skirt wearing medals, holding silver plates, and wielding heavy-looking trophies.

I ring my girlfriend at lunch.

"Beth says she saw you at Belladonna last night."

"Keep your voice down, Bubble. There's no need to shout."

"And that you were with Bianca Stein. At the very time I was texting you to wish you luck with your essay."

"Sheesh, Harriet. I'm not deaf. You can say these things at an ordinary decibel level, and I will hear them just as clearly."

"Well, were you?"

"Of course I was, what do you think?" she says harshly.

"I—I don't know what to think! Which is why I'm calling!"

"I was getting the lowdown," she murmurs. "On whether she's playing the doubles at Tawney."

"Oh," I say, giddy with relief. "And is she?"

There is a pause. "She's considering it. She wanted to know if I could recommend any players who weren't partnered up yet. So I gave her a couple of bum steers. Nell Kee from Riverston, for example."

"Oh, Edie, you didn't." Nell Kee is a previous Tawney Shield winner whose game dropped considerably after an ankle injury two years ago. "But why didn't you tell me what you were doing?"

Edie lowers her voice. "Because it's a dirty game I'm playing, Bubble," she says darkly. "And I knew you wouldn't approve. Besides, I don't want you implicated. Ignorance is the best defense in these situations, okay?"

I am touched by her concern, though still not entirely happy. She is right. I don't approve. But if she is so keen to play this so-called dirty game, she shouldn't be taking on all the risk herself.

"Bubble? Are you still there?"

"Promise me, Edie, that if you decide to do this again, you'll tell me first."

"Of course."

"I don't like it when you lie to me."

"You know you're my lucky charm, don't you?" she says, soft and sweet, and I think about lying in her arms in the tall grass beside the tennis courts at Tawney last year: my head in her lap, her hand stroking my hair, our fingers entwined.

"Don't you forget it," I say, smiling. "I'll call you after school."

✺ ✺ ✺

We have resolved things, we love each other, Edie and I are rock solid. But after I get off the phone I feel strangely hollow. Then I remember: I haven't had lunch yet! Dear me—what a crazy cat I am.

I am on my way to the cafeteria when I decide, on a whim, to take a left turn toward the newsroom. I promised Will I would steer clear, but I have a sudden urge to tell her about the emails I sent. I am feeling guilty about not clearing them with her first. When I reach the newsroom door, though, I notice something bizarre going on behind the mottled glass. There is a lot of thumping, like someone is playing dodgeball, only the balls are heads, and there are two of them, and they seem to be doing the opposite of dodging each other.

The door opens and out bursts Will. Her face is flushed. She adjusts her dress and, just before she pulls the door shut, I see a glimpse of Natasha Nguyen behind her, adjusting hers, too.

Surely not.

Will looks up. "Holy shit! What are you doing here?"

I put a hand on the wall to steady myself.

Her eyes widen. "Hey, are you all right? You're as pale as a ghost."

"Perfectly fine," I say, inhaling deeply. "Just a bit of a head throb, that's all. It happens when I haven't eaten for a while."

"I need to talk to you, actually," Will murmurs. "Buy some food and I'll meet you in the storeroom in five."

I nod.

Will casts her gaze up and down the corridor. "You are such a weirdo, Harriet Price," she says in a loud voice, before abruptly walking away.

✳ ✳ ✳

I walk to the storeroom via the cafeteria deliberately slowly, processing what I have just witnessed. Will and Natasha? It doesn't make sense. I wonder if Will's boyfriend knows what is going on between them.

When I finally reach the storeroom, Will is lounging in her padded chair with her feet on the armrest reading *American Portraiture in the Twenty-First Century*. "Feeling better?" she asks. Closing the book, she places it on a meter-high stack of art books beside her chair.

"Whose are those?"

Will threads her fingers together. "They're art books, and I'm reading them, and they don't belong to you, so..."

"Don't you have room for them at home?"

"I brought them *from* home. So I could read them here. What's got up your nose?"

I squeeze some of my hand sanitizer on a tissue and wipe the other chair with it without looking at her. "Thanks for calling me a weirdo." I sit down.

She shifts in her chair. "You know I didn't mean it. It was

a cover. I had to do it because you broke our deal. No loitering around the newsroom, remember?"

"It was hurtful."

"I'm sorry," she says, her voice softer than before.

I peel the plastic off my turkey-and-Camembert wrap in pointed silence.

"Come on," Will coaxes. "I'm really glad you came and found me. And hey, I'm not even mad about the emails you've been sending without telling me. I actually wanted to say, nice work. After that assembly speech by Davids yesterday, I got nervous. You're right. We've got to throw people off the scent. Speculation about your emails was rife in the common room at break."

This cheers me somewhat. "People are already talking about them?"

"Yep. At first everyone was like, 'It's Millie! Millie Levine's Amelia Westlake!'" Will waves her hands around hysterically. "Then they're like, 'No, it's Janine Richter!'" She leans back in her chair and waves her feet around. It looks like she is trying to pedal a bike, but not particularly effectively, which is no surprise given Will Everhart is not exactly fitness oriented. "Then they're all, 'It's Nakita! It's Nakita!'" She has a strange full-body roll thing going now. "So I think we're in the clear. For now, at least," Will says, "which is great. Because I have another idea, which is what I wanted to talk to you about. You know the wall behind the science building? I want to paint a mural on it. I want Amelia to. I'll come up with the drawings again, and you can help with the concepts, just like we've done before. If they won't let us publish cartoons in the school paper, this is what we can do instead. It'll be like a cartoon on steroids. What do you think?" She looks at me expectantly.

"I don't understand. Why a mural? What would it be for?"

"To expose Hadley, of course. It'll be the same theme as our first cartoon. I'm working on a two-by-two-meter stencil of his face."

At the very thought of a giant Coach Hadley peering down from a wall, my stomach drops like a stone.

"We need to keep pressing this Hadley issue since the school isn't doing anything about it," Will says. "We wouldn't even have to buy the paint. Nat's uncle owns a paint shop, and she keeps spare tins for me in the newsroom in case I need them for an art project...."

"Oh, great idea," I say, my heart beginning to pound. What an idiot I've been. If I'd known the situation between Will and Natasha, I would never have embarked upon Amelia Westlake in the first place. "And while you're borrowing her paint, why don't you just tell her that you and I are Amelia Westlake? Or have you done that already?" I ask.

"I would never tell Nat without checking with you first," Will says emphatically. "Yes, we're friends, but that doesn't mean—"

"*Friends*, are you?" I meet her gaze. "I know you don't think much of me, but I'm not entirely stupid. I just wish you'd told me. I spent an entire evening sending emails to cover our tracks when the biggest potential leak is *you*."

Will looks confused, before comprehension breaks across her face. "You thought you saw something through the newsroom window today."

"Didn't I?" I cry.

She bursts out laughing. "Yes. You saw Nat and me moving a filing cabinet."

"Oh! I thought you were..." Relief sweeps through me like a cool breeze through a hot room.

"No." Will looks uncomfortable. She clears her throat. "I mean, not that we *haven't*...you know...before...or aren't..." She sighs. "To be honest, things between us are a little complicated right now. All I'm saying is that today we were moving a filing cabinet."

So I was right all along. I feel a sharp heat in my throat. "Then my point remains," I say as coldly as possible, even though a sickly warmth has started spreading through my body.

If Will and Natasha are together, how can I trust Will to keep Amelia a secret? Suddenly my head feels so tight that my eyes begin to tear up. "And tell me, Will," I press on. "How on earth are you going to paint a mural without anyone seeing? We'll be expelled on the spot." My voice is shrill. "Anyway, haven't you got a major work to complete? Shouldn't you be expending your creative energy on that?"

Will looks appalled. "You know what, Harriet? Sometimes you can be a really condescending bitch."

I gasp.

Her lip lifts like a cat's to show her teeth, and I have an extremely frightening vision of her leaping on top of me in attack.

There are moments in one's life of sudden clarity, moments when you recognize you've been stumbling along, happily admiring the landscape, only to realize there are sharp rocks below your feet, the surrounding plants are heavy with poisonous berries, and the path you're following is no ordinary path; it's a sociopath called Will Everhart. Why am I spending so much time with an attention-seeking, untrustworthy troublemaker, plotting, planning, and sneaking around, only so Coach Hadley can continue being celebrated as a role model and we can be threatened with suspension, or worse?

It might be fine for Will—she has nothing to lose. But for me? I'm putting in jeopardy a stunningly bright future, an amazing girlfriend, an incredibly fulfilling life!

I wrap up the remains of my lunch, my head pounding. "You know what, Will? This whole thing is getting entirely out of hand. Do what you like. I don't care anymore. I quit."

chapter 15

WILL

I watch Harriet storm out the door. Okay, storming isn't the word. Storming implies hunched shoulders, noisy limb movements, menacing bulk. No. What Harriet does is more like what a floating tissue might do to express its displeasure: a weightless twist here, a wispy turn there.

As soon as the door shuts, I know she isn't coming back.

The point is not whether I want her to stay. For starters, I'm perfectly fine with spending the rest of lunch on my own. I'm comfortable with isolation, unlike some people I know who sweat at the temples if Snapchat is taking too many seconds to load.

The point is not that Harriet has decided to quit Amelia Westlake. What do I care? If she steps aside, I can choose my own projects. I can do anything I want, although I'd probably draw the line at arson.

Of course, it's easier with two of us. It's the perfect number: not too many people to let the secret out, but enough for us to each have an alibi. Best of all, no one has any reason to suspect her. You'd have better luck pinning a double homicide on Big Bird than accusing Harriet Price of being Amelia Westlake.

The point is this: Harriet has spent the last two minutes shooting accusations at me like arrows, and the very moment I've finally loaded my own bow and drawn back, she's shot out the door. So I do what any self-respecting person would: I go after her screaming.

I get within three meters of her before Her Highness deigns to acknowledge me. At the sound of my screams, she breaks into a run. Still making a fair amount of noise, I run after her, which is tricky, what with her being an elite sportsperson and me being an elite couch potato. Since the screaming and the running aren't working, I change tack and begin moaning instead.

This gets her interested. There's no prefect bait like a person in distress. Her about-face is so swift that I barely have time to wince and fake a limp before Harriet's at my side, offering me an arm to lean on and a freshly ironed handkerchief.

I blow my nose on it loudly.

"Sick bay's just down this path."

"Oh no! I'm fine. It's just a sprain." I grip my ankle bravely.

"Are you sure?" Harriet asks. She sounds genuinely worried, and I almost feel bad.

"Positive. Anyway, I've got a test after lunch I have to be there for."

"Then I'll help you walk back to the main building. Only if

you're okay being seen with me in public, of course," she says pointedly.

"You've just quit Amelia Westlake, so I guess it doesn't matter anymore."

It takes so much effort faking a sprain all the way back to the main building that I almost get a real one. Having Harriet Price's arm around my waist for an extended period is also weird enough to send my lower back into a series of disturbing spasms, but at least it gives me the chance to set her straight about some things.

"Just for the record," I say between concerted grunts of exertion, "and not that it's any of your business, but you need to understand something about me and Nat."

"Okay."

"What do you mean, 'okay'?" I ask.

"Nothing. Just okay."

"Well, it certainly sounded like something more than okay."

"Well, it really wasn't," says Harriet, flustered.

"The thing between me and Nat is just—just one of those casual things between good friends," I improvise. "Anyway, it doesn't mean I'm going to tell her what the two of us have been getting up to."

Harriet turns pale. "What on earth are you talking about?"

I glance around. "Amelia Westlake, I mean," I murmur.

Flushing from the neck up, she nods quickly. "Of course." She pauses. "Does your boyfriend know about this... casual thing between friends?"

"My *boyfriend*?" I burst out laughing.

Harriet looks uncertain. "You don't have a boyfriend?"

I shake my head, still laughing. "Boyfriends are not my thing," I say. "Sure, I know that some people like to swing in multiple directions. Which is great, if that's what you're into. Nat's like that. But I'm not."

It takes Harriet a while to process this, and it clearly places a strain on her usual brain function because the next thing she says is even stranger. "If you don't have a boyfriend, or anyone else, then you mustn't be very keen on Natasha if you want to keep things with her...casual."

Trust Harriet to make a judgment in the absence of any knowledge whatsoever. "Of course I'm keen on her!" I say. "What's not to be keen on? She's very attractive. She has a political conscience, a love of culture, and the clarity to see Rosemead for the elitist brainwashing factory it really is. We don't see eye to eye when it comes to music—she's obsessed with garage punk—but other than that we have heaps in common. We're practically the same person."

"I'm not sure that clears things up," says Harriet stubbornly.

We're passing the oval. The hockey players are in a scrum in the middle, jostling against each other, shoulder to shoulder. Someone pushes too hard and the whole scrum collapses. I think about shifting the conversation in another direction, but Harriet needs to have the full picture. "I like her. I do. A lot," I say. I sound as convincing as a rookie real-estate agent.

"But?" Harriet prods.

"Just perhaps not in that way," I admit, realizing it's true.

Nat is my friend and I love her, but I don't want to be with her. Just because we get on as friends and both happen to like girls doesn't mean we have to be together.

The more I think about it, the more certain I am that Nat feels the same way I do. We gave it a try, and it hasn't worked, but we're both too worried about offending each other to break it off.

Of course, I should be having this conversation with Nat instead of Harriet Price. But it feels good to finally be talking about it with somebody.

"It's ridiculous, really," I tell Harriet. "Personality-wise, we're far more compatible than I was with any of my previous girlfriends."

"Exactly how many other girlfriends have you had?" asks Harriet.

I pretend to count in my head. "Four or five," I lie. It's more like a couple of kisses with Sami Farouk at the end of art camp in the year-nine summer holidays, but Harriet doesn't need to know that. "I've lost count, to be honest. Why? How many boyfriends have you had?"

Harriet pauses. "No boyfriends. Just, ah, Edie. Who I'm seeing now. She's captain at Blessingwood."

"Oh! I didn't realize," I say, keeping my eyes firmly on the hockey players.

Harriet Price has a girlfriend? Why didn't I know this? Her tendency to play by the book has clearly fucked with my usually impressive intuition in this field. I already had her married off to a chump with a square jaw and a receding hairline. I clear my throat. "Not that every romantic relationship has to be utterly electric." I look at her. "Of course, I'm sure you and—Edie, is it?"

Harriet nods.

"I'm sure you guys have a whole truckload of fireworks going off whenever you're—"

She drops her arm abruptly. "Will, I'm sorry I mentioned your major work earlier," she says. "Where you are up to with your schoolwork is absolutely none of my business."

Talk about an unsubtle change of topic; clearly Harriet doesn't want to discuss Edie with me. I wobble to regain my balance. "It's fine," I tell her, and it is. I don't feel so angry anymore. The exhaustion of walking a kilometer on one foot has expended my emotional stores.

We reach the end of the oval, and I pause to rub my ankle. Fake injuries are the worst. With my hand on Harriet's shoulder, I make a performance of moving my foot gingerly in a slow circle. "I'm sorry about what I said to you earlier. About being a condescending bitch."

Harriet flinches.

"I didn't mean it. I'm just a bit sensitive right now about my major work. I have a bit of a block about it at the moment," I explain.

"What kind of a block?" Harriet asks, holding my hand to help me balance.

"I can't work out how to explore what I need to explore, I guess."

"Which is?"

"A sort of phobia-type thing that escalates the closer I get to, um, airports."

"You have a fear of flying?"

My parents aside, this is not something I've talked about to anyone. But Harriet deserves to know why I lost it earlier. "A few years ago, we went to India for an art festival Dad was keen to go to. On the way home we hit some major turbulence. We got here okay. But while it was happening..."

I'm not sure what to tell her. There are the facts, of course: How the lights went out and the oxygen masks dropped down. How the guy sitting next to us hit his head on the ceiling and got concussed. How a woman three rows behind us broke her arm when she landed on the floor.

But how can I describe the feeling—the sense that everything was ending? The sudden knowledge that I was a speck in the universe and that death could be as fast and simply executed as someone flicking a switch? Even worse, that in my time on the planet I'd done bugger all worth speaking of. I would die and be forgotten. End of story.

"We landed safely in the end. But it freaked me out. Plus, all these explosions and disappearing flights in the news lately..."

She is gazing at me.

"What?"

"Your voice is shaking," Harriet says.

"So?"

"I'm surprised, that's all. You don't seem like the type of person who's scared of anything."

I grunt.

"It's true," Harriet says. "You're always standing up to teachers. Protesting for causes you believe in even when you know it will get you into trouble. Choosing to study subjects like art that have no market value..." She drifts off. "I couldn't imagine what I'd do if I couldn't fly," Harriet says.

"Those charcoal pajamas they give you in first class are really something, hey?"

Harriet blinks. "It's more that my grandma's in Brisbane and can't get down much. She doesn't have any family up there so I like to visit her a couple of times a year. I help her with shopping and house repairs, that kind of thing."

Okay, so maybe Harriet isn't quite the selfish trust-fund brat I pegged her for.

"Why don't we sit down for a minute?" Harriet points to a bench near the main building. "Give you some rest?"

I consider the response that is most consistent with my hypothetical level of pain. "Great idea."

When we reach the bench, I sit down with a gigantic sigh, as if being off that darned ankle is the best thing that's happened all year. From here the hockey players on the oval are tiny battery-operated action figures, programmed to run back and forth until their motors give out.

When I think back on that plane trip, that's the overwhelming sense I have—one day my motor is going to give out. I'll be dead, and I need to make a mark on the world before that happens.

"My dad lives in Perth," I tell Harriet. "So I never get to see him anymore. He knew about my phobia and still chose to move there."

"Are you two close?"

"We used to be."

Harriet is silent for a moment. She gives me a serious look. "I think you'll get there. With your major work, I mean. The hard stuff inspires the best kind of art."

"You sound like you know what you're talking about."

She looks at her hands. "There's something I didn't tell you. About the first cartoon we did."

"Oh?"

She takes a breath. "I'm being silly. Never mind."

Something in the tone of her voice makes my ears prick. I realize I've been waiting for this. "Did something happen with Hadley? Is that it?"

"Oh no." She shakes her head. "Not really. Forget I brought it up."

I consider dropping the subject. But only for a moment. If that creep has done something to her . . . "Whatever it is, you're still thinking about it. I'm sure it would help to talk it over."

"You'll think I'm completely overreacting."

"Try me."

Harriet crosses her legs, then uncrosses them. Then she crosses them back the other way. "It was at the end of last year, and I was coming out of tennis practice after school. I'd been chatting with my tennis coach about something so I was late getting to the change room." She clears her throat. "It was just after Edie and I started dating, and everyone had recently found out about us. The whole Sports Department knew."

"I see."

"Anyway," says Harriet quickly. "You know the corridor you have to walk through to get down to the change room? The one with the blue grip on the floor?"

I nod.

"I was walking through there, and I saw Coach Hadley coming in the other direction. It was just the two of us in the corridor; there was no one else. As he approached, I smiled at him. Generally, we'd stop if we met like that and have a bit of a chat. He's always—was always—so nice. But this time, instead of smiling back he gave me this kind of, I don't know, lewd grin."

I make a face. "Gross."

"And he was looking me up and down in a way that he'd never done before. He's *looked* at me before, certainly. He often used to say nice things about my hair or my figure—"

"Are you serious?"

Harriet wraps her arms around her chest. "Anyway, this time as we passed each other he leaned in and said something in my ear."

"What did he say?"

She flushes. "He said, 'What a waste.'"

Something curdles in my stomach.

"I'm probably overreacting," Harriet rushes on. "But it just made me, oh, I don't know...so..." She is struggling to find words. "I'm not sure why I even keep thinking about it. It's probably a compliment, in a way, I suppose."

"A compliment?" I lean forward, almost forgetting about my fake ankle sprain. "Are you kidding me? Did it feel like a compliment? Being judged by a sleazebag?"

"No," says Harriet in a small voice.

"No. Because it's not a compliment. It's a fucking disgrace.

In my view, coming from a teacher, it's also a sackable offense. Who did you go to?"

"Go to?" She seems confused.

"Who did you tell? Bracken? Watson? Who?"

"Oh! No one like that."

I sit back. "Why not? You didn't want to cause trouble? Or...?"

"I don't know." Harriet prods her hairline with her fingers. "I guess I didn't think it was important enough to cause a fuss about. I mean, it's not like I'm the only one. I've seen him say far worse things to other girls. We all have. I did tell Beth and she said—she said..."

"What did she say?"

"That I wouldn't be so upset about it if I were, you know, into guys."

Beth Tupman. I could kneecap that girl. What a piece of work. So she thinks the straight girls are all doing just fine with his inappropriate behavior, does she? I have a feeling Ruby and Nakita and Trish and Anna and all the others he's had a go at might see things differently. Hadley is a sexual predator, and Beth Tupman is a fool who probably thinks he should be forgiven because nine hundred girls in uniform is too great a temptation. Or that it's just the way of the world, so get used to it. Whatever Beth thinks, she's not helping.

"And how has he treated you since?" I ask.

Harriet grimaces. "Oh, I don't know."

"It sounds like you do," I say.

"It's hard to know." She shrugs. "I mean, he's certainly

making me do extra laps in the pool more frequently than he used to. But then, he makes lots of people do extra laps."

I reach for Harriet's hand and squeeze it. "Listen to me," I say. "Beth's wrong about this. You're not overreacting. You need to tell somebody."

Harriet shakes her head vigorously. "I'm not telling anybody."

I try again. "What about your parents, at least?"

"My parents?" Her eyes are wide. "No. We don't talk about that kind of thing."

"Then what the hell do you talk about?"

"School and Tawney, mainly. When we do talk. Look, Will, it's fine," she says, pulling her hand away.

But I'm not letting this go. "You really need to talk to somebody."

"Will, I've made up my mind. I'm not doing it," she says firmly.

I can't believe this. "But don't you see, Harriet? This is the problem with this school. It's conditioned us so completely that nobody even considers questioning what goes on here anymore."

"I don't think that's true."

I remember my recent meeting with Croon and how she shut down everything I implied about Hadley. *"This* is why we have to keep doing what we're doing," I say. "This is what Amelia Westlake is all about. Changing how this place operates. It's not about protecting Rosemead's values, like you pretend it is. Rosemead's true values are rotten to the core. And things are only going to change if people learn to stand up for themselves. Right now, we're all being crushed."

Harriet looks incredulous.

"You know it's true," I say. "Otherwise Hadley would be out on his arse by now."

"I'm sure Principal Croon is investigating. These things can take time...." She peters out.

I search for her gaze until she meets mine.

"If anyone can show them how to stand up to the school and its warped values, it's Amelia Westlake," I say quietly.

Harriet watches me, her teeth clenched. She firms her mouth. "Then what's our next move?"

chapter 16

HARRIET

Will's idea is a series of pranks in quick succession. Major enough for people to take notice and regular enough to make it difficult for Rosemead to respond before another begins. I suggest a code name for our new accelerated phase and Will agrees.

So begins Operation Volley.

VOLLEY STAGE ONE
LOCATION: DUMPSTER BEHIND
COMPUTER LABS

Will spies the dumpster one lunchtime while taking a prohibited shortcut from the main building to our storeroom. In it are about fifty desktop computers, destined for landfill.

"No more than a couple of years old. In perfect working condition," says Will. "I was using one of them in the lab just a few weeks ago! Rosemead decides to upgrade its equipment and can't think of anything better to do with the old stuff than throw it out? It's outrageous."

By the time my free period (and the class Will is truant from) has ended, we have a plan.

I buy fifty sheets of neon-pink card stock that afternoon. We divide them up the next day. The day after that, we meet at the storeroom before dawn. By the time the sun has crept above the Performing Arts Center roof, a trail of neon-pink arrows tacked to the pathways leads from the front staircase of the main building through campus and up the lane to the dumpster. Glued to the side of the dumpster, a neon-pink notice glimmers in the early light.

Dear Rosemead,
You could TRASH the environment
and TRASH the dreams of the less
fortunate while you're at it,
OR
you could DONATE this "waste"
to kids in need.
Love, AW

At break, the lane is so choked with students who have followed our trail of arrows that the gardeners trying to get through to the rose garden have to back up their utility truck and take a roundabout route.

At assembly on Tuesday, Mr. Reynolds, the computer teacher, announces that the school has decided to donate ten desktop computers to a western Sydney community center and forty to a municipal library. The news is greeted with considerable applause.

✶ ✶ ✶

VOLLEY STAGE TWO
LOCATION: PERFORMING ARTS CENTER'S
LOWER HALL

One thing I have noticed since Will and I started frequenting the storeroom is the underutilization of the PAC's Lower Hall. It's smaller than the Upper Hall, and on the shadier side of the building, so teachers tend not to book it for activities, meaning it is only occupied a few hours a week. This is despite its being an acoustically designed facility with an orchestra pit, sound-and-lighting box, and a seating capacity of five hundred.

Will and I compose a template letter and print out five variations on Rosemead letterhead that Will has "obtained" from the school office.

Dear Principal [insert surname],

I am writing to you and the other local school principals to let you know about our Lower Hall facility. The Lower Hall, located at the back of our recently renovated Performing Arts Center, is a state-of-the-art facility with an impressive audience capacity.

I would be more than happy for you and your students to make use of the Lower Hall, at no cost, if and when you require it. Please let me know if you are interested, and I will arrange a booking.

Sincerely,

Principal Croon

Rosemead Preparatory School

We send off five letters to nearby primary schools. Within a fortnight, a notable number of local schoolchildren are regularly filing back and forth from the Lower Hall to the main car park.

It does not take long for the other students to notice.

"What's with all the mini freeloaders?" Beth asks in the common room one break. "Have we ceded the Lower Hall to the state government or something? Is this a form of tax avoidance?"

"There was a sign on the Lower Hall entrance—" says Ruby Lasko.

"Really, though," Beth interrupts. "What's the point of going to this school if we still have to mix with the poors?"

"What did the sign say, Ruby?" asks Liz Newcomb. She opens the common room fridge, takes out an opened tin of condensed milk that has white fur growing on it, and throws it across the room into the trash. It is an impressive display of hand-eye coordination, but if Little Miss Tawney Shield Captain wants applause, she is not going to get it from me.

Ruby squints into the middle distance. "I'm trying to remember the exact words. *Dear local school student, Amelia Westlake welcomes you to Rosemead. Please enjoy the facilities.* Something along those lines."

"Genius," say Liz.

With the hours I am spending adhering neon-pink arrows to brickwork, mailing envelopes, and placing notices in the Lower Hall, it is no wonder my teachers begin querying my commitment to schoolwork.

Ms. Bracken: "Harriet, is everything okay at home? I ask because I haven't seen your Medici essay yet, and the only other time you've been late with an essay was when your brother required emergency surgery after slicing his finger on a guitar string."

Mr. Porter: "Look, I hate to bring this up with you, Harriet, because it's never been a problem before, but I noticed you were distracted during the class quiz. The answer to question three is eight hundred forty-six. Instead, your workings suggest you were trying to multiply fifty by 'however much A4 sheets of card stock cost.'"

Mr. Van: "What have you got there, Harriet? We're discussing reptiles. A Rosemead letterhead is not a reptile."

※ ※ ※

VOLLEY STAGE THREE
LOCATION: LIBRARY

One Thursday afternoon a camera crew is expected on campus. They're shooting a live segment for the early news about Rosemead's recent success at the National Schools Robotics Competition.

The robotics team consists of seven year-twelve physics

and math students, and Deputy Davids is the team's coordinating teacher. She has invited a spokesperson from the team's company sponsor, SNARC Electronics, which funded the robot build, to be part of the live broadcast.

What the student team doesn't know until midafternoon is that despite being the ones who won the competition, *they* won't be on television.

Will hears Zara Long complaining about it at her locker during lunch. "We won the comp, not SNARC," Zara mutters. "We should be the ones in front of the camera. SNARC just wants to use the airtime to push their brand."

"It's completely unfair," agrees Palmer Crichton. "We should at least get to demonstrate how to operate Mr. Buddy. We're the ones who invented him!"

After a quick reconnaissance trip by Will to the library between classes, we devise a plan for her to carry out. At five o'clock, when the TV segment is scheduled to take place, I retreat to the storeroom to live stream the early news on my phone.

The segment begins with a beaming Deputy Davids. She is standing next to the SNARC spokesperson. The journalist asks them questions about the competition. The SNARC spokesperson talks a lot about SNARC. The two of them then move to the side of the shot to reveal Mr. Buddy.

"So, what can this little fella do?" asks the journalist.

"Oh, lots of things," says Deputy Davids, keeping her smile wide for the camera. "He can travel in all directions, throw boulders, go under tunnels, go over bridges."

"Fabulous. Let's see some of his moves."

Deputy Davids hands a remote control to the SNARC spokesperson. "Why don't you do the honors?"

He smiles. "It would be a pleasure." He points the remote at Mr. Buddy.

Nothing happens. Nothing continues to happen for one and a half minutes. Nothing at all. Unless you count the SNARC spokesperson's fingers whitening from pressing hard on the buttons, and the color on Deputy Davids's face deepening, and the journalist laughing uncomfortably before announcing a commercial break. Just before the live scene ends, the camera catches the spokesperson flipping the remote in his sweaty palm. On the back in white marker are two large letters: *AW*.

A fast-food jingle starts. I hear the click of the storeroom door. Will comes in, panting.

"You were right," she says. "The remote was just sitting there on a shelf. I went in through the other door and slipped it out while they were schmoozing with the news team in the corridor. All it took was a coin to get the back open. Done in seconds."

She opens her palm. On it sit two button-cell batteries, shiny as jewels.

✼ ✼ ✼

VOLLEY STAGE FOUR
LOCATION: VARIOUS

One morning I am staring unseeing at one of the Rosemead banners hanging at the top of the main stairs when my eye catches on our school motto: *Qui cherche trouve.* For those not au fait with French, it translates as "Whoever seeks, finds." It occurs to me that a game of hide-and-seek is exactly what is called for.

Over the course of a week, when the coast is clear, Will and I remove every Rosemead banner on campus. There are eight in total: the one above the main stairs, the three hanging in the PAC, the two in the Assembly Hall, the one in the gym foyer, and the one in the staff building foyer. Each banner has the motto embroidered in cursive writing along the bottom.

I deliver the banners to a company that can destitch—and restitch—embroidery. They complete the job within a week. It takes another week, and a couple of near disasters (who knew Ms. Bracken smoked cigarettes in the staff foyer after hours?) to return the banners to their rightful homes.

The stitching has been matched so well that you can hardly tell the difference. But the difference is significant. Instead of the French motto sits another phrase in English, hiding in plain view.

And so the waiting game begins.

* * *

"Okay," Will says, when Operation Volley has been going for five weeks. "These pranks have been great. We're shedding some serious light on the elitist crap that goes on around here. But it's time we ramped things up. I say we draw the op to a close and shift focus." She places a flyer on the storeroom table.

It is less of a table than a slab of wood on a milk crate. I have no idea where it came from. Why is it that every time we meet here something else has materialized? Along with the chairs we started with and the pile of art books, there are now a pair of molting velveteen cushions, a blanket that reeks of campfire smoke, a plastic kettle plugged into the baseboard power outlet, a coffee press, a vacuum pack of coffee, a box of stinky tea bags, and half a dozen mugs with bad slogans on them. Is Will living here part-time? Has she moved in? I don't want to know, but I am fearful her paraphernalia is turning the storeroom into a firetrap. I make a mental note to buy a fire extinguisher.

I notice she has tacked copies of our *Messenger* cartoons to the wall. Then there is the flotsam from Operation Volley—leftover neon-pink card stock and a pile of stationery bearing the Rosemead letterhead. We really need to clean things up around here.

I pick up the flyer.

"You've seen it?" Will sips coffee from a mug that reads *Friday is my second-favorite F word*.

"I'm secretary of the Sports Committee. Of course I've seen it."

The flyer is an advertisement for Rosemead's Buy a Tile project. It is an invitation for parents to donate to the school's latest major building work. This year, at Coach Hadley's suggestion, we are raising money to build a twenty-five-meter outdoor swimming pool. We already have the Olympic-size indoor one, of course, but other top-tier schools like Edie's have a second pool where the B-grade teams can train. I have lost count of the number of times Coach Hadley has bemoaned the absence of a second pool. Rosemead might have a top-tier coach, he argues, but we can never be a top-tier swimming school without a second pool.

Parents who donate enough money will be rewarded by having their child's name inscribed on one of the wall tiles of the new pool complex.

"So how much time and money goes into a fund-raiser like this, do you think?" Will asks, her expression suspiciously serene.

"As a matter of fact, I've seen the budget," I say. "The promotional costs alone are quite a lot. Then there is the parents' cabaret dinner they're putting on, with silent auction prizes to raise more money, although parents donate most of those. A luxury weekend away at Parnell's Heritage Resort is one of this year's big-ticket items." Graham Parnell's daughter, Lucy, is a year-nine student whom I tutored in math for two years. "We're expecting at least two hundred parents to come. It's just as well, because the school is hoping to raise about thirty thousand dollars. And of course, we can't forget the fund-raising envelopes they print to go out with every monthly newsletter to the entire school community. They get a lot of contributions that way. The mailing list has over two thousand recipients."

Will puts her mug down. She has a mischievous sparkle in her eye that would be very appealing if I didn't know better than to trust it. "These charity cupcake sales you run from time to time. Who are you raising money for?" she asks.

"Lots of different charities. This year we've donated to cancer research, Amnesty International, and St. Vincent de Paul."

"And how much money goes into organizing a cupcake sale?"

"Each student who volunteers buys her own ingredients and bakes her own cupcakes. That's basically it."

"The school never puts in anything?"

"No."

"And how much money do you usually raise?"

"On a good day? About three hundred dollars." I frown. "Where are you going with all this?"

"Oh, I was just thinking," Will says casually. "Wouldn't it be great if the school put as much time and energy into raising money for charity as it does into building a *second* swimming pool for itself?"

I pause. "I've never thought about it like that before."

"You've never thought about the fact that if Rosemead made the same kind of commitment to charity events as it did to fund-raising for its own coffers, you'd be handing over five-thousand-dollar checks to Amnesty instead of three-hundred-dollar ones?" Will gives me the look of hers that I am getting to know well—the one that implies I am more or less an idiot.

I swallow. "When you put it like that, it's quite a disparity, isn't it?"

"I'll say it is. And I reckon there's a way to make that point and, at the same time, hit Hadley where it hurts."

"Really?" I feel suddenly nervous.

"There's an easier way to get to Hadley, of course," Will says after a moment. "Have you thought any more about telling the school what he said to you?"

"No," I say quickly.

She reaches into her pocket for her phone. "Then I take it you haven't seen the message Amelia Westlake received via Instagram last night?" Will taps her screen a few times and hands me her phone.

Someone from an account named @RosemeadStudent has tagged Amelia Westlake in a stock photo of a swimming pool. I read the words beneath the photo.

> Just wanted to say thank you @amelia.westlake for the cartoon about Coach Hadley. People need to know what he's really like. I've known for about a year now and wish I didn't. I really wish I could stop thinking about it. Maybe you know how that feels. Anyway, thanks.

I feel a lump in my throat. "Who wrote this?"

"A Rosemead student," Will says. "That's all it says on the account. There's no other information. Not even a photo. The profile was probably set up just to write the note."

I take a deep breath. "For someone to have written this, it makes me think Coach Hadley has really . . ."

We look at each other, neither of us willing to form the words. Will nods.

"What should we do?"

Will takes another sip of coffee. "We write back to her. Perhaps we can encourage her to make an official complaint. If Coach Hadley's . . ."

I rest my forehead on my palms. "I don't even want to think about it."

"I know." Will leans forward. She sighs, and her coffee-scented breath warms my neck. "I know it's a confronting thing to consider, but if you were to make your own official complaint to the school about what he said to you..."

I shake my head. "It is not worth reporting. Anyway, I already told you I don't want to."

"But, Harriet, don't you see?" She puts a hand on my arm. "If you did, it might convince other people he's harassed or... who knows what... to come forward."

"If only we knew who wrote this..."

"But we don't. We may never know."

I try to assess the logical options, but for some reason Will's hand on my arm is making it difficult to think logically. I wait until she takes it away. "Let's write back, then," I say. "We'll suggest to her that she make a complaint and see how she responds."

It's as if Will is about to say something else but changes her mind. She nods.

I add a comment beneath the swimming pool picture.

> @RosemeadStudent I'm really glad you wrote to me. I am very sorry to hear you are having a bad time. The best thing you can do is make a formal complaint to the school. In fact, I urge you to do so. The school will be able to help you and maybe others as well. Any time you want to chat, you can reach me at this address.

I add the email address I set up for Amelia Westlake when I created her Instagram account. I show my comment to Will.

She looks me straight in the eye. "It's good advice, you know. To make a complaint."

I focus on the screen. My finger hovers over it, presses down. "It's done," I say, not looking up.

We say nothing for a moment.

"Maybe she'll email," I say. "Maybe if we start a correspondence..." My words drift into the air.

Will clears her throat. "So. This fund-raising business," she says. "Do you want to help Rosemead raise some serious money for charity?" She stands up and tacks the fund-raiser flyer next to the cartoons on the wall.

chapter 17

WILL

It's simple. All we need to do is hijack the fund-raising letters for the Buy a Tile project that go out with the monthly school newsletter. According to Harriet, the school outsources the printing and distribution of both the newsletter and the donation requests.

"First we find out which printing company has the job. Then we arrange for the company to change the details on the donation letter to those of a worthy charity," I explain. "That way, we leverage the school's massive mailing for good instead of evil."

"Raising money for a new swimming pool is not exactly evil," Harriet says.

"Self-interest, then."

Harriet's brow creases. "Let me get this right. You're saying we call up the printing company and ask them to replace the text on the letter?"

"Exactly. We choose a worthy cause, describe it, leave the usual space for people to fill in their card details, and include the charity's address so that people can mail donations to them directly. I was thinking we could choose the Fund for Australian Women. Its focus is on supporting women and children who are victims of domestic violence. *And* its initials double as Amelia Westlake's calling card. By the time the mailing has happened, it will be too late for the school to do anything about it. Sure, a lot of people will ignore the letter, but some will donate. And it will send a message to Rosemead that its uncharitable ways haven't gone unnoticed."

"But how are we going to convince the printers to change the details?" Harriet asks.

"We'll call them up and pretend to be someone from the school. I'm pretty good at putting on a mature voice," I say in a mature voice.

"I guess all that leaves is finding out who the printing company is."

"Oh. I assumed you'd know," I say, disappointed.

Harriet shakes her head.

Damn. This could be the one detail that holds us back. "Are you sure you've never heard a name mentioned in a Sports Committee meeting?"

"Not that I remember," Harriet says. "Although it would make sense for Rosemead to use the same company it uses for other projects. Has Natasha ever mentioned who prints the *Messenger*?"

"Possibly, but the name doesn't spring to mind. Although I bet the information is somewhere in the newsroom."

"Why don't you look around next time you're in there?" Harriet suggests.

✳ ✳ ✳

I try this on Wednesday. I figure I'll find the name on the boxes of undistributed *Messengers*, or the contact details on one of Nat's Post-its. But I don't. I even try casually opening the filing cabinet, but Nat's warning stare stops me. "Don't touch my shit, Will. It's taken me months to arrange those files."

"We need to find a way to get into the newsroom when Nat's not there," I tell Harriet when we meet up at the storeroom later.

"How about when she's in class?"

"During school hours is too risky. She'll skip class if she has a deadline to meet, and anyway, there's too much foot traffic in that corridor. Someone will see us."

"Then we sneak back one evening."

I shake my head. "Nat's there most nights."

In fact, the only time of year you can depend on Nat *not* being in the newsroom is during September, the month before deadline for Rosemead's annual literary journal, *Falling Leaf.* It's the time of year Nat hates most. For four weeks, Nakita Wallis and her team of budding literati take over half the newsroom to sort through poetry and short stories, sip coffee, and argue the comparable merits of haiku and pantoums.

Exam time aside, it's the only time of year Nat spends more hours out of the newsroom than in it. But it's only June. So how are we going to get in there alone?

It's Harriet who works out a plan.

⚹ ⚹ ⚹

My mother is standing in the door to my room. She's been doing this a lot lately—loitering there with her hip on the frame. Sometimes, to mix things up, she'll pick at one of the nuggets of poster putty on my door. Sometimes she'll hum a line or two from a Sia song. When I finally stop whatever I'm doing and bark *"What?"* she always says the same thing.

"How's your major work coming along?"

This has been going on for weeks.

The truth is, my creative juices are not exactly flowing—not in the direction of my major work, anyway. Yes, I'm thinking about its subject matter, but this is less from conscientiousness and more from my anxiety disorder. Every time a plane flies over the house I think about it. For example, I think about how supposed experts always claim that air travel is ten times safer than other modes of transport when actually this is only when you measure deaths per kilometer. When you measure deaths per journey, it becomes clear you're safer playing hide-and-seek with a jaguar in heat than getting on a plane.

Luckily, the fund-raising prank has me preoccupied. The potential impact of our latest operation is bigger than the others put together. We'll be hitting Rosemead's coffers directly, possibly to the tune of thousands of dollars. It's the Robin-fucking-Hood of heists.

I hear Mum's fingernail scraping at the timber.

"What?"

I ready myself for the major work question.

Mum's lips part.

Here it comes.

"Who's Amelia Westlake?"

"*What?*"

"Amelia Westlake. I've never heard you mention her before."

"Who told you that name?"

Mum looks at me strangely. "She did. She's on the phone for you. Or should I tell her to call back?"

I grab the phone from Mum, heart slamming in my chest. "Hello, Will speaking?"

"Hi," murmurs a voice. "It's me, Harriet."

I breathe out.

"I know we promised not to call each other. So I thought I better use a . . . well . . . fake name." She gives a half laugh.

"Where did you even *get* this number?" Nobody calls our landline except for Dad, Mum's boyfriend Graham, and a persistent market researcher named Atari.

"On the year-twelve contact list."

"There's a year-twelve contact list?"

"I needed to talk to you urgently, and you weren't answering your mobile. I just checked the Rosemead student's Instagram account," Harriet says. "The swimming pool picture and the comments beneath it are gone."

I had a feeling this would happen. "But the account's still there?" I ask.

"Yes," Harriet confirms. "Do you think we should send her another message?"

Mum is still loitering. I give her the thumbs-up before closing the door. "If you think it would help."

"What should we say?"

"The same thing again, I guess. That she should make a formal complaint," I say.

There is a pause on the line. I don't know what Harriet expects my advice to be, if not this.

"There was another reason I rang, in fact," says Harriet at last.

"Oh yeah?"

"I've worked it out. I've thought of a way to get Natasha out of the newsroom."

"I'm listening."

"Remember you were telling me about Natasha's musical taste? It was when you sprained your ankle. You said something about her being obsessed with garage punk."

"Ye-es," I say.

"It's given me an idea. Have I ever told you about my little brother, Arthur? He's in a garage punk band. And they have a gig on Saturday."

Harriet has a brother in a garage punk band? "I don't know. Nat's taste is pretty specific."

"I'm not saying I know that much about their music, but they're quite successful. Not as big as Doktor D or anything, but then he's hip-hop, not garage—"

"I've heard Nat mention Doktor D."

"They've played gigs with him before."

"Where at?"

"On Saturday they'll be at Deep Fryer in Surry Hills."

Only the best bands play at Deep Fryer on Saturdays. This little brother of hers is clearly pulling her chain.

"If you're unsure, why not come over and check them out?" says Harriet. "They're rehearsing at our place right now."

✳ ✳ ✳

Mum is on the couch watching *Midsomer Murders*. She's a sucker for formulaic, predictable crime shows. "I'm going out for a bit," I tell her, flipping my wallet in the air and catching it again.

She looks up. "You're in a good mood."

"No, I'm not. Is it okay if I take the car?"

"Where are you going?"

"Just to see someone from school. About an assignment. I'll be back soon."

"Your major work?"

"Kind of."

"Don't tell me you've made another friend at school." Mum's eyes widen in exaggerated shock.

"You can be a real cow sometimes. Have I ever told you that?"

She smiles. "I'm pleased for you, honey, that's all. Anyone special?"

"Mum!"

"What? I just happened to notice you're wearing your favorite T-shirt."

I look down. "This isn't my favorite T-shirt."

"That's not what you said last week."

"I've moved on since last week."

Mum raises an eyebrow. "So which one's your favorite now?"

Harriet Price's house is the most insane place I have ever been to in my life.

First, due to the number of cul-de-sacs and one-way streets in Mosman, it takes ages to find. When I finally drive down the part of the street where it's supposed to be, there doesn't appear to be a house at all. It's as if the block has been compulsorily acquired for a medium-sized nature reserve. Then I spy a sleek red letterbox bearing the number 18 nestled between two bamboo fronds.

Beside it, a timber path lit by louvered lights winds its way through the trees. I start up it. The sound of mating frogs chokes the air. There's a squawk; a bat shoots out of the darkness. I stop to watch it flap across the sky.

I finally reach an opening where I find Harriet waiting for me in front of a Palladian monolith. The doorway is twice her height. She's in her school uniform still, with a pair of shiny white slippers. "Come in!" she says. "They're in the central atrium."

The central atrium. Of course. Where else would the next generation's most subversive band choose to rehearse?

I follow Harriet through a hotel-style lobby, up a hallway the width of the school gymnasium, and to the doorway of a glass-walled room the size of our flat. Inside it are three boys on keyboard, drums, and guitar, making a freakload of noise.

We listen for almost an entire song before the guitarist notices us and comes to the door. "Hey!" he greets us.

"Will, this is Arthur," Harriet says.

This is Harriet's brother?

Arthur Price is not what I expected. His vibe is relaxed. His clothes are fashion forward. He has excellent hair. He looks like Harriet, only, well, *cooler*.

"And that's James on the keyboard. And Bill on drums."

James is a lanky guy with bright blue eyes. Bill has bushy eyebrows and a head the size of a planet. I like them immediately.

Arthur is glancing between Harriet and me. "You two are friends?"

"In a way," Harriet says uneasily.

"Associates is probably closer to the mark," I say.

Harriet turns to me. "So what do you think? Is this the type of music Natasha Nguyen likes?"

Bill looks at James. "Hey, I know that name. Doesn't Nat Nguyen hang out with Duncan?"

"You guys know Duncan Aboud?" I ask.

Bill and James exchange glances and grin. "Everyone knows Duncan," says Bill, scratching his leg with a drumstick.

Harriet tugs at my elbow. "Let's leave them to it. Carry on, boys. Sorry to disturb!" She pulls me back into the hall.

The music starts up again with a high-pitched wail from the guitar.

"Well?" Harriet asks.

Above the guitar racket I can hear footsteps. Someone's coming down the hallway. A blond woman wearing a skirt suit and heels appears. It's either a Harriet clone with slightly older facial features or Harriet's mother.

"Hello," she says when she reaches us.

"Mum, this is Will."

"Hello, Will." Her expression is cool. "Are those friends of Arthur's still here? I have two apicoectomies scheduled at eight tomorrow morning, and I need an early night. I really think it's time they went home."

Harriet gives her an efficient nod. "I'll have a word with him."

"Lovely to meet you, Will," says Mrs. Price's mouth while her eyes wish me a thousand frozen winters.

I watch the back of her heels strike the tiles until she reaches the end of the hall.

"So, the band," says Harriet when she's gone, completely unaware of this wordless exchange. What I'm beginning to learn about Harriet is that sometimes things happen in her line of sight that she simply doesn't see. It's like she walks around blindfolded half the time. And yet, just when I'm about to write her off completely, she'll share a thought or an idea that totally nails everything. The problem is, there's no way to know what you're going to get: the smart stuff or the dumb stuff. You just have to flip the Harriet coin and wait to see which side it lands on.

"I reckon Nat would like them," I say. "But I'm still not clear how we're going to make sure she goes to the gig so we can get into the newsroom. I could invite her to go with me while you raided the newsroom, I suppose...."

"You inviting her is absolutely not what I had in mind." Harriet sounds panicked by the thought. "The invitation has to come from Amelia, obviously."

And there it is: The spinning silver has landed on smart. I smile. There's no way Nat will pass up an invitation from Amelia Westlake.

HARRIET

On Saturday night I shower early and dress by six. Arthur has sound check at seven, and I have offered to drive him to the venue. That way I can park, find some dinner nearby, and return in time for their set.

It is usually Dad who goes to Arthur's shows—venues won't normally let him in without an accompanying adult, even when his band is the lead act—and anyway, Dad rather enjoys it. In his predentist days he had his own band. He likes to boast they almost made it big. How truthful this is, given they mainly played Doors covers, I don't know. But tonight Mum and Dad have a teeth-related function to attend.

I have a couple of essays due that I should be working on instead. I have already missed a recent biology essay deadline because of Amelia Westlake. But I have no option other than to attend Arthur's show to ensure the success of Operation

Newsroom. My presence at Deep Fryer will mean that if and when Natasha Nguyen shows up, I can let Will know the coast is clear.

A little after six I am in the kitchen preparing a preouting snack of balsamic-glazed pecans with rosemary and sea salt when Mum comes in.

"Goodness, Harriet. What on earth are you wearing?"

I look up from the stove. "You've seen this shirt before." It is black with a few deliberate tears in the lower stomach region held together by oversized safety pins. "Arthur loaned it to me. I'm going to his concert tonight, remember? I need to blend in."

Mum frowns and opens the fridge door. She takes out a tub of hummus and a carrot. "That friend of yours. The one I met on Thursday. Will she be there?"

I shift the pecans in the pan with my wooden spoon. "Will Everhart? No."

Mum lays the carrot on the chopping board and slices it down the middle. "I haven't seen Edie for a while," she says.

"She's been very busy."

"Edie is a lovely girl, Harriet. And she's a perfect friend for you while you're finishing school."

"We're a little more than friends, obviously."

"Mmm," says Mum, chopping the carrot carefully. "Being a teenager is a very intense time. And experimentation is a healthy part of the maturity process." She dips a sliver of carrot into the hummus. "Edie is such a good role model for you. Not to mention your best chance to win Tawney. It's not like you have the talent to win the singles event. Really, you are lucky she chose you to be her partner. Very lucky. Which is why I wouldn't want to see you taking your experimentation in another...direction." She looks at me intently. "Do you understand what I'm saying?"

To be honest, I am not 100 percent sure. Is she talking about experimentation in the bedroom? How embarrassing! She has no cause for concern, though. Edie and I have already agreed to keep things at second base until the Tawney Shield and exams are over. We are both of the view that it is important to avoid unnecessary distractions in the lead-up to the competition. I am fine with this arrangement. I can wait. I tip the pecans from the pan into an earthenware bowl. "Don't worry, Mum. You've got nothing to worry about."

"I'm glad to hear it." Mum pats my hand.

* * *

After dropping off Arthur at Deep Fryer, I walk to the restaurant strip around the corner. I have just ordered some rice paper rolls and a prawn crepe in a sweet little place halfway down the block when a shadow looms across the tablecloth.

"Harriet Price." Natasha Nguyen puts her palms on the table. "What a lovely surprise."

She is dressed in a leather jacket and drainpipe jeans. Her jacket is covered in zips. The metal studs along the sleeves look sharp enough to puncture a bike wheel. I nervously dab the corner of my mouth with my napkin. "Natasha! What are you doing here?"

She looks around. "This *is* a Vietnamese restaurant. Where else would I be on a Saturday night?"

"Oh," I stammer. "Right!"

Natasha's expression darkens. "That was a joke, Price. I could probably tell you my father runs this place and you'd believe that, too. Because what else could a Vietnamese refugee do other than run a restaurant? For your information, Dad's a management consultant, and his spring rolls taste like shit." She rolls back on her heels. "The bigger question is, What are *you* doing here? Alone? Wearing—oh my—a retropunk T-shirt? Off to the opera, are we?"

"Not that it's any of your business, but I'm going to see the Sphere at Deep Fryer tonight," I say calmly.

"Is that right."

"Yes. It is."

"What an amazing coincidence."

"Are you seeing them, too?" I ask, feigning surprise.

Natasha smirks. "Like you don't already know."

"Why on earth would I already know?"

Natasha straightens her shoulders. Leather creaks. "Christ, Price, you're a piece of work. Just come out and say it. Isn't that why you asked me here? For the big reveal? Or have you changed your mind?"

Why didn't we think of this? Natasha thinks my presence here has something to do with her invitation from Amelia Westlake! "I didn't ask you anywhere. I have no idea what you're talking about."

She considers me broodily. "Fine. Play it that way. Because your pretense at being a garage punk fan has me completely convinced." She starts on a slow lap of my table. When she has done a full circle, she starts on another, like a matador psyching out a bull. The whole performance is making me a tad light-headed.

"All right. I'm not a garage punk fan," I admit.

She stops in front of me again. "Does this mean you're going to talk turkey? Or that you've come up with an excuse? Don't tell me: You're going to the gig to test out some new earplugs. Or for a sociological experiment. Oh, I know. You're an undercover cop, and you're doing a sting. *That* I would believe." She bares her teeth.

"My brother's in the band. He plays the guitar."

Natasha Nguyen does something I've never seen her do before—she giggles. "*Your* brother is the guitarist in the Sphere?"

"Yes."

"Are you seriously trying to tell me that you're related to Art Juice?"

"It's a stage name, obviously."

"Oh, this is perfect. You'll have to introduce me, then, won't you?" Natasha Nguyen smirks.

⁕ ⁕ ⁕

Outside Deep Fryer, a cold wind rattles the awnings along the street. Shivering in the line, Natasha zips up her front zip, her arm zips, even her pocket zips. "Why did I forget my Pussy Riot balaclava?" she complains. "Hey, if your brother's in the band and everything, shouldn't we be able to skip this damn queue?"

Maybe she's right, but I don't want to interrupt Arthur's preparation time. He likes to sit in a corner, think of his power animal (a squirrel), and hum the tune of Yeah Yeah Yeahs' "Heads Will Roll." Then again, it is only eight o'clock. The Sphere won't be on until ten at the earliest. If I call Arthur now, he will still have plenty of time to prepare before playing.

I try his mobile. No answer. "Come on," I tell Natasha.

A security guard I have not encountered before—a six-foot muscle man with a shaved head and metal-tipped boots—stops me with a hand. I explain who I am. He reaches for his phone. "I've got a Harriet Price downstairs," he says into it. "Says she's related to Art. Yep, the Juice Man." There is a pause. "Yep. Nah. Yep. Nah. Yep." He hangs up. "Okay. You can go in."

"How the hell did you pull this off, Price?" says Natasha as we climb the stairs to the greenroom.

"I told you. My brother's the guitarist."

"Yeah, and I'm the Dalai Lama."

"Then maybe you are."

"What, because I'm Asian? We all look the same to you, don't we?"

"That's not what I meant!"

"Harri!" calls a voice from above.

Arthur is leaning over the banister. He already has his show gear on: a leather jacket over a white shirt, army pants, and commando boots. I run up and give him a squeeze.

Natasha, wide-eyed, looks from me to Arthur. "Well love me tender and call me Elvis."

"Natasha, this is my brother, Arthur. Arthur, Natasha."

Arthur smiles, and a funny thing happens to Natasha's face. All the pinched parts suddenly go smooth.

"Natasha Nguyen?" says Arthur. "You're the one who knows Duncan."

Her eyes look glazed. "Everyone knows Duncan."

"Right." He gives her his goofiest grin. "You want to meet the rest of the band?"

* * *

With Natasha safely occupied meeting the Sphere, it is time to call Will. I go downstairs and into the hallway. Along the walls, which are painted black, a series of large canvas paintings hang in intricately gilded frames. They depict various gory scenes: the sacrifice of a goat, a man being gutted by a giant sword, a human head on a stick, etc. Above a polished oak hallstand and a crystal vase of fresh, long-stemmed crimson roses is a gigantic beveled mirror. I stop in front of it, tidy my hair, readjust my T-shirt, and take out my phone.

Within seconds Will's face is on my screen, up close and furious. "Oh, it's you."

"Who did you think it was?"

"Never mind. Why are you FaceTiming me? Wouldn't it have been simpler to just—? Um—okay, wow." Her face looms on the screen as she tries for a better view.

"What?"

"Your outfit." She grins. "You should wear that T-shirt more often."

My T-shirt is certainly getting a variety of responses this evening! I pat my burning cheeks. "I can switch to audio if you don't like FaceTime."

"Nah. Don't do that. FaceTime is fine," Will says quickly.

"Are you sure you're all right?" I ask. "When I first called, you looked like something bad had happened."

Will groans. "Nothing worse than usual. I've just been on the phone to my dad, that's all. He's having a big birthday bash for his fiftieth."

"Oh, that sounds fun."

"Yeah, if I were going."

"Why aren't you going?"

"It's in Perth."

"Oh, Will."

Will looks away from the screen. "Are you at Deep Fryer yet? Is Nat there? Should I do it now?"

"Yes, to all of the above."

"Okay. Here goes."

The screen wobbles. I hear the sound of a car door slamming. Will holds the phone up so I can follow her along the school path to the newsroom. With the gardens in darkness and the solar lamps between the camellias casting ominous shadows, it's a bit like watching a police raid on *Australia's Most Famous Hoarders*. When the door comes into sight, Will wags her plastic photo ID before the camera. "Watch this."

I watch as she slots the card between the door and the frame.

"Hang on. You don't have a key?" I ask.

"Why would I have a key?" The screen view dips to show the dimly lit walkway. I hear a grunt and a click. "Bingo," says Will as the door swings open.

A group of punk fans stalk past me in the Deep Fryer hallway. I turn around so they can't see my phone screen, which now shows Will going through the shelves of the newsroom cupboard. An International Roast tin twice the size of her head crashes onto her shoulder and she swears. I quickly turn the volume down.

"Can you see anything?" I murmur.

There is a second tinny crash through the phone speakers, and a third, and then Will is waving a piece of paper triumphantly at the screen. "An invoice from Parsons Printing for five hundred copies of the *Messenger*. Dated two months ago."

"Thank goodness. Now get out of there as fast as you can."

Will swears again.

"What is it?"

"This bloody door. It won't open!"

Oh God. This can't be happening. "Can't you use your card again?"

"I'm trying that. It's not working from the inside."

"Are you serious?"

Will's face fills the screen. "No, Harriet. I'm pretending to be locked in the *Messenger* newsroom for your personal amusement."

I feel a hand on my arm. "There you are! I've been looking all over for you."

I jump.

In the Deep Fryer hallway, Natasha Nguyen is standing in front of me. I quickly flatten the phone against my beating chest. "I'm just speaking to my mother. Won't be long!"

Natasha glances at my phone. "You want me to buy you a drink?"

"Sure!"

"What would you like?"

"Anything! You choose!"

"Okay." She looks at me curiously. "I'll be in the bar."

When Natasha is gone, I bring the phone screen back up to my face. "I've got to go. Just get out of there as fast as you can, okay?"

"Piece of pie."

"Good-oh. Speak soon."

✳ ✳ ✳

I return to an extraordinary scene in the bar: Natasha Nguyen waving at me from a booth in the corner, almost as if the two of us are friends. "Here, I got you a vodka and lemonade," she says, chirpy as a parakeet, pushing it across the table. "I figured it's the kind of thing you drink." She is nursing a dark brown stout. "I want to apologize to you. I got the wrong end of the stick tonight. I thought you were involved in something you're obviously not. Please. Sit down."

I slide across the ripped vinyl, careful not to catch it on my skirt. Is Natasha bluffing? It is a distinct possibility. If she saw Will on my phone screen . . .

I decide to play along. "Is that why you were so hostile at the restaurant?" I say.

"Yep."

"And kept asking me all those strange questions?"

Natasha nods.

"You were convinced I had something to reveal to you."

"Uh-huh."

I think of slow-dawning things—the sun on the lip of the

ocean, a rattling kettle, a tulip crowning through snow—and then speak. "You thought I was Amelia Westlake, didn't you? You guessed I made up this whole 'Art Juice is my brother' story as a cover for some Amelia Westlake activity."

Natasha gives a hysterical cackle. "You? Amelia Westlake? How funny. No. God, imagine the headlines. 'Harriet Price, Rosemead Prep mascot, Tawney Shield prefect, throws perfect life down drain for antiauthoritarian hoax.'" She swills the beer in her glass before taking a mouthful. "No, of course not *you*. But I figured you were going to tell me who Amelia Westlake is. My job at the *Messenger* is at stake if I don't help Croon catch the culprit. So, are you going to spill? I've had my money on your friend Liz for weeks, you see."

"Liz Newcomb?"

"That's her."

I pause. "We're more acquaintances."

"Really? Anyway, when it comes down to it, Liz is one of the few people I can think of who is motivated and smart enough to pull off this whole Amelia Westlake caper."

I bite hard on my straw. "That's an interesting perspective."

Natasha grins. "Tell me what you really think, Harriet Price, sister of Art Juice. I'm feeling uniquely open this evening. I'm in a positively generous mood."

She really is. Someone has slipped aside the gift ribbon, torn off the paper, and unwrapped her like a present. A shiny one, with an LED light that glows from within. I realize she has no idea what Will and I are up to. Even so, I have to be careful.

"Apart from Liz, who else is on your list of suspects?" I ask lightly.

"So far, I've managed to knock out about sixty percent of our year group based on who was in class when the essay swap happened," Natasha says.

Which leaves me in the other forty percent. I gnash at the straw between my teeth.

"And I've narrowed down the list further after considering who and what types of issues the pranks have targeted. It's all a bit speculative at this stage, to be honest, but I'm hoping to change that."

I try not to overreact to this expressed hope of hers. Polite interest is the key. "Really. How?" I say.

Natasha leans forward conspiratorially. "Duncan's uncle is a forensic handwriting specialist." She sits back and waits for me to respond to this startling piece of news.

"He is?"

For someone usually stone-faced, Natasha looks ecstatic. "Yep. Talk about good luck. Between Duncan and me, we've just about finished collecting handwriting samples from everyone in the year, which his uncle will then cross-check against the cartoons."

I freeze. Will may have penned the pictures, but it's *my* handwriting on those cartoons. "How on earth have you managed to collect samples from everyone?" The question comes out shriller than I was aiming for.

"We've been taking photographs of stuff people have put up on noticeboards around school. You drew up the Formal

Committee sign-up list that's in the year-twelve common room, didn't you?"

"Um, I'm not sure..."

"The one with the handwritten paragraph at the top about the formal being the 'pinnacle of the Rosemead experience'?"

I take a long drink of vodka.

"Thought so." Nat grins. "If all goes to plan, we should have solved the puzzle by the end of term. Which not only means I'll be in the clear with Croon, but also that I'll be able to write my exposé for the *Messenger* over the holidays."

I don't want to hear any more. I need to tell Will about this latest development. Preferably immediately. "I just have to visit the bathroom," I tell Natasha.

"Sure," she says. "I'll get us another round."

✶ ✶ ✶

Will is still in the newsroom. Behind her head I can see the corkboard, with page drafts hanging limply, and a decrepit-looking couch.

"Oh dear, Will! You're still stuck in there?"

"I think I've found a way out."

"Thank goodness. Listen, I've got some bad news. It sounds ridiculous, but Natasha says she's employed a *forensic specialist* to analyze our cartoons. They've already got my handwriting sample—What on earth are you doing?"

The picture is shaking, and Will is grunting like she's lifting weights. I bring my face closer to the screen.

"I'm pretty sure this window isn't actually locked," Will

says. "Some crappy painter has painted it to the frame. If I can...just..."

Will upends the phone onto a flat surface and the screen goes black. I hear another grunt and the sound of breaking glass, followed by Will screeching.

I hold the screen to my nose. "Will? Will! Are you all right?"

"I think I've cut my arm."

"Oh my God!"

Finally her face fills the screen. She is breathing deeply, and I realize I am, too. "You're still there," she says.

I nod. "Are—are you okay?"

"There's quite a lot of blood."

I feel a pulse in my throat. "Will," I say as calmly as possible. "I'm going to come and pick you up. We need to get you to a doctor."

Will runs a hand across her gleaming forehead. "Don't be silly. It's just a graze."

"I can see that's not true," I say, suddenly breathless. "I'm leaving now."

"Really, Harriet, you don't have to do that," Will says as I'm about to end the call. "I've got a handkerchief. I'll put pressure on it to stop the flow—"

"It's not enough—"

"And as soon as I get home, I'll get Mum to look at it. She's a nurse."

I hesitate. "I didn't know that."

"There's a lot you don't know about me. Don't worry." She smiles reassuringly.

"I really think I should come. And I need to talk to you about this handwriting issue—"

Will interrupts me. "I'll be fine," she says firmly. "I need you to stay there. Just make sure Nat stays within sight." The screen goes blank.

✂ ✂ ✂

When I return to the booth, Natasha is halfway through her second beer. A fresh vodka and lemonade stands on my half of the table.

"Feeling better?"

I wave a nonchalant hand, hoping she can't see it shaking.

She rests her cheek on her palm and gazes at me quizzically. "Art Juice's sister. Who would have thought?"

I'm getting tired of this refrain. "Why do you find it so surprising?"

Natasha laughs. "Are you kidding me? Because he's awesome! He and the rest of the Sphere are musical genii. They're pushing the boundaries of punk the whole time. You don't exactly have a reputation for pushing boundaries, Harriet. All that blind faith you place in Rosemead..." Seeing my expression, she peters out. "I'll give you this. You're not as bad as those evil twins you hang out with."

"You mean Millie and Beth?"

Natasha nods.

"They're not twins."

"They may as well be. They're a pair of stuck-up, racist brats."

I redden. "They're not that bad."

Natasha snorts. "They look down on anyone who isn't as

rich or as groomed as they are. They're always calling in favors from their wealthy parents to get ahead. And you know Beth calls me Ning Nong, don't you?"

I reach carefully for my drink. "That's . . . not very nice."

"Have you ever said that to Beth?"

"I . . ." I shift in my chair.

Natasha narrows her eyes. "Then you're no better."

I swallow. I've never thought of it that way before. I look at my lap. When I look up, Natasha is swilling her beer and studying me. She appears to take pity on me, because the next thing she says is, "Luckily for you, you have a hot brother."

"I'm sorry," I say, confused. "I don't think I heard you properly. Did you just say you find Arthur attractive?"

"Hoo yeah."

This is astounding. "Even with that haircut?"

Natasha nods. "Especially with that haircut. It's been a while since I looked twice at a guy, especially a younger guy, but he's something, all right. He's not single at the moment, by any chance?"

I have no idea what to say.

Natasha pushes her empty glass away. "Does my question surprise you?" She looks amused.

"Oh! It's just that I didn't realize you were, ah—" I stammer.

"You didn't realize I was what?"

"Single yourself."

Natasha looks uncomfortable. "I'm not sure if I am or not, to be honest."

"That sounds . . . complicated," I say carefully.

Natasha looks toward the window and back again. "You know when you're with someone? And it's fine? But not amazing? But you're mates? And you don't want to jeopardize the friendship by—" She stops and shakes her head.

She's talking about Will. She has to be. A heady beat starts up in my chest.

"God, I shouldn't be saying any of this. Forget I spoke." Natasha rubs her face. She slides out of the booth. "Your brother's on in ten. You coming?"

"I'll, ah, just finish this drink."

"Suit yourself."

I watch her stalk across the room.

A sudden urge overtakes me. I need to see Will. To see if she made it out of the newsroom okay. To tell her not to worry about Natasha. About anything to do with Natasha at all.

I wait until Natasha is out of sight, then send Will a quick text:

> How are you? Do you need me to do
> anything? I can drive over right now. I have a
> first aid certificate! And do not worry about
> Natasha returning any time soon, she is deeply
> preoccupied. Let me know. H XXX

Her response is swift. Very swift.

> All good. Speak later.

I stare, disappointed, at the text.

I put away my phone. I try to think steadily about Natasha's comments. Perhaps it is not my place to relay this particular news to Will.

If only the two of them would talk to each other!

Like a lasagna fresh from the oven, I let the situation settle on the metaphorical countertop.

If Arthur likes Natasha as much as Natasha clearly likes Arthur, she could help mend Arthur's heart. And that could resolve Will and Natasha's delicate . . . situation . . . delicately.

I should not say anything to Will about what Natasha said to me.

But it occurs to me: If *Amelia* can solve this particular problem of Will's, maybe it isn't all she can solve.

chapter 19

WILL

I am climbing into a taxi with Harriet Price. On a Sunday. Before coffee. Life, it's safe to say, has become weird.

Mum's in the front yard with her bum in the air, tackling a weed. Does she garden every Sunday morning? I'm never up before eleven on Sundays so I don't have a clue. It's strange being awake this early: the street so quiet, the air so crisp, the sunlight refracting off roof tiles. If I were to ever commit a robbery, I decide, now would be the time of day to do it.

The weed comes free; Mum crashes onto the lawn, dirt spraying across her sweatshirt. I turn away from the taxi window in embarrassment and slot my seat belt into its holder as we ease away from the curb. "Are you going to tell me where we're going?"

"I told you already. It's Amelia-related business," Harriet says.

"So I'm giving up my Sunday because . . . ?"

What I'm supposed to be doing and, in fact, have promised a couple of people I'll be doing (Mrs. Degarno, for example, and Mum) is mapping out my major work. I even pocketed a utility knife from the Drama Club's set design stores to size my canvas.

Harriet reaches over and gingerly touches my bandaged arm. "How is it feeling? Is it healing okay?"

She's wearing jeans. This is new. On school casual clothes days she always wears skirts with various rotating knitted items. Today she has on a yellow cardigan, but also skinny jeans and yellow Converse sneakers. The outfit is working for her.

I inhale the smell of stale cigarette smoke and bottled air freshener. "It stung for a while, but it's fine."

I try to gather clues about where we're going from the stuff she has with her. On the floor are a medium-sized satchel and a small cotton bag. This doesn't help. She could have a baby ferret inside each of them for all I know.

"Does today's adventure have anything to do with the handwriting business you mentioned last night?"

Harriet pauses. "Sort of, yes. But before we get into that, I checked Instagram again, and Amelia Westlake's email account." She is picking at the stickers on the inside of the door. "Still no word from that girl."

"If only somebody—a well-respected person in a leadership position at the school, for example—could demonstrate it was okay to come forward," I say.

Harriet says nothing.

The taxi trundles through the quiet streets, past shops and

rundown warehouses. They're not streets I often go down. But then, I usually catch buses, and they follow the main roads.

At the next corner I notice a green arrow sign, and on the green arrow, a picture of a little white plane.

My chest feels suddenly tight.

Another corner. Another green arrow. Another little white plane.

I could kill her.

I look at Harriet. She has placed a hand on my arm and is leaning toward me. Her mouth is moving, I can feel her breath on my face, but the pounding in my ears makes it hard for me to hear what she's saying.

It's always hard to hear things on a plane. The noise of the engine mutes everything else: stewards asking for meal orders, the rustle of food being opened, screams. That's how you know you're not in a disaster movie. In movies you can hear every word people speak. In real life it's all chaos and engine roar and your own mad heartbeat.

Harriet is talking to me about Chuck Close. Have I heard of him, she's asking. *She's* asking *me*. About *Chuck Close*.

Of course I've heard of Chuck Close. I've seen his paintings at the Museum of Contemporary Art. I've pored over books of his portraits that my dad owns.

"The American portrait artist," she says as we round another corner, sliding closer on the plastic-wrapped seat of the taxi. "He works with photographs and grids. He puts one grid on the photograph and one on a giant canvas and copies the photograph cell by cell."

My heart has begun to pound against my rib cage.

"Each cell is an artwork of its own. But when you put the cells together they make up the portrait perfectly. It's so intricate, the work he does, that the finished product is almost indistinguishable from a real photo."

Her voice rings high over the drone of talk radio. We turn another corner, following the arrow sign in the direction of the little white plane.

My glands fizz.

"Do you know why he does it? What keeps him so motivated?" Her smile is bright. "He has a condition called face blindness. He doesn't recognize faces, even the ones of people he knows. By studying a person's face so carefully, by tackling it piece by piece, by absorbing it in small morsels, he gets to know the face so intimately that he overcomes his condition."

The taxi drives into the shadow of an overpass. Above us is a sign that reads DOMESTIC TERMINALS 2 AND 3.

Blood is thick in my ears.

"So what I've done," says Harriet, rooting in her backpack as the taxi slows to a halt beside the terminal's revolving doors, "is booked us on a flight to Brisbane. There and back. Just for the day. I thought it was best to start with a relatively short distance. We can make some Amelia-related mischief when we get there, perhaps send a postcard or two. And my grandmother is expecting us for lunch."

I feel my stomach heave.

Harriet places the cotton carry bag on my lap and squeezes my arm. "Here you go." She empties out the contents: a magazine, an iPod, a plastic-wrapped muffin, and a small stack of note cards. "Don't you see, Will? You can do this. All you have to do is break down each moment, just like Chuck Close does. To help you, I've written out the steps. You can follow my instructions, see?"

I open the taxi door and vomit into the gutter.

The terminal boardwalk is crowded with people, most of them pulling bags on wheels. I don't look up to see if any of them have noticed. Instead, after wiping my face with the tail of my shirt, I undo my seat belt and make a beeline for a concrete pillar. I lean heavily against it, shielding my eyes with a hand.

Harriet rushes out of the taxi. She puts a hand on my arm again. "Are you okay?"

I look at her for a long moment.

"What the fuck does it look like, Harriet?"

"Oh. I—"

It takes willpower not to retch again. I gulp it down. "You think it's easy, do you? You think you can fix this 'problem' of mine with a set of *note cards*? Like my fear of flying is some sort of public-speaking exercise? Is that it?"

Her eyes widen. "I just thought—"

I press my hands to my knees and lean forward, panting. "Don't you think if it was that easy I'd have done it already? Sucked it up and gone to Perth? He's my father! Of course I want to see him. What is wrong with you?"

"I was only—"

"Do me a real favor and stay the hell away from me."

I stumble past her to the taxi line.

It's not until the taxi's winding back through the warehouses of Sydenham, leaving Harriet Price in her little bubble of ignorant perfectionism far behind, that my muscles finally unclench. My heart rate settles. We drive past a neighborhood park where the early sun's turning dew into mist and play equipment into molten silver, and the whole foggy, glittering scene is like the Yosemite Valley of a California impressionist, or even better—those dreams where an angel comes down to tell you your destiny, his wings backlit by heaven's high beams.

Only this isn't the Destiny Angel but the Angel of Revealing the Bloody Obvious.

I should never have started a hoax with Harriet Price. There are so many reasons it was a bad idea. I tick them off.

She's a meddler.

She's patronizing.

She's snobbish.

She's uptight.

She's straitlaced.

She's overly ambitious.

She has zero personal style.

She's clueless.

She's as half-baked as a bloody lamb roast.

She chooses half-full over half-empty every bloody time.

She's a joiner. Joiners are the worst.

She's unbelievably repressed.

She has a grating enthusiasm.

She says meaningless things like "Everything happens for a reason" and "There's no *I* in team!"

She wears a weird-smelling moisturizing cream.

By the time I get back home I regret having given her my number. Eighteen missed calls. I add "obsessive" to my list of her negative personal characteristics and go to my room.

Screw Harriet Price and the prestige car she rode in on.

What I need to do is get back to the things that matter, like my major work. I take out my oversized canvas and draw a line down one side. With the stolen utility knife I slice the canvas with the precision of a microsurgeon. Now all I have to do is decide what to paint.

I consider my ideas one by one. A stalling aircraft—but how do you pictorially represent that? The toxicity of the smoke spiraling from the burning upholstery of first-class seats—again, difficult to draw. I finally settle on a jet engine ingesting a flock of Canada geese.

Somehow, though, I keep picturing a confounded Harriet Price standing by the automatic doors at the domestic terminal of the airport.

* * *

Clearly the best thing is to avoid Harriet from now on. I'm calling an end to Amelia Westlake. We've achieved a lot, but continuing it isn't worth the hassle of dealing with the prefect from hell. I begin by blocking Harriet's number from my phone and deleting it.

At school on Monday, I steer clear of the year-twelve common room, the staff building, and the PAC storeroom. Given the number of times Harriet has cornered me outside the newsroom, I decide to avoid that, too.

"Rotten tooth," I explain to Nat during English while Fowler is defending Ernest Hemingway's sexism.

"Huh?" Nat says.

"I've been visiting sick bay for painkillers. It's why I haven't been around the newsroom at lunchtimes lately. For some reason the pain always kicks in at noon."

"Sounds awful," she says, her gaze drifting.

Since when does Nat lose focus when I speak to her?

She turns back suddenly. "Listen, I've been meaning to talk to you." She sounds serious.

I sit up.

"I think it's best if we put a pause on the … extracurricular stuff for a while," says Nat. "Things are getting busy with overdue study, and deadlines are tight at the *Messenger*. . . ." She trails off, watching for my reaction.

This is unexpected, but to be honest I'm relieved. I suspect she's reached the same conclusion as I have—that there's simply no chemistry between us. It's her gentle way of saying as much, and coming from Nat, who is usually the opposite of gentle, I'm especially grateful for it.

I smile to reassure her. "That makes sense." I pause.

"Really?" She gives me an apologetic grimace.

"Totally." I nod. "I'm really busy right now, too."

"Okay, great," Nat says. "I mean—that works out, then. For both of us." She looks embarrassed.

I try to think of something else to talk about. "Hey, random question, but did you know Harriet Price had a girlfriend?"

As soon as the words leave my lips, I regret them. Nat snaps to attention. "Why are you asking me about Harriet Price?"

I think fast. "I heard recently she's dating the captain of Blessingwood, that's all," I say.

Nat studies me broodily for a while, and then her expression relaxes. The dreamy look she wore a minute ago returns. "Everyone knows that," she says mildly. "It's just that you happen to live under a rock."

"Right," I say, nodding. "If you say so."

As Fowler and Nakita Wallis lead an open discussion on the albatross as a metaphor, I steal glimpses at Nat. What's going on with her? She looks uncharacteristically content— happy, even—almost as if one of life's great truths has been revealed to her.

"I'll try to make it to the newsroom today, but I'm not promising anything," I tell her when class is finished.

"Don't worry about it," Nat says. "We've had to move out anyway."

"How come?"

Nat rips the paper off a stick of gum. "The place got broken into, and there's glass everywhere, and the police don't want us to disturb anything."

I stare at her. "The police?"

"They're taking fingerprints, DNA, all that. Some of the glass has blood on it so they reckon that whoever broke in cut themselves on the way out. Not that we can work out what's been taken."

I finger the sleeve that covers my bandage.

Nat looks at me strangely, almost like she's never been so pleased. It makes no sense.

Unless she knows about my involvement in Amelia Westlake.

Oh crap. That's it. She saw Harriet at the Deep Fryer gig and worked it all out. And my question just now about Harriet confirmed it for her.

Of course.

She is reveling in her secret knowledge before confronting me.

I try to remember what Harriet told me about Nat's recent investigations. I was trapped in the newsroom at the time and was kind of preoccupied. I didn't get a chance to follow it up in the taxi, either. Something about handwriting? Nat collecting samples? Analyzing our cartoons? I'm pretty sure that was it.

Shit.

If only I knew for certain. If I could just quiz Harriet for a minute, I could ask her exactly what Nat told her that night, so I'd know how to handle her. Otherwise, Nat might trick me into telling her everything, just when I'd hoped to pack Amelia Westlake into a neat little box and send her off to deep-freeze storage.

I'm going to have to break my Harriet ban. Instead of skipping biology to avoid her—our only class together now that our swimming rotation in phys ed is over—I'll pull her aside and we can shore up our alibis.

* * *

I take my usual seat at the far right of the lab counters. I keep an eye on Harriet's usual seat: at the front, in the direct line of Mr. Van's desk.

The class files in.

Palmer Crichton is sitting behind me. She leans over and murmurs in my ear. "Have you placed a bet yet?"

I turn around. "Is this the Amelia Westlake sweep I've heard about?"

She nods. "Even if you've bet, you may want to place a new one. Some new information has come to light."

I wonder what's she on about. "Oh yeah?"

"Prisha Kamala has come forward about a trip she took to her local stationers last month to get some materials for a class project," says Palmer, close to my ear. "The stationers was short on neon-pink card stock. Apparently another Rosemead student had bulk bought fifty sheets of the stuff the day before." She tilts her head. "Want to guess where Prisha's local stationers is?" But Palmer doesn't wait for an answer. "Mosman," she gloats.

Crapping maloney. Has Harriet really been so stupid?

Palmer is clearly pleased with herself. "It's definitely shortened the odds on some of our contenders, let me tell you. There are only six people in our year who live in Mosman. Prisha, Beth Tupman, Lorna Gallagher, Harriet Price—"

I bite the inside of my cheek. "Does Nat Nguyen know about this analysis of yours?"

Palmer nods. "She's cross-checking our findings against some tests of her own. She's pretty confident we'll be able to narrow it right down. Which means we're only taking bets for another two days. Come on. It's your last chance."

"I don't have any change on me, sorry." I turn back to the front.

Beth Tupman, who is Harriet's lab partner, is one of the last to arrive. Usually they arrive together, but she's by herself.

Mr. Van begins class. Still no Harriet.

Twenty minutes into the lesson, her empty seat stands out like a human ear grafted on a mouse.

Where is she?

✳ ✳ ✳

She isn't in biology on Tuesday. I do a few walk-bys of the year-twelve common room. Nothing.

Where the hell has she disappeared to? Is she sick? Injured? Did something happen at the airport after I left? Is that why she tried to call me eighteen times? Maybe she tripped over a baggage carousel and shattered her kneecaps. Maybe she was abducted by a drug cartel to smuggle illegal substances inside her body.

Or maybe she's been at school the whole time but with a new haircut so I haven't recognized her. Has she finally seen sense and ditched the Butterscotch Blonde?

The other possibility is I've forgotten what she looks like. I think about it. Other than the hair, I can't remember any particular facial features. Has all her talk of Chuck Close triggered some kind of empathetic face blindness?

I want to ask somebody if they've seen her—Beth Tupman, Millie Levine, anyone—but with so many people on the Amelia Westlake trail, not to mention Palmer's new damning clue, the question would be suspicious.

On Tuesday afternoon, out of sheer desperation, I take a casual walk down to the tennis courts. They're empty, so empty that it feels like the sign of a coming apocalypse. I'm beginning to feel desperate enough to text her. Then I remember I deleted her number.

I climb into the umpire's chair to think. From up here you can see the whole school empire: the gymnasium, both ovals, the classrooms, the Performing Arts Center, the architectural-award-winning staff building, girls wandering down pathways and across lawns in pairs, in groups, alone. None of them is Harriet.

I take my phone out of my pocket.

To be clear, Instagram is for narcissists. The only reason I keep a personal profile there is to follow the feeds of my favorite art magazines. Other than to check out Amelia Westlake's feed, I haven't been on it for months. I'm hopeful that Harriet does not share this mindset.

I type in her name and voilà, up she pops, plenty of personal information freely available for any ax murderer to see. Harriet Price: *Sydney, Australia* | *Rosemead student* | *Tennis tragic* | *The Sphere fan*. Followers: 1,096.

Like anyone could possibly know that many people.

I look at her profile picture. She's in her Tawney Shield tennis whites with her arm around a girl in matching gear, presumably School Captain Edie.

Harriet's face looks so familiar on the screen that I wonder how I forgot it. I study Edie. She is pretty, but to be honest— okay, honest and extremely superficial—I reckon she's punching above her weight.

See? This is why I hate social media. It turns you into a horrible person.

It's probably just a bad photo of her and a really good one of Harriet. Or maybe it's because I know Harriet and that makes me see her as more beautiful.

Beautiful in a bland, preppy kind of way.

After dinner at home I look at a few more Instagram photos of Edie and Harriet, just to be sure.

Then I look at a few more photos of just Harriet.

Then I log out of Instagram and image search Harriet through a couple of different search engines and look at those pictures. Harriet on skis. Harriet in tennis gear. Harriet with Arthur and their horrible-looking Ken and Barbie parents.

I hear the key in the front door, which means Mum is home after a night out with Graham. I check my watch.

How can it possibly already be eleven thirty?

I hit FOLLOW under Harriet's profile and go to bed.

* * *

I check Instagram as soon as I wake up the next morning. Nothing. At lunchtime, in a last-ditch effort to hunt Harriet down, I decide to go to the storeroom on the off chance she'll swing by. The first thing I do is check out the shelves for any sign she's been there recently.

Everything looks to be in order: my tea and coffee, my novelty mugs, and my art books. Harriet's weird little collection of trinkets: air freshener, a selection of health bars, a fire extinguisher, and a fire blanket with the price tag still dangling from it. On the bottom shelf are the embroidered cavalry jacket, vest, pants, and shirt in a pile that have been there all along. I settle into my usual chair to wait. I start eating my falafel roll.

It's strange being here by myself. As infuriating as Harriet is, I guess I've become used to her.

I'm dabbing hummus off my chin when I have a thought.

I look at my pile of art books again. *American Portraiture in the Twenty-First Century* is missing. It was definitely there last week.

Okay. This can't be a coincidence. If I remember correctly, there's a chapter on Chuck Close in it. Harriet must have taken it to research her little taxi speech.

Why haven't I thought of this before? Harriet clearly has no personal interest in art. She must have looked up all that stuff. What Harriet did was work out a topic that would interest me as a way of getting me to think about my phobia.

Which is completely deluded. But kind of nice.

Something on the bookshelf catches my eye. A set of note cards. The top one is stained on the corner. It looks like vomit.

I pick them up and take a sniff.

Definitely vomit.

I read the twelve cards one by one.

CARDS FOR WILL
TOPIC: HOW TO FLY ON A PLANE IN TEN SIMPLE
STEPS
1. Arrive at the airport.
2. Go through security.
3. Buy a coffee and drink it slowly.
4. Go to the boarding gate.
5. Complete this crossword (see over).
6. Board plane.

7. Read magazine (enclosed).
8. Listen to playlist on iPod (enclosed).
9. Eat snack (also enclosed).
10. Get off plane.

I can see what she's done. Or tried to do. She's broken it down for me just like Chuck Close breaks down his paintings. It's nice. Really nice. In fact, I can't think of a nicer thing anyone has ever done for me.

She was nice, too, when I pretended to sprain my ankle. And the night of the newsroom break-in, offering to come around and administer first aid, texting me to make sure I made it home all right.

I finger the bandage on my arm.

If I wasn't so certain that we weren't friends, I'd say Harriet Price is one of the best friends I've ever had. Over the last couple of months I have shared more with her than I have with anyone.

Suddenly I can't think of why I've been angry with her. I overreacted when she was simply trying to help me out. What I want, I realize, is to make things up to her, and it's burning a hole in my chest.

I hear a click and the door opens.

* * *

In the summer before year ten, Dad took me to see the Great Barrier Reef. I insisted we needed to visit before the short-sighted interests of successive money-grubbing governments made it extinct. On the second day, I snorkeled too far down and had to paddle like a demon to reach the top before I ran out of breath. I still remember breaking the surface, that first clean taste of air. It's the kind of relief I feel now.

She's wearing tracksuit pants and a polo shirt with the Tawney Shield emblem on it. Now I understand why I haven't been able to find her. Tawney Shield prematches take up a good part of a week and are held off campus. "I've been looking all over for you," I say.

She opens a Tawney Shield sports bag and begins to fill it with items from the shelf.

"Harriet, wait."

I put a hand on her arm. She flinches.

"I wanted to apologize. I overreacted on Sunday."

Harriet is still facing the shelf.

"What you tried to do for me at the airport—it was completely ridiculous and embarrassingly naïve. But also sweet."

Harriet throws her air freshener into the bag.

"More than sweet. *Really* sweet."

Harriet throws her health bars into the bag.

"Kind of amazing, actually."

Harriet throws her fire blanket into the bag.

"Can you look at me for one second? Please?"

I touch her arm again. This time she throws it off so violently that my fingers hit metal shelving. I wince. "Harriet..."

I hear a click.

Someone's coming in.

In the whole history of our secret storeroom meetings, nobody has ever come in.

Harriet turns in surprise. I glance around the storeroom.

A pile of leftover neon-pink arrows is on the shelf in plain view. Our cartoons are up on the wall. We're here as well, among it all. Whoever walks in the door in five microseconds, four microseconds, three microseconds, will know everything at a glance. They'll know who we are. They'll know who Amelia Westlake is. Harriet Price and Will Everhart in a storeroom together—it's so unlikely that there's no other possible explanation.

Unless.

Two microseconds. One.

The door opens and in comes Duncan Aboud, and I throw Harriet Price against the wall of cartoons and kiss her on the mouth.

PART THREE

chapter 20

HARRIET

Madame Chair, adjudicator, audience.

Today I will be arguing the topic "my life is over."

"My" pertains to me. "Life" refers to the general or universal condition of human existence. "Over" in this context means ended, finished, utterly extinguished.

My life is over because a week ago it was ruined by the actions of one selfish and possibly deranged person called Will Everhart.

First, Will Everhart involved me in an elaborate hoax. Second, through this hoax she implicated me in an illegal enterprise. Third, to disguise said enterprise she placed me in a compromising situation. The consequences have been irrevocable. Put simply, the life I once led is done with.

Ladies and gentlemen: In contemporary society, great emphasis is placed on academic success, sporting prowess, and the maintenance of stable relationships. Four months ago, I had all these boxes ticked. Today, my school marks are average at best, my sporting goals are unlikely to be reached, and I have no relationship to speak of.

I ask you, Who is to blame? Is it my teachers, who have made it their life's work to educate the youth of today? Is it my tennis coach, who has trained me in the art of the backhand and the volley? Is it Edie Marshall, future prime minister and love of my life?

Distinguished guests, the answer is *no*. Will Everhart is the reason for all of it.

My life is over because Will Everhart cajoled me into a ridiculous series of activities that distracted me from my life goals.

My life is over because she then decided it would be a good idea to kiss me in a storeroom in the presence of a school journalist.

My life is over because unsurprisingly, news quickly spread that Will Everhart and I were having an affair.

My life is over because as soon as the news reached my girlfriend, she broke up with me. BY TEXT MESSAGE.

I ask you, Madame Chair: How much havoc can one person wreak? When is enough enough?

But it doesn't end there. The day after Edie dumped me, she messaged to say it would be best for both of us if we were no longer doubles partners in the Tawney Shield. Instead, she has partnered with Queensland's under-sixteen champion, Bianca Stein.

As a result, my lifelong dream of winning the Tawney

Shield doubles, something I have been working toward for the last six years, has been completely obliterated.

I come now to the arguments put forward by the opposition. While I acknowledge the point that I am still technically breathing and that consequently my life has not in fact ceased, I reject this argument on the basis that it is a truism and therefore invalidated by the rules of this debate.

My opponent further argues that kisses are a metaphor for life, as in the kiss of life featured in such fairy tales as *Sleeping Beauty*. He reasons that I should therefore interpret Will Everhart's kiss not as an ending but a beginning. In response I refer him to Ralph Vaughan Williams's three-act opera *The Poisoned Kiss*, to Michael Corleone's kiss of death in *The Godfather: Part II*, and to the kiss of Judas described in Matthew 26:47–50, which led to the demise of Jesus Christ.

Besides, how is anyone to take anything my opponent says seriously when (a) his key goal in life is to play guitar for a garage punk band and (b) he is, since Wednesday, literally in bed with the enemy, Natasha Nguyen—the head of Rosemead's predatory student media—who aided and abetted the prime culprit to ruin me forever?

In conclusion, as a result of the actions of Will Everhart and her accomplices, my life is totally and completely fucked.

Thank you.

chapter 21

WILL

I should have let her keep the art pen. That's where this all started. That day in detention, when she held it ransom, I should have upped and walked. Instead, like an idiot, I did a deal with her—the devil in pastel—a stupid deal about a stupid cartoon. And now here we are.

Did I mention how shitty my life is? Here's another tale. Add this to the long-winded name, the pet fatalities, the faulty hair dryer, the charlatanizing parents, and the flying phobia: I kissed Harriet Price.

It's not your sympathy I'm after. What I need is a life raft.

We kissed, and it was wonderful.

Please send help.

chapter 22

HARRIET

"Harri, can you hear me? Harriet!"

I open my eyes onto broken light. The world is a shadow box, and each square holds a different thing: a flying bird, a wavering palm, a scrap of sky. Someone is tapping their foot in another room. Or is it a hand slapping my cheek?

I stretch my legs the full length of the lounge chair and remove the straw hat from my face.

"Harri," says Arthur, peering down at me. "Are you drunk?"

His head is freshly shaven at the sides. Gel glistens in the ferrety bit running down the middle of his scalp. He looks worried, but I don't care.

"Go away." I cover my face with my hat again.

"Is there vodka in this juice?" I hear him pick up the glass and slurp from it. "That's vodka all right." An arc of liquid hits the grass. "Sit up and talk to me."

Talking to Arthur is the last thing I want to do. He will only tell me that everything will be okay, when it won't be, and that I will get through this, which is a lie. Even so, I struggle into an upright position, all the while keeping the hat brim over my face.

"Look at me," Arthur says.

"But the glare off the pool—"

Arthur swipes the hat from my head. "That's better."

I squint at him. Witchetty white he is, king of the darkened music halls, my bandman brother, my little troglodyte. Art Juice, player of tunes, wooer of snarly women.

"Harri, you're muttering. Drink this."

I look at the glass with disdain.

"Drink."

Oh, the boredom of water. I take a teensy-weensy sip.

"What are we going to do with you?"

I prop myself up on one elbow and face him. Why can't he just act like a self-absorbed kid brother rather than trying to fix my life? If he wants to do something useful, he should break up with his new girlfriend. She is the one who sent her cub reporter to spy on Will Everhart and me and then plastered the news all over the school paper's gossip pages.

Natasha Nguyen. What a callous bitch.

Her only saving grace is that she hasn't published her findings about Amelia Westlake yet. I wonder what the holdup is. If she's carried out the handwriting tests like she said she would, then she knows the truth by now, or at least half of it.

Perhaps she has decided that ruining my life twice in one fortnight is a step too far.

Like she would ever be that thoughtful. Ruinous cow.

I pull my sarong across my shoulders. "Leave me alone, Arthur." I roll onto my back again.

"Come on, Harri. Things aren't that bad."

"Not that bad? My Tawney chances are ruined."

"Not necessarily."

"My school marks—shitted on."

"The mouth on you, girl."

"Not to mention Edie and me—"

"She didn't deserve you," says Arthur, pushing the glass of water toward my lips again.

"Nice try." I turn my face away from it.

"Think of it this way. Now you're going out with Will, you guys can double-date with Natasha and me."

I sit up again. "I am *not* going out with Will Everhart. We've been through this already. And I want nothing to do with Natasha Nguyen. She can rot in hell for all I care."

"Okay. You're not going out with Will. But you could if you wanted to."

I scoff. How little he understands. "Will didn't kiss me because she's *interested* in me. She had other motives," I say.

"Like?"

"It's sort of complicated and difficult to explain. Anyway, I'm not in the mood."

Arthur makes the awful cackling sound he always makes when he doesn't believe me. Like an evil mastermind with laryngitis. "*I* like her," he says. "That night you brought her round? She seemed really great."

If only Arthur knew how far off the mark he is! "Really great" people don't deliberately set out to ruin others. To think what Will did after all the ways I tried to help her! And how she repaid me for my generosity: by desecrating my entire existence.

"She was about a million times more chill with me than Edie's ever been," Arthur adds.

"So that's what you've got against Edie."

"It's one of the things. I know Mum likes her, but as far as I can see, that's just because she wants you to win Tawney. She hates that Edie's your girlfriend."

I shake my head. My vision blurs. "That's not true."

"Sure it is. If you brought any other girl home—hey, don't look so mortified. Who cares what Mum thinks, anyway?"

I clutch at my hair. "Why is everything so terrible? Why?"

Arthur flicks my shoulder playfully. "It might all seem overwhelming now, but it's term holidays. You've got two weeks to sort everything out before you even have to face anybody at school."

I groan and reach for the bottle of vodka stashed beneath my chair. "What are you looking so smug about?"

"No reason. Hang on. What's that?" says Arthur, pointing across the grass.

I follow his finger.

Suddenly I feel his arms beneath my knees and back, lifting me up.

The treetops blur. Cool air breathes at my feet.

Splash!

The world turns cold and liquid.

I make my way to the surface of the pool in the shade of his silhouette. I swear the little grub is grinning. Wiping the water from my eyes, I look up at him.

"Arthur, you're dead."

chapter 23

WILL

Dear diary,

Do people even write that? "Dear diary"? I've never kept a diary in my life. To be honest, I've always thought diaries were completely cheesy—the kind of thing people who like ponies and Hello Kitty are into. But that's the amazing thing, diary! In the last seven days, cheesy things have felt right....

It makes no sense. It's been a crappy week. The cut on my arm from the newsroom fiasco got infected and swelled up like an eclair. Mrs. Degarno gave me a lecture for being behind with my major work. Nat published a gossipy piece on Harriet and me without so much as a heads-up. I am no longer returning her calls.

But despite everything being fucked up, I feel so happy to be alive!

Take Thursday, for example: I smiled at a baby. A *baby*. On Friday I downloaded the *Finding Dory* soundtrack.

I know.

Then yesterday afternoon Mum was wearing a pair of those socks that are like gloves for feet—the ones with a separate bit for each toe, where each toe is a different color. We're talking more cheese than a four-cheese pizza here. But instead of making a snide remark about them like, "There's a five-year-old out there with frostbite," I said, "Cute socks."

And when Mum asked whether I wanted to watch *Twilight* with her because it was on TV, I was like, "Sure."

I am on record for hating that film. (My review is on Rotten Tomatoes under Willanthropic.) Remember the part in the movie where Bella and her creepy vampire boyfriend dance at their school formal together? That's when I usually throw something at the screen.

This time, when the scene came on, I welled up. Tears literally ran down my face.

Mum put a hand on my forehead. "Are you feeling okay? Cripes. I put too much chili in the vegetable curry, didn't I?"

"I'm fine." I swiped roughly at my tears. Imagine getting emo over a school formal scene! It was the kind of thing the girls at Rosemead would do. "Hey, Mum. Can I ask you something?"

"Of course."

I brought my knees to my chin. "Why were you so keen for me to go to Rosemead?"

Mum grabbed another cushion for her back. She was probably remembering the last time we had this conversation—it had taken a while. "Do you really want to go through this again? You know why. You remember the problems you had at your old school."

"Yes, but why Rosemead?"

Mum paused. "I wanted to send you to a school with better resources, and a more nurturing environment—"

I snorted.

"What?"

I was tempted to tell her about my meeting with Croon and how she'd made it clear that Rosemead would prefer not to have me anywhere near its environment, but I knew it would upset her, so I held my tongue. "Nothing."

"And I wanted you to have the opportunity of a first-rate education," Mum said.

"The teachers at my old school were heaps better than the ones I have now."

"Maybe they were," she conceded. "But the classes were twice as big, the sports facilities consisted of one field that turned into a mud bath every time it rained, and there was no Art Department to speak of."

I grunted. "Yes, but it wasn't a snob factory like Rosemead."

She knew this was one of Dad's lines. "Your father went to a school very similar to Rosemead, you know."

"And he hated it."

"But as a result of going there, he got to become what he wanted to be." Mum tapped the coffee table in time with her words. "He got the marks for the degree he wanted, and the first job he had in the arts industry was through the father of a high school friend of his. He likes to think it was all on his own merit, but he is living his dream because of that school. Whereas only fifty percent of my public high school year even graduated."

"My old school wasn't like that," I said. "I know the facilities weren't great, but at least I didn't have to deal with the stuck-up bitches at Rosemead, who will get to rule the world because of the size of their family's stock portfolio."

Mum let out a sigh. "You can't blame me for trying to give you a fresh start, can you? For giving you a chance to be happy?"

Of course I couldn't.

"You've got Natasha now. And what about that new friend of yours, Amelia Westlake?"

"Er, sure."

"Look, Will." Mum turned to me. "I have no doubt you're right about the stuck-up girls at Rosemead. But they can't all be that bad. We've talked about this before. You have such high expectations of people. Not everyone can have fully formed opinions about politics and current affairs like you do."

"Why not?"

She shook her head, smiling. "Give people time to grow, Will, and they'll do the same for you."

We sat quietly for a moment watching *Twilight*.

"I'm sorry we don't have a family stock portfolio," she said when the next ad break came on. "It was remiss of us."

Now she was making fun of me. "You know that's not what I meant."

She smiled. "You could still make your mark, you know. You're a bright girl. And we may not have the type of money your classmates have, but I'd like to think your dad and I gave you a decent grounding in other ways."

"Your point being?"

She clasped her hands together. "Put it this way. You are passionate and creative, and you have a lot of knowledge to back that up. And knowledge is a form of power—a tool you can use to change the status quo. 'Down with capitalism and all that bullshit,' right?"

I grumbled into a cushion.

We watched the end of the film, and Mum switched off the television. There was the tick of the screen cooling, then silence.

While usually I'd prefer to stab myself in the eye with a cocktail umbrella than actively pursue a heart-to-heart, we were going so well that I figured there was no reason to stop.

"You know what's always puzzled me?" I said.

"What?" Mum asked.

"What you see in Graham."

"Will," Mum said crossly. "What did I just say about not judging people?"

"Sorry," I said, trying to look apologetic. "But it's true. He's so . . . I don't know . . . boring, I guess, in comparison to you. It just makes no sense to me."

Mum raised an eyebrow. "It doesn't need to make sense to *you*. It needs to make sense to *me*. Anyway, I *like* how different Graham and I are. Our differences are what make things interesting."

I considered this. "Can I ask one more thing?" I said.

"Could I stop you if I wanted to?" said Mum drily.

"When you started seeing Graham, did you know Dad was having an affair?"

She cleared her throat.

"You don't have to answer me," I said.

"No. I didn't. In fact, I'm not sure that he was," Mum said carefully. "Not then. It's hard to put a definitive date on these things. Your dad and I had been disconnected for a while." She watched me to see how this landed.

I bit my lip. "You make it all sound so... *inevitable*."

"Not everyone is meant to be with just one person for their whole life. I'm not saying it was wrong that your dad and I got together to begin with or that I regret our years together, because I don't. They were good years. I just mean that our time was up."

"So when you found out about Naomi, were you relieved?"

"No. I was very hurt. I felt rejected."

I pulled a cushion to my chest. "Even though you'd rejected Dad first?"

Mum flushed. I could see she was struggling to explain it. "Feelings are complicated. I felt really guilty about cheating on your dad. I know it hurt him as much as his affair hurt me. It's not like our infidelities canceled each other out. I hated myself for what I was doing. What I was doing to you, most of all. I was splitting up our family. I know how hard it's been for you with your dad moving out."

"'Moving out' is putting it mildly."

"It breaks my heart to see you fighting with each other

when you used to be so close." She reached out and brushed my hair with her fingers. "You are so much like him, you know."

It had been a while since she'd done that, the fingers-in-the-hair thing. I usually batted her hand away, but this time I snuggled in beside her like a joey into its mother's pouch.

Go ahead, diary: Vomit in your mouth.

✱ ✱ ✱

Now I slide my diary to the side of my desk and turn our conversation over again in my mind. I think about what Mum said about her and Dad splitting up. What surprises me is that she didn't try to justify anything. I respect her for that.

She was right about one thing: Feelings are bloody complicated.

I think about what she said about her relationship with Graham and how it works because of their differences, not in spite of them.

It makes me think of Harriet.

Then I try *not* to think of Harriet.

But the truth is, I *like* thinking about Harriet. And ever since that kiss...

I wasn't even aiming for anything. It was just meant as a cover. A way to hide the truth about Amelia Westlake. But she kissed me back, with her hands on my face and her lips apart.

I don't know what to do. It's not like we'll be kissing again. She made that clear seconds later, by acting outraged in front of Duncan.

Anyway, she has a girlfriend.

Although apparently not at the moment. Because of Nat's *Messenger* exposé.

Why am I even considering this? Harriet being single is irrelevant. We'll never be together. Can you imagine? Me and Harriet Price? Besides, going after someone who's on the rebound is never a good idea. And she and Edie were made for each other.

I open my laptop and find her profile pic online—the one with both of them in it. Edie. Look at her. Well-groomed. Good posture. A two-hundred-dollar haircut. Her face is so damn clear it looks photoshopped. Nothing like oily-skinned, slouchy old me.

For the first time since the storeroom, my mood dips.

Great. Now I'm getting jealous about some privileged, overachieving girl from Blessingwood. This is ridiculous. Damn Harriet Price for putting me through this.

And that's when I work it out. I've been happy all week, but it's a delusional state. As pathetic as some smiling kid who gets a letter from Santa in the mail.

Just tell the kid he doesn't exist! Get it over with! Rip off that Band-Aid, fast!

That's what I need to do, I realize. Rip off the Band-Aid.

So I leave the house.

I grab Mum's car keys from the counter on the way out.

⚹ ⚹ ⚹

It's late afternoon by the time I make it to Harriet's. She opens the door wearing nothing but a swimsuit and a beach towel.

This is going to be harder than I thought.

Vodka fumes waft off her. Her hair drips water, like she was caught in a flash flood minutes before I showed up.

Seriously, universe, what do you have against me? I swallow. "You're shivering."

"What do you want?" Her eyes are wild, violent.

"Shouldn't you put some clothes on or something?" My voice is unsteady, like *I'm* the one who is standing half-naked in the cold.

"Just say what you have to say," Harriet says, impatient.

Droplets cling to her skin. I swallow again. "I can wait while you get a sweater."

She gives a curt shake of her head and stays where she is. I gaze at her and my thoughts start to wander. Perhaps she doesn't own any sweaters. I know cardigans are more her thing. There are pimples of cold on her shoulders. Should I rub them smooth?

Of course not.

Her reflection jitters in the door glass, she is shivering that much.

"I'm here to apologize," I press on when she fails to move. "I tried to save our butts except I got us into a whole other pile of shit instead. I know that. I'm sorry I even tried. I promise that what happened in the storeroom won't happen again."

There. I've done it. I wait for a word from her. A sound. Anything.

"Okay, that's all," I say finally. "You really should get dressed." Gingerly, I reach out a hand to coax her.

Harriet's fingers bat mine away; my skin buzzes at her touch.

We stand there looking at each other. A metronome keeps a dizzy pace deep in my chest.

My thoughts float back to the storeroom. Our hands on each other. The warmth of her breath.

A sharp heat rises up my neck.

Harriet sways toward me and her arm grazes mine.

It's happening.

She reaches out her hand. Our fingers meet. She presses her palm to my cheek.

She sighs, and my belly jolts.

She takes her hand away. Steps back. "You need to leave," she says coldly, and slams the door in my face.

chapter 24

HARRIET

Under the glare of the bathroom light I slap my cheeks with
water and wipe them dry. I stare at my reflection in the mirror. My eyes are as pink as a rabbit's. My hair is a mess. Everything tingles, like I've just had oral surgery and the anesthetic is wearing off.

Why won't Will Everhart leave me alone?

In for four, out for six, I recite, breathing deeply. Or is it in for six, out for eight? Or in for seven, out for five? Every time I try to concentrate, Will's face floats up before my mind's eye like a helium balloon. Her lips on mine in the storeroom...

Clearly this is what happens when you spend too much time with one person. We did a whole unit on Stockholm syndrome in Ms. Bracken's class so I know there are historical precedents. It is a type of lunacy, this distraction. The way her breath seems to linger on my neck. How I can still feel her fingers on the small of my back.

Maybe, like stains on a table, she can be wiped off. I rub at my skin with damp hands. I try to smooth off the memory of her touch with heavy strokes.

It makes things worse. The friction creates an unbearable heat. I need a clean break from Will, that much is certain, but how can I have one when she insists on showing up at my door?

So much for the restorative power of swimming pools. Arthur is right about one thing, though. It is time to right the wheelbarrow and mend the fences. To cleanse my life of its impurities, of all the things that are keeping me from achieving my goals—Will Everhart, for example.

I drink some Gatorade. I blow-dry my hair. I put on my favorite jeans and merino cardigan and give each of my cheeks a hearty pinch.

"You are a winner!" I whisper to the mirror.

"You are a success!"

"You are heading for abundance!"

I practice smiling and leave the house.

✳ ✳ ✳

I drive to Edie's with my foot down, red traffic lights glowing in my rearview mirror. Where has all this pent-up energy come from? I go straight across her yard and climb the frangipani tree outside her bedroom window. It is a way to avoid her parents and also win points with Edie for the romantic gesture.

I reach the highest branch and crane my neck to look in.

Edie's lamp is on. She is sitting on an ergonomic chair in her Wimbledon pajamas. Above her, our collection of Tawney player profiles stare out from the wall. Her computer screen spills white light across the room. In front of it, Edie is massaging her forehead with her fingers.

I knock on the glass.

She comes over and pushes up the window halfway. "What do you want?"

"You." I redden. I haven't had much practice in this type of talk. Edie and I have never really gone in for it, and besides, it is difficult to be suggestive when you're gripping the slippery trunk of a frangipani tree with both hands to stop yourself from plunging down a three-meter drop.

"Expand," Edie demands.

"Aren't you going to let me in?"

She puts her elbows on the sill and her chin in her hands. Her hair flashes auburn in the lamplight. Even angry she is magnificent.

"Let's hear what you have to say first."

I dig into the trunk with my fingernails. Sap oozes. "I miss you."

But Edie is unmoved.

I try again. "I swear I had no idea Will Everhart was going to kiss me," I say with feeling. "She led me into that storeroom on spurious grounds."

Edie looks unconvinced and even a little hurt. "How do you even *know* her? I hear she's a total freak."

"Eccentric, maybe—" I say, faltering.

She sticks her hands into her pajama pants pockets. "You've got to stop collecting strays, Bubble. They're a waste of time. You and Arthur are both the same. You know it drives your mother crazy."

I feel a flash of irritation. I try to stay focused on the reason I am here. "*You're* the one I want to be with."

"Really." Edie regards me coolly.

"We're perfect for each other."

"How so?"

I think about it. "Both of us are academically successful. Both of us are superior sportspeople. We are equally ambitious, too, don't you think? Not only that, we have a very similar worldview."

"Similar in what sense?"

Apart from the fact I am clinging to a tree, this is beginning to feel very much like a job interview.

I outline our underlying optimism. Our firm belief that we can make a difference in society. Not that we've ever talked about sharing such a belief. Not in as many words.

Surely Edie cares about making a difference, though. She puts on functions for refugees. Surely that means she is a good person.

Now she leans a little farther out the window. Her ponytail flops forward over her shoulder. "Bianca Stein is a killer player, you know."

I readjust my grip on the trunk and the bark squeaks. "What's her backhand like?"

"At a rough guess? Twenty-three percent more effective than yours."

Ouch. "Please believe me when I say I never want to see Will Everhart again."

Edie rubs her hairline, where I can see the beginnings of a bruise. I remember the massaging she was doing earlier. "You were having a bit of trouble, when I knocked on the window?"

She looks uneasy. "Just preparing for the National Public Speaking Competition, that's all."

This is my chance. "You know I could help you with that. I could do notes for you on debate cards like I did for SpeakOut."

She regards me shrewdly.

"Bianca Stein might be the best player at Tawney this year," I continue. "But she can't win the doubles if she's up against you and me, not even if she manages to find another first-tier player to play with. And with me as your public-speaking coach, you have a good chance of winning the National Public Speaking Competition as well."

Edie gets the look she gets when she's decided to smash an overhead from the baseline: a risky shot, but when she pulls it off, deadly. "Fine. If you agree to help me with this speech, consider it a deal."

✳ ✳ ✳

I am back in the game. There is only one more thing to square off. I have to make clear to Will Everhart exactly where we stand. I was so muddled with cold earlier. If it means driving out to her house, so be it. I am up for the trek.

I arrive at her place a little after eight. The Everharts' flat is at the back of the complex: a small, freestanding, cottagey building set beside the garden. A hedge of lillypillies grows under the front window. Next to the door is a potted fig, neatly trimmed. Other than a length of dangling gutter and some fairly horrid aluminum windows it is all rather, well, lovely.

"I want to let you know that Edie and I are back together," I say when Will opens the door. "Just so you know. All's well that ends well and all of that."

She has her hands tucked into the pockets of a plain green hoodie, and Ugg boots on her feet. She looks cozy—even cuddly—not that that is at all relevant. She knocks an Ugg boot against the step and it makes a hollow sound. For a long moment, she doesn't say anything. "That's great, Harriet. I'm pleased for you." She sounds tired.

"Thanks," I say.

"I'm glad I didn't, you know, ruin things too much for you."

"Me too."

"It's good of you to drop by."

"Don't mention it."

"See you after the holidays, I guess." She begins to close the door.

"Yes, see you then," I say, lingering. The driveway looks horribly dark. The lamp on the porch is giving off such a welcoming light.

Will looks at me in that wry way she has. She takes her hands out of her pockets. "Unless you want to come in?"

I follow her along a short and narrow hallway, past a coat-rack, a stacked umbrella stand, and a crowded bookshelf. On the shelf a stick of incense is burning, filling the hall with the scent of sandalwood. At the end of the hall is a small living room and inside it, a woman perched on a couch watching television with the sound turned down, holding a glass of wine.

"Mum, this is Harriet."

Will's mother puts the glass down. She stands up and hugs me, which is a little awkward given we have never met.

"It's lovely to meet you," she says, smiling. "Will's told me nothing about you, but then she never tells me anything, so that's no surprise. You dropping by makes me sorry I have to go out."

"You're going somewhere?" I ask, eyeing her full-length bathrobe.

"What a surprise," says Will, not sounding at all surprised.

"Don't worry," her mother says to me. "I'm sure Miss Sarcasm here will look after you. She might even offer you a cookie if you ask her nicely."

Will blushes, which is more of a surprise than anything. She moves into the kitchen and takes a packet of Tim Tams from a corner cupboard. "You eat these, Harriet?"

I nod.

"We'll leave you to get ready, Mum."

I follow Will back across the living room and down the hall. We reach the front room.

Her bedroom.

This was possibly a bad idea.

She leads me through the door, held open by a pile of art books like the pile in the storeroom.

Why am I suddenly thinking about the storeroom?

A wooden easel stands in the corner. A framed Prado poster hangs crookedly above the bed. Will eases herself onto the mattress and leans up against the headboard. "You can sit wherever you want," she says, opening the cookies.

I perch carefully on the edge of the desk. "I like your mother."

"I think she likes you." She looks amused.

"I mean it. My mother's not friendly that way."

Will looks like she's going to say something but doesn't. She holds out the cookies.

I take one and peer around. On her desk stands a shadow box filled with trinkets—toy cars, vintage buttons, a miniature cactus in a pot. On the wall are dozens of postcards, clippings, and photographs—so much swirling color! Will takes a bite of her cookie, her brown eyes gazing at me. Her voice is low, almost a murmur. "Come and sit up here. You'll be more comfortable." She nods at the portion of the mattress next to her.

"I don't know...." Now I'm the one blushing. Why am I blushing?

The mattress dips with my weight, and she falls lightly against me, her arm against mine. Heat blooms on my skin like a flower. Will glances at the open door. Does she want me to say something? I can hear the close rhythm of her breathing. I am aware of the rise of her chest. I stare at a crumb of chocolate on the corner of her mouth and suddenly feel disoriented.

What was the question again?

chapter 25

WILL

This is the state of things: Harriet is killing me. Preppy Harriet with her perfect teeth and her perfect hair with more shine than a jar of honey. Sports star Harriet with her breath that smells of peppermint and her skin that smells of peppermint and her peppermint-smelling legs that are long and toned from all that tennis.

Her arms, too, are tennis-player arms. Then there are her Tawney Shield tennis-player shoulders. So much about her is Tawney, and Tawney is everything I'm against.

So why can't I stop thinking about her?

There is so much about Harriet to dislike—her pretentious vocabulary, her French-polished nails, her sockettes. But as much as I try to dislike them, somehow I *love* how much I hate them. And it makes things worse.

Is this what Mum meant about differences making things

interesting? Nothing about this situation makes sense. Harriet herself makes no sense. Ever since the storeroom, there's been no correlation between what she does and anything she says. Asking me to leave and then driving to my house. Saying she's back with Edie and then spending two hours loitering in my bedroom. Nothing happened—not a goddamn thing—but what does it matter? Every time I see her I crash deeper into madness.

✳ ✳ ✳

So it is that two days after her evening visit I'm halfway up the path to Harriet's front door again. I don't even have a game plan for when I get there. All I know is that I have to see her. I'm like a junkie risking life and limb for the sake of another hit. I push a bamboo frond aside and, lo and behold, there's Nat Nguyen ambling toward me.

I've never seen Nat amble in all my life. She's more inclined to march swiftly, dictator style. Seriously, what's going on with her? And what's she doing at Harriet's house?

Nat ambles to a halt in front of me. "This is unexpected."

"I'll say."

"Really, though. I'm surprised to see you. I heard Harriet and Edie are back together."

Natasha "finger on the pulse" Nguyen. Of course she's heard. It crosses my mind to ask her which leg, left or right, the premier puts through his underwear first in the mornings.

"I guess I assumed the storeroom thing was a one-off." She says it so matter-of-factly, like the "storeroom thing" is no big deal. Like I could have kissed the president of Russia and it would be of total irrelevance to her. Like we didn't spend last term doing our own "storeroom thing" in the newsroom.

Let her think she knows what the "storeroom thing" is all about, I decide. It's better than her knowing the truth about Amelia Westlake, not to mention the other truth: That Harriet is the tune stuck in my head. That every waking thought I have is shadowed by the thought of being with her again.

Deflection seems the preferable approach. "Aren't you even going to apologize for the appalling piece in your gutter press?"

Nat shreds a bamboo leaf with her fingers. "I'm a journalist."

It's a callous response, even for Nat. "That's your answer?"

"We stumbled on to a good story. We ran with it."

"*Stumbled?* That's a funny way to describe sending Duncan out to corner us."

"Duncan was picking up some items of his that he stores there. He can't store them at home because his parents are ultra conservative and wouldn't approve. He found you guys by pure chance. What were we supposed to do? Our circulation numbers depend upon those gossip pages. And our existence depends upon our circulation numbers."

"No, it doesn't," I snap. "It's a bloody school paper, Nat. Circulation numbers have nothing to do with it."

Nat shrugs. "Then I knew that a piece about you and Harriet Price would be something people would want to read about. Come on. What kind of a professional would I be if I let my friendship with you get in the way of breaking a story?"

"A nice one?"

That makes her chuckle. "You still haven't answered my question. Are you and Harriet a thing?"

"Don't be ridiculous. It was a moment of madness, that's all."

"Then what are you doing here?" Nat asks.

"I could ask the same thing of you."

Just then a flock of swallows explodes out of a nearby tree. I hear footsteps on the timber path. Arthur Price appears wearing black jeans, a Teengenerate T-shirt, and gardening gloves. He's carrying a pair of pruning shears. "You're still here!" He puts the shears down and gives Nat a squeeze. "Hey there, Will!"

I wait for Nat to throw off his hand, but she doesn't. Instead, she kind of nuzzles into his neck.

I stare at them. "You two are...?"

Nat coughs. Arthur grins.

So that explains her strangely pleasant demeanor these past two weeks.

Nat's face suddenly clouds. "Hang on." She turns to Arthur. "How do you know Will?"

"We met a few weeks ago when she came around to see our band rehearse before the gig," says Arthur.

This is not good.

Nat frowns. "What gig?"

"The one Harriet invited you to at Deep Fryer," says Arthur. "The night we met, remember?" He nudges her playfully.

Surely Harriet never told Arthur she invited Nat. I hope to God she didn't.

"Your sister didn't invite me to that gig," Nat corrects him. "I thought she did at first, but in fact we just ran into each other on our way there."

"Oh. My mistake," says Arthur.

I breathe out in relief.

"It's just that I remember..." He shakes his head. "Never mind."

There are more footsteps. Harriet emerges from between two plants in her tennis whites, her racket case slung over one shoulder like some Golden Hollywood–era goddess off to challenge Grace Kelly to a game. God, I worship her.

Seeing us, she slows. "Hello."

"Hey, sis," says Arthur. "Look who's here!" He nods in my direction.

Harriet turns a deep crimson. "I'd love to stay and chat," she says with an attempt at breeziness. "But I'm just off to Tawney practice. With Edie," she adds pointedly.

Nat glances between us. "Let me get this straight. You guys aren't a thing? You've never been a thing?"

"Never!" Harriet shakes her head vigorously. "We don't even like each other!"

In an effort to absorb this punch to the heart, I exhale slowly through my nose.

Something appears to occur to Nat. "Art, you were going to say something about why you thought I was at the gig at Harriet's invitation."

Bloody journalists. Like dogs with bones. *Let it go*, I will her.

"Oh. It was just that the night Will came around..." says

Arthur, wavering a little, since at this point Harriet is doing a great impression of someone choking on her own intestines, "the night Will came around you asked her, didn't you, Harriet, whether she thought Nat would like our music?"

"I don't remember that," I say emphatically.

Arthur looks surprised. "Yeah, you do. We had that chat about Nat knowing Duncan."

"Hang on," Nat interrupts, looking at me. "If you and Harriet have never been a thing, what were you even *doing* at Harriet's place that night?"

I glance at Harriet. "Um, I—"

"And for that matter, why are you here right now?"

Harriet opens her mouth to speak, but Nat stops her. "No. I think I'm beginning to piece it together myself." Her eyes grow wide. "That was the same night the newsroom window got smashed."

I scoff. "What's that got to do with anything?"

"The person who invited me to that gig," says Nat, a look of discovery blooming on her face, "was Amelia Westlake. Only she never showed up. When I got back to the newsroom, someone had broken in. Coincidence? I think not." She breaks into a smirk.

"Who's Amelia Westlake?" asks Arthur.

"Well you might ask," says Nat.

"Why are you looking at me?" I say.

"I'm looking at both of you, actually," says Nat smugly.

"Now, just stop right there," Harriet says.

"Come on. It makes perfect sense. I've been working off the assumption Amelia Westlake is a single person. That's why I ruled Harriet out. When Duncan's uncle ran the hand-writing tests and the results pointed to her, I figured he'd made a mistake. Besides, the newsroom break-in was clearly Amelia-related, and there was no way Harriet could have broken into the newsroom when she was with me at Deep Fryer. Or so I thought." She is looking at us with wonder and something close to admiration. "You decided, for whatever reason, that you needed me out of the newsroom. Harriet suggested Arthur's gig as a possible lure and asked Will over to check out the band to see if they played my kind of music."

"This is pure speculation," I say. "You haven't given us an ounce of proof for this crazy theory of yours."

"The cartoons were my other sticking point," Nat muses. "I could find no evidence that Harriet could draw. Obviously, Will is one of the few people in our year with the technical skills needed for those cartoons. But Will swore she had nothing to do with them. And I believed her. Partly because I didn't think she'd lie to me. Partly because the cartoons were too witty."

"Excuse me?"

"Oh, come on," Nat says. "Tedious, drawn-out polemic is more your style."

"That is an outrageous and completely ridiculous—"

"But what if you had someone to help you? Mandy Delaqua from Blessingwood, who Harriet debated in the year-ten finals, once told me that Harriet was known for making terrific jokes when you least expected it."

"Sounds like a complete fib to me," I say. "No offense, Harriet."

"And the English-essay swap," says Nat. "Again, Will's

connection is obvious, but I ruled you out because I was in legal studies with you when it occurred. But what if you were working with someone else who happened to have a free period?" She turns to Harriet. "You have a free period on Thursday mornings, don't you?"

"I don't think so," Harriet says shiftily.

"I'm waiting for some actual evidence here," I say, my voice turning shrill.

Nat pauses. "You're right. Actual evidence of your involvement is lacking, Will, even though the pieces fit. Even the storeroom kiss makes sense to me now. It's a perfect alibi. But it *is* hard to believe the two of you could have come up with a collective idea given your historical lack of rapport. I've got nothing concrete to pin you down. Unless—"

She springs toward me.

Harriet shrieks.

"Nat, what are you doing?" Arthur cries.

I bat her away. "Get. Off. Me."

Nat grabs at my left sleeve and yanks it up my arm. She lunges for my right sleeve and wrestles it up past my elbow. There, in plain sight, is my pus-stained bandage. "Did you have a run-in with a glass window recently, by any chance, Will?"

"I—um—it's—" I say.

Harriet groans.

"Gotcha," Nat whispers.

⁕ ⁕ ⁕

In the Prices' ballroom-sized lounge room we each sit on our own pristine cream leather couch.

"Coffee, anyone?" Arthur asks.

"No, thanks," Harriet says.

"How about tea?"

"We're fine, babe," says Nat.

"We've got herbal, black, green, rooibos—"

"No," say the three of us together.

"I'll leave you to it." He gets up quickly.

We watch him go. For a long moment, none of us says anything. What's left to say? Nat has worked it out. This is the mission she's been on since the beginning.

"Congratulations," I say at last. "You may as well write up your scoop. Get Croon on speed dial. Ruin two lives."

Nat regards me, her expression serious. "Don't worry, I am well aware of the consequences of going public with this."

"Which in your professional opinion are what, exactly?" Harriet asks nervously.

"Will broke into the school and damaged school property. Which means, if I publish, she gets expelled."

She's right. It's that simple. Rosemead will have no qualms in taking that type of action against me. I'm an average student. I have no special skills. I have a long history of making trouble. Croon has already threatened me with expulsion. What does she care that we have only sixteen weeks until final exams and that expelling me now could have a significant impact on my future after school?

It's strange. I've been looking for ways to ditch Rosemead since I started. But now that it's a real possibility, the thought of what it means, including how my mother will react, makes me want to bring up my breakfast.

"And me?" Harriet asks impatiently.

"You'll be fine," Nat says, giving a dismissive wave of her hand. "They'll protect you because they need you. You're Rosemead's greatest hope for winning Tawney, and you'll bring up our year's average exam results substantially. If they can paint Will as the ringleader, you could get off virtually scot-free. Which is completely unfair, obviously."

"Unfair enough to make you reconsider going public?" I ask. I can't believe how long she is dragging this out.

Nat runs a stiff hand through her hair. "We've just been through this. What sort of a journalist would I be if I let my friendship with you get in the way of breaking a story? Besides, you know my deal with Croon. This is my chance to hang on to the paper."

"It seems you're in a bit of a quandary," Harriet says.

"The problem I have is this," says Nat, swinging her feet onto the couch. "The whole point of journalism—for me, anyway—is to expose the truth."

"I hear a 'but' in that sentence," Harriet says, hope in her voice.

"*But*," Nat says obligingly, "I have good reasons for believing that this particular exposé will have the opposite effect."

I glance at Harriet, then at Nat. "How come?"

Nat sighs. "Because I have doubts about Croon's motive for wanting to know who's behind Amelia Westlake. What if it's less about finding out the truth about Hadley, and more about shutting down the hoax and sweeping everything it's drawing attention to under the carpet? Everyone knows sexual harassment by teachers is notoriously underreported. If

Croon was acting responsibly, she'd make some proactive investigations."

Harriet bites her lip. "You can't possibly be saying Principal Croon's motive is to protect Coach Hadley."

"It's a distinct possibility," Nat says. "Protecting him is the same as protecting herself. Hadley is one of the greatest assets the school has. Parents enroll their kids on the basis of his medal-winning reputation. And Amelia Westlake has been causing Croon all sorts of headaches. That computer donation debacle, for example. And the robotics competition screwup on live television. Of course, I don't know for sure that I'm right about this. It's no more than a gut feeling. That said, I can't help but feel that by handing you over to Croon, I'd be playing into her hands. There is shit going down at Rosemead that needs exposing. And as much as I hate to admit it, Amelia Westlake is the only one making any progress on that front."

We are silent for a moment.

"So what are you going to do?" Harriet finally asks.

"Hold off saying anything to anyone on one condition."

"Being?"

Nat looks at us both. "I want in."

chapter 26

HARRIET

Involving Natasha Nguyen in Amelia Westlake is obviously a terrible idea. Will tries to talk her out of it immediately. "You can't be serious. What if we get caught? What about your future journalism career?"

"As long as I don't do anything like breaking into school property, for example"—Natasha looks pointedly at Will—"Croon's hands are tied. The way I calculate it, punishing me means punishing Harriet, and she'll avoid that at all costs."

Will appears as conflicted as I feel. She meets my eye, and I shrug helplessly. I don't see that we have a choice.

Will sets her jaw. "If you're in, then we need your help with something."

"Shoot," says Natasha.

Will glances at me again. "We have a plan to leverage Rosemead's newsletter mailing list to raise money for charity."

Natasha nods slowly and grins. "I like it. Talk me through the details."

"We want to hijack the Buy a Tile fund-raising envelopes," Will says.

The three of us draw into a huddle. "We want to get them printed with the details of a charity, so that the money goes to the charity instead of the school."

"Which charity?"

"The Fund for Australian Women. It helps victims of domestic violence."

Natasha's grin fades.

"What?" Will asks.

Natasha breaks the huddle and falls back against the couch cushions. "Fighting domestic violence is a worthy cause, but I've heard some less-than-positive things about Australian Women. Apparently, they have a pretty exclusive idea about who they consider to be 'Australian.'"

This is extremely alarming news. "What have you heard?" I ask.

"That they've turned away women who are on temporary immigration visas."

I look at Will. From the panic on her face she is clearly as concerned as I am. "But they're the ones who often need the most help!" I cry. I know this for a fact. It was on *Four Corners*. "Especially if they're relying on a violent partner to gain citizenship. Did you know about this, Will?"

"I had no idea," she admits. "I chose the charity for its initials, to be honest." She wipes her face with a hand.

I wish we had done more research. It's just as well we have

Natasha to consult. "Can you think of an alternative charity?" I ask her.

"How about the Domestic Violence Australia Network?" she suggests. "They have a special service to assist women who need help with immigration issues. And a lot of other culturally specific services, too."

"Sounds perfect," I say. Thank God she's on board.

Natasha nods. "Good. Now, what part of the plan did you need my help with?"

I explain that we need to get in touch with the company that prints the envelopes for the newsletter mailing and that we're hoping she could give us the name of her contact at Parsons Printing.

Natasha looks confused. "I don't get it. What does Parsons have to do with this?"

Will and I look at each other. "We assumed that since they print the *Messenger*, they must print the school newsletter as well," Will says.

Natasha shakes her head. "You assumed wrongly. I arranged the printing deal with Parsons for the *Messenger* myself. We're the only school group that uses them. I know that for a fact."

So the ruse of Arthur's concert, the newsroom break-in, and Will's arm injury were all for nothing.

"Fuck," Will says with feeling. "Then we need another plan."

✶ ✶ ✶

"I reckon we get Liz involved" is Natasha's first suggestion when we meet at the *Messenger* newsroom on the first day back at school. She pitches a handful of pistachio shells toward an open window and misses.

"Liz Newcomb?" I am standing in the middle of the room, making sure not to accidentally touch anything. The place smells of rotting food and dead cockroaches. I swear the couch Will is sitting on is more moldy pastry than upholstery. "We have enough people involved already," I say firmly.

Natasha cracks open another nut and chews it with her mouth open. "Liz is a huge fan of Amelia Westlake, and more importantly, as Tawney Shield captain she's got a key to the gym staff room. If Hadley's organizing the fund-raising, he's bound to have the printer's contact details in there."

I shake my head. "No way. Not Liz Newcomb."

Will, who has been staring at me on and off in the most distracting way for the last ten minutes, raises an eyebrow.

Natasha grabs another handful of pistachios. "Why not? We don't have to tell her who's behind Amelia. We can just recruit her on Amelia's behalf."

"We simply can't trust her," I say, turning to Will for help.

Will bites into a pistachio. "I agree with Nat," she says.

Traitor.

"How else are we going to get into the gym staff room?" Will continues. "It will be easy. We get Liz to leave the key for us somewhere. She doesn't even have to know who we are."

"It's too risky." I fold my arms.

"Come on, Harriet," Will coaxes. "The only reason you don't like Liz is because they made her the Tawney team captain over you."

"That's ridiculous."

"No, it's not."

"It really is."

Natasha is watching us like a line umpire at the net. "Are you sure you guys aren't together? You're definitely bickering like a couple."

Will glances at me and I look away quickly. "Fine," I say. "Ask Liz Newcomb. See if I care."

✱ ✱ ✱

At the end of lunch, Principal Croon accosts me beside the filtered-water fountain. "Harriet! A brief word?"

Her office is as tasteful as I remember: a large bay window, cucumber-green walls, and the scent of fresh potpourri. On the floor sprawls a mammoth rug, rumored to have come from an Ottoman palace.

"First of all, I wanted to thank you, Harriet, for all the hard work you are doing this year." Principal Croon's teeth flash. "It really is extraordinary what you girls can achieve on top of your study." She looks at me expectantly.

"Oh. Thank you." On the sideboard, an orchid's slim stalk is bent forward as if listening to us talk, and with the recent upgrades to Rosemead's security features, maybe it is.

Principal Croon folds her hands together, her burgundy nails shining like blood. "I have high hopes for you at Tawney this year, of course. You and Edie Marshall winning the doubles would be such a combined coup for Rosemead and Blessingwood. So good for morale. And we're incredibly grateful that on top of all this you've managed to keep a hand in organizing fund-raisers and events as well."

You have to admire the woman. She runs the whole of Rosemead, dresses like royalty, and still has time for tête-à-têtes with students.

"I understand you are chair of the Formal Committee."

"Yes," I say.

"Dish is a fine choice of venue. It is in such a beautiful spot, right there on the harbor. And I understand you've organized buses to take guests there from Rosemead's front gates?"

"I have."

"A very sensible arrangement. I'm sure it's going to be wonderful. I for one am very much looking forward to making the welcome speech on the night." She sits back in her chair. Abruptly, her smile vanishes. "There is one thing I want to make clear."

✳ ✳ ✳

I walk back from Principal Croon's office with a high-pitched ringing in my ears. I am not even sure what just happened in there. The conversation I was apparently a part of does not seem remotely possible.

I drift through the rose garden, only half-aware of the climbing Iceberg that is about to flower, and hardly noticing the Blushing Lucy in full bloom. I am preoccupied by a memory of the first time I saw Principal Croon.

She was standing at the top of Rosemead's main staircase, poised and graceful, as a sea of students filed past. I watched her meet a young girl's eye and smile at her. How I wished to be that girl! To be in the orbit of this majestic figure who seemed more powerful, even, than the stone lions that flanked her, more luminous than the sun-kissed sandstone.

It is a memory that has stayed with me through the years, complete with the orchestra of emotion I felt at the time: the desire to belong to the world she embodied, the hope that one day I would be a part of it, the deep admiration for the woman herself. Now the whole ensemble falters.

Did she really just say what I heard her say? Could Will and Natasha be right about her after all?

Will. I feel a sudden need to talk to her, which makes absolutely no sense. This has nothing to do with Will.

All right, that isn't strictly true. She is one of the few people in our year whom Principal Croon's pronouncement *is* relevant to—she and possibly Natasha. But the person it is my duty to tell before anyone else is Edie.

✳ ✳ ✳

Edie is due for dinner at six. When she arrives, my mother, whose clinic appointments finished early, shows her to my room. But rather than returning promptly to her study as she usually does after an interruption, she hovers in the hallway. "It really is so wonderful to see you again, Edie."

"You too, Mrs. Price. That's a beautiful shirt you have on."

"This old thing?"

"And where did you get those shoes?"

My mother presses a hand on Edie's arm. "You darling. I am so pleased you and Harriet are friends."

"If you don't mind, Mother . . ." I say, irritated.

Edie and my mother look at me with surprise.

"Sorry," I mumble.

Edie steps past my mother into my room. She turns around. "Will I be seeing you before Harriet's formal, Mrs. Price?"

My mother looks confused. "You're going to Harriet's formal?"

"Of course."

"Oh," says my mother, fiddling with a button on her sleeve. "I'm not sure we'll be around that evening. . . . Anyway. I'll leave you girls to it." Without looking at me, she gives Edie another brief smile and closes the door.

Edie groans. "I thought she was never going to leave. It's been too long, Bubble. I've missed you." She reaches out a hand and pulls me onto the bed. I feel the warm press of her hip. I yelp.

"What's wrong?"

"Something's digging into my side. Hang on." Freeing myself from Edie's grip, I empty my pockets onto the bedside table. "I had a ballpoint pen in there. Silly me. It's out now."

"Are you ready, then?"

"Ready."

We resume.

We've been kissing for a few minutes when Edie stops. "Are you okay, Harriet?"

"What do you mean? I'm fine." I am trying very hard to put my conversation with Principal Croon out of my mind. "I'm enjoying myself," I assure Edie. "Us, I mean. This. Let's keep going."

As Edie descends on my neck, I do what I sometimes do

on these occasions to keep focus, which is to imagine that I am Ryan Gosling and Edie is Emma Stone.

For a while it works well. I have a firm picture of myself as Ryan lifting Emma in my muscular arms before pulling her to my toned chest. Then the picture wavers. It is not Emma Stone I am pretending to be with, but Will Everhart. It is Will's pressing hands that are getting me through this, Will's bare neck, Will's mouth.

Oh—her mouth.

I sit up.

"What is it?" Edie asks in an exasperated tone.

I let my head drop. "I've got to tell you something."

Edie raises herself up on one elbow. "You're behind on my National Public Speaking notes, aren't you?"

The notes for her competition—I'd completely forgotten about them. The topic is "poverty is a state of mind," and I promised I'd have a first draft to her by the weekend. I shake my head. "It's not that."

"What, then?"

I inhale. "Principal Croon called me in today. She told me I can't invite you to our formal." The words catch in my throat like a hook.

Edie looks at me blankly. Then she gets it. She laughs. "Are you serious?"

"That's what she said."

"Is this a joke?"

"Apparently not."

Edie combs her fingers through her hair. "What's the story? Not even Blessingwood is that conservative, and we're as stuffy as it gets. And it's not like Rosemead is a religious school."

"Apparently it has something to do with one of the school board members," I say. A sudden anger flames inside me. "He's the head of a 'family-oriented' association. He also happens to be a big financial supporter of Rosemead. And so the board passed a motion."

"This is unbelievable."

"Principal Croon has asked me to speak to everyone individually—all of us in our year who she thinks might bring girlfriends, that is."

"How many people is that?"

"Not many, as far as I'm aware," I say. "Two. Maybe three." Although when I consider it, Natasha will probably bring Arthur. And I have no idea what Will is doing.

I taste salt in my throat. I wipe my eyes with the back of my hand.

"Bad hay fever? Here, blow on this." Edie digs into her blazer pocket and hands me a crumpled paper napkin.

The high-pitched ringing has started up again. I hope this isn't another one of my migraines. I breathe out slowly. "There's got to be a way to get them to reverse their decision or, I don't know, change their minds somehow."

Edie takes her hair out of its ponytail and makes a higher one. "If it would be easier for me not to come..."

"Excuse me?"

"I said, if it's easier if I don't come to your formal..."

"That's not the point." I struggle to keep my voice calm. "I've been dreaming about the school formal ever since year seven. What's more, I've organized the whole thing, practically by myself!"

Suddenly I'm thinking of Will again and imagining how she would react. She would use crass language, absolutely. She would say something along the lines of "we're being crushed," far too loudly, before miming (badly) getting violently crushed by some form of heavy machinery. Then she would formulate a plan to do Rosemead over once and for all.

Not that it helps matters to be thinking about Will right now.

"You and I have bought complementing dresses," I remind Edie. "And what about your ballroom dancing lessons? We can't let them go to waste!"

"Then let me know if I can do anything." Edie smooths her hair with a palm. She stands up and straightens her dress. "And about those public speaking notes. Any chance they might be ready by lunchtime on Saturday? I've got this family lunch to go to on Sunday, and it would be good to look over them on Saturday afternoon."

I line up my teeth carefully. "I'll see what I can do."

chapter 27

WILL

At four thirty on the day of our planned break-in, I'm standing outside the gym entrance, my whole body thrumming, taking in the heady scent of rubber, talcum powder, and sweat. I'm in a tracksuit and sneakers, trying to look like wearing sports gear is the kind of thing I do all the time.

The tracksuit I have on, its pocket heavy with Liz's staff room key, is Harriet's. I'm not going to lie: It's a turn-on. Despite all the talks I've given myself, I'm having an extreme amount of trouble getting her out of my head—or getting anything else in there, for that matter. Right now, my cranial real estate is pretty much wall-to-wall Harriet.

What was I saying again?

That's right. My outfit.

I've borrowed the sneakers from Nat, who can't be here due to a *Messenger* deadline and whose feet are the same size as mine. As long as no one who actually knows me wanders past, I look no more out of place than a Rosemead alumna in the halls of an uptown law firm.

It's the perfect time in the afternoon because most of the staff have left for the day but security hasn't yet locked the building. Soon, thanks to Liz leaving her key taped beneath a basin in the PAC bathrooms as Amelia Westlake asked her to, I'll have the details we need about the printing company. Then we can pull off the prank to top all pranks. The Domestic Violence Australia Network will have cash for their cause. Amelia Westlake will reign among the gods.

I think through the plan again.

We know from Harriet that the Sports Committee meets at four, which means Hadley will be out of the gym staff room for at least another half hour before returning for his things. The only teacher still around is the head of netball, Miss Kinton. As soon as she's gone, I'll go in.

I peer through the heavy glass doors. My eye is drawn to the school banner hanging on the foyer wall. I grin, remembering that Harriet and I had the French motto removed and another phrase stitched in its place. So far, nobody seems to have noticed our handiwork.

Suddenly there is movement. Miss Kinton appears carrying a sports bag and a pile of netball bibs. She leans on one of the heavy glass doors until it opens. The air fills with the stench of sweaty athlete.

"Hello..." she says when she sees me. She looks uncertain, as if she's never seen me before in her life. This makes sense. Two years ago I managed to wag our entire semester of compulsory netball by feigning a condition called labyrin-thitis, which I thought I'd made up but, it turns out, actually exists.

I'm glad she has no idea who I am. "It's Wendy," I say cheerily.

She gives an embarrassed smile. "Of course. Good night, Wendy."

"Night, Miss Kinton."

I wait until she's disappeared down the path before mes-saging the others.

> Coast clear. I'm going in.

Nat messages back with a thumbs-up. Harriet's reply comes through soon after.

> Thank you, Will. Much appreciated. Coach
> Hadley is here with me at the Sports
> Committee meeting. Standing by for further
> reports. Harriet.

Have I mentioned she's *killing* me?

Once I'm inside I make a beeline across the foyer for the gym staff room. It takes three seconds to lift the key from my pocket, slot it into the door, and turn the handle.

The door swings open and I step inside.

I'm in.

Man, it stinks in here. I guess jocks are immune to the reek of stale perspiration. I scan the room for what I'm looking for.

Not the stacked hockey sticks in the corner. Not the regulation Rosemead sports caps in a pile on the desk. Not the halved oranges in a Tupperware container on one of the chairs. If the printing company details are going to be anywhere, they're going to be with the paperwork on the bookshelf.

The problem is, the shelf is *full* of paperwork, spewing out of rows and rows of plastic binders, many of them unmarked. It could easily take me hours to sift through it all.

My gaze drifts to a corkboard hanging by the window. It's worth a look.

I walk over and scan the notices pinned to it: some class rosters, a list of emergency phone numbers, and an invitation to Miss Watson's thirtieth birthday party (no thanks). Then I see it.

There, on a tiny square of paper sharing a pin with a flyer about the swimming pool fund-raising dinner, is a handwritten note:

Newsletter printer: Peak Printing. 9828 7354

Bingo.

From outside the door, I hear the sound of the heavy glass doors creaking open.

Shit. I grab the note, pin and all, and make a dash for the door. In my rush I clip the chair with the container of oranges on it; the chair spins. The container slides off and lands on its side on the carpet.

There's no time to pick it up. I can already see Miss Kinton walking across the foyer.

I slip back through the staff room door, close it behind me, and quickly stash the note and Liz's key back in my pocket.

Just in time.

I try to look casual as I walk toward the head of netball.

"Hello, again," she says when we reach each other, her voice loaded with suspicion.

"You're back." I shoot her a friendly grin, as if the opportunity of seeing her twice in the space of ten minutes has made my day.

"I forgot the oranges for my evening game," she says.

I nod. "Orange you glad you didn't leave without them?"

She doesn't laugh.

The oranges belong to her? That means as soon as she sees them on the staff room floor she'll know I've been in there.

I've got to get out of here.

But Kinton is standing in my path. "What are you still doing here, Wendy? All on-campus training has finished for the day."

"I'm—I'm looking for the sign-up boards, as a matter of fact," I say. "You see, I'm really keen to join one of your netball teams."

This piques her interest. She considers me. "Have you played netball before?"

"Oh, I've been playing for years. But not for Rosemead. I play in a, er, highly competitive local competition."

The head of netball pivots to face me properly. "We're looking for a new player, as a matter of fact. What position are you?" She fiddles with the whistle around her neck.

"I'm in a great position. I'm fit, and I'm available pretty much every weeknight."

"I meant what position do you play?"

Dammit. "Left wing?"

Kinton levels a stare at me. "Left wing is field hockey."

"Wing attaché, sorry."

"You mean wing attack?"

"That's the one."

She purses her lips. "Perhaps you should be getting home."

"Good idea."

As soon as I'm past her, I hurry toward the glass doors at full speed. If I can get away before she realizes I've been in the staff room, maybe it will be okay. She hasn't a clue who I am, after all. I turn my head to see her slot her own key into the staff room door. I turn back just in time to see the heavy glass doors an inch from my face, but not in time to stop myself from ramming straight into them.

⚹ ⚹ ⚹

Time dissolves. I feel the imprint of a cold, hard surface. I see a tint of green. I hear the sound of vibrating glass: an endless, bassoon-low note. I taste saliva, sour, in my throat.

⚹ ⚹ ⚹

I don't know how long I'm out for, but I know it's the pain that brings me back. My head aches where it collided with the doors. My right hand, which I raised too late in an attempt to protect my face, throbs like an electronic dance beat.

The first thing I see when the fog parts is the ripple of a cream silk shirt. A pair of sheer stockings dazzles in the late-afternoon sun. French perfume clogs my nostrils. A shadow slips across me and I startle.

"Hello, Wilhelmina," says Croon.

chapter 28

HARRIET

At Sports Committee, the first item on the agenda is the new swimming pool complex. Coach Hadley waits for everyone to take a seat, then draws a diagram of the complex on the whiteboard.

"This boundary line will flank the second oval," says Coach, drawing a straight line with his marker.

I text Will to let her know I have him in my line of sight.

"And this one will meet the side of the gym where the staff room is." He outlines the swimming pool, the lanes, and the bleachers. He erases parts of the boundary lines and draws squiggles to represent the gates. He caps his marker. "Any questions?"

Giddily, I think of asking him how many legal-advice clinics, social worker salaries, and health services could be funded with the money we're raising for the pool. But I don't. We will find out soon enough.

"Will the new complex have its own change room?" asks Zara Long.

She is sitting at the front beside Kimberley Kitchener. I've noticed Coach Hadley has been paying both of them a fair amount of attention lately. Last month, he appointed Zara captain of the softball firsts when Eileen Sarmiento had to pull out of the season after breaking her wrist. As for Kimberley, she has become his student trainee coach for the middle school swim squads. I have seen the way he walks along the edge of the pool with her, his arm draped loosely around her shoulders, intermittently whispering in her ear.

"What would be the point of a change room?" Coach Hadley says. "We're all friends here," he adds with a wink.

Zara and Kimberley laugh raucously. The rest of the committee members give uncertain smiles. I feel a heavy weight in my jaw. Coach sees my expression and mimics me with an exaggerated pout. "It's a joke, Harriet," he says. "Of course there will be a change room." He uncaps his marker and draws a rough box in the corner of the whiteboard, like he was planning to all along.

I blush, but it's not embarrassment I feel. There is a granite-hard lump of outrage in my throat. I wish I'd never agreed to be on this committee. When Coach Hadley first asked me, it seemed like such a privilege, but what is so privileged about doing administrative duties free of charge that the sports staff should be doing themselves?

There is a knock at the door and Natasha Nguyen bursts in. Never have I been so pleased to see anybody in my life.

She crosses the room swiftly without even a glance at anyone else and bends at my ear.

"You've got to come," she murmurs, low enough so that no one else can hear. "There's been an accident. They've called an ambulance for Will."

"An *ambulance*?" I cry out.

Everyone in the room turns.

Coach Hadley clears his throat. "What is the cause of this unexpected interruption, Miss Nguyen?"

"Family emergency," says Natasha smoothly.

Coach Hadley nods at me. "We'll catch you up on the minutes later, Harriet."

Natasha ushers me out.

✳ ✳ ✳

"She crashed right into those bloody gym doors," Natasha tells me when we're safely up the hall. "Gave herself a concussion. Looks like she's broken some fingers as well."

"Oh my God." I stop dead beside a bank of lockers. At the thought of Will prostrate on a gurney, I feel faint.

"But that's not all. Croon was on the scene." Natasha reaches out beyond the railing and yanks roughly at a tree branch. Yellow leaves rain down. "When Will slammed into the door, Miss Kinton was there. She must have called Croon. She was there within minutes."

I lean heavily against a locker door. "What do they know?"

Looking around, Natasha lowers her voice. "Nothing specific. Only that she was up to something in the staff room."

"Where are they taking her?" I ask, steadying my shaky hands.

"Royal North Shore."

"Someone should have gone with her."

"Why do you think I'm here?" says Natasha, reddening. Suddenly she won't look at me. "I offered to go, but she said that she wanted you."

✶ ✶ ✶

I find her on a bed in the emergency holding area. At first I almost don't recognize her—someone has tied her hair up in a strangely symmetrical knot. There is no mistaking her hand, though, wrapped in a bandage the size of a sourdough loaf and propped on a tower of pillows. Her face is pale, her skin damp. I feel a trembling in my chest.

I draw the curtain around the bed and put down my school bag. "Are you okay?"

"Dandy." She looks glazed.

"Does your mum know you're here?"

She nods. "She's out getting takeaway and then she'll be back." She glances over. "You don't have to stand, you know."

I pull up a metal chair.

I can't remember the last time I was in a public hospital. It was probably when Arthur had his guitar injury. That was only twelve months ago, but I had forgotten how much I hate these places—the linoleum, the lighting, the smell of illness and despair. I have a sudden urge to get Will out of here. Then I remember it is not my place to want anything for, on behalf of, or in relation to Will.

She sees me eyeing her bandage. "Don't worry. It looks far worse than it is. Just two fractured fingers and some bruising."

"Are you in much pain?"

"Not anymore. They've got me on morphine." She nods at the drip cord, grinning, but her grin abruptly vanishes. "I should warn you that Croon grilled me. She even asked if the accident had something to do with an Amelia Westlake prank. Don't worry, I denied everything. But she knows from Kinton that I was in the staff room, and she didn't waste any time exacting her punishment."

"Her punishment?"

Will nods. "It's funny, really. It's the opposite of a punishment as far as I'm concerned."

"What is it?"

"She's banned me from going to the formal." Her voice is flat.

"Oh, Will." I reach out my hand.

"Like I give a shit about the formal," she mutters, drawing her hand away. "It's not like I had anyone to go with." She stares hard at the bedsheet.

"The formal has been ruined anyway," I tell her with a sigh.

Will looks up. "What do you mean?"

"Principal Croon has prohibited girls from inviting other girls as their dates."

Will sits forward with such violence that the drip needle almost dislodges from her hand. "That bigoted bitch," she growls.

I try not to smile.

"Where the fuck does she get off?" Will continues. "Hasn't she heard of the Anti-Discrimination Act? We should take her to court."

I give her good hand a gentle tap. "You should probably keep it down," I whisper.

Will draws up her knees, making a mountain of the starched white hospital sheets. Her bread loaf of a bandage rolls miserably on the pillows. "This gives us all the more reason to screw Rosemead over."

I reach around to the back of her head.

"What are you doing?"

I find the elastic band and wrangle it out so that Will's hair falls back into its usual lopsided position. "It looked wrong the other way."

She smiles at me curiously.

My phone buzzes.

> Starting work on my NPS speech tonight and
> still waiting for those notes, Bubble. Currently
> looking for 3 examples of famous poor-but-
> happy people. Any ideas? Thx

"Edie?" Will asks.

"My, ah, brother." I put my phone facedown in my lap. I fidget with my fingers. "Will. You know what this means, don't you?"

"No. What?"

I bite my lip. "We have to put Amelia Westlake on hiatus for a while."

We look at each other as the truth of it sinks in.

"I suppose you're right," Will says eventually. "Talk about a bloody cock-up," she adds, her tone bitter.

"A hiatus may even be understating it," I say carefully. "Principal Croon is squarely on the Amelia Westlake trail now. She'll be watching you like a hawk."

Instead of disagreeing, Will moans. "It's not fair. We've got so much unfinished business."

My stomach sinks as I realize it's true. We put an extraordinary amount of time and effort into the charity prank, only to leave it incomplete. If only it hadn't been such trouble finding out the details of the printing company! I think of all the ways the money could have been used had we managed to pull it off—the lives improved, the help given. I imagine the other pranks we could have done had we succeeded with this one.

"I know we do," I say. "But there is too much risk. And I'm not just talking about Principal Croon. This is the second time you've seriously hurt yourself because of Amelia Westlake."

Will looks pained. "Maybe if I'm more careful..." She peters out.

"You know as well as I do that there isn't going to be a next time, Will," I say gently.

We sit in silence, or in as much silence as exists amid the beeping machines, moans of discomfort, and panicked shouts of medical staff.

"Maybe it's for the best," I suggest finally. "It's probably time we focused on other things anyway. We've got midterms soon, and I've got Tawney...."

Will looks at me. "So our one attempt at helping the wider

community comes to nothing. And the money that could have gone to women and children in need instead gets sunk into a superfluous swimming pool at Rosemead."

"I'm afraid so."

"Well, that sucks balls," Will says. She claws at her bandage.

I look at her face and see her despondency. I feel it myself. No more brainstorming. No more sneaking around. No more secret meetings in the storeroom. Amelia Westlake was changing things, but now it's over. That knowledge makes me ache.

"Nat will need to know, of course," says Will.

"I'll talk to her," I offer.

Will sits up suddenly. "We've still got to find a way to get in touch with that girl," she says.

"What girl?" I ask.

"The one who wrote to Amelia via Instagram about Hadley. We have to convince her to make a complaint."

Why is Will bringing this up? I don't want to get into it again. Not now. It has been an incredibly overwhelming day already. "But how can we reach her if she's not answering our Instagram messages and we don't know who she is?"

My phone buzzes again.

> Still waiting to hear from u about Arthur's
> keyboard player. Formal's really soon!!! B xx

When I look up from the phone, Will has me in her gaze. "Can you tell me exactly what's stopping you from making that complaint?"

I take my time putting my phone in my bag. I think about the Sports Committee meeting earlier, and Coach's innuendo about the new change room. I grimace. "I've already told you. So many things," I say to Will.

"Like?"

I cross my legs and uncross them again. I straighten the sheet on her bed. "Mostly it just seems petty," I say. "It was such a minor thing. I'd feel so...*vexatious*. He's said plenty of worse things to other girls, and no one else has complained. And besides, what's the point when I know the school won't do anything about it anyway? Except for making my life difficult. It's like what you said about our charity bake sales. It's not worth the bother."

"I can't remember saying that about your bake sales," says Will. "But if I said that, I was wrong. And I think you're wrong now." She readjusts her hand on the pile of pillows. "To begin with, just because it seems like a minor thing in comparison to more horrible things, that doesn't make it right. That's like saying breaking and entering is okay because murder exists. Secondly? It matters that you speak out because if you don't, this kind of thing will keep happening. Not to you, maybe, but to other students. Possibly worse things. You realize that, don't you?"

"Of course," I say softly.

"It might not always feel like it, but you've got power when others don't," she says. "Which means that even if what Hadley said to you wasn't haunting you, which it clearly is, and even if there was no one else at risk, when there clearly is, you're in a position to say something where others aren't."

If only it were as simple as Will makes it sound. "I still don't know," I murmur.

Will bounces her head against the pillows to the rhythm of the hospital monitor. Beep. Thud. Beep. Thud. Beep. "I'm sorry for getting so heavy on you," she says. "I just hate it when things drag on without a resolution."

She is gazing at me again and there is heat in her voice. "I know it's crazy." Her words have thickened. "I don't even know why I feel this way. You annoy the shit out of me most of the time."

A thudding starts beneath my rib cage. Everything I've been concertedly trying not to think about presses obstinately against my skull. "Will. Don't," I whisper.

"It makes less sense than pretty much anything." She laughs before a shadow of gloom sweeps across her face. "Oh, what's the point? I wish you and Edie a very comfortable life."

My heartbeat quickens. Why have I put myself in this situation again? I should never have come to the hospital. Why did I rush over before thinking it through? "I should get going. My mother is expecting me home for dinner." I pick up my school bag.

"You never talk about her, you know," Will says.

I place the bag over one shoulder. "My mother?"

"That's not who I meant."

"If you mean Edie," I say, not meeting her eye, "I talk about her all the time."

Will shakes her head. "I didn't even know you had a girlfriend until I specifically asked you. And when you do talk about her, it's all—logistical—like you're in a business partnership or something. 'I have to meet Edie at five.' 'Edie and I have training this afternoon.' 'I promised Edie I'd pick up muffins for her fund-raiser.' That stuff doesn't count."

"I don't see why not." My mouth feels dry.

"If you told me you'd devised a cartoon so she wouldn't be marked down in English—that would count. Or if you told me you cornered her at lunchtime every day outside a place you knew she hung out—that would count. Or if you told me you planned an entire ruse involving an American photorealist and domestic air travel to help cure her of a weird-ass phobia—"

"What are you trying to say?"

"What do you think I'm trying to say?" Will's words are fierce.

"I—I do stuff for Edie as well."

Will pounds the starch from the sheets with her functioning fist. "Okay. You're nice to everyone. I get it. But when Edie does this, how does it make you feel?" She grabs my hand and tugs me toward her, bringing her face so close to mine that our noses are practically touching. I feel her breath on my lips, and she looks at me with such strange softness that my heart crashes against its cage. And the most peculiar thought occurs to me.

If I could only remain in this moment, if everything else could be cordoned off somehow, if all the other portions of my life could just drop away . . .

But it is impossible. Will Everhart is impossible.

My phone buzzes again. I pull back.

chapter 29

WILL

My fingers will be fine. The doctors say there's no serious or long-term damage. But while the breaks are healing I can't grip a paintbrush without wanting to injure someone. My major work will have to wait.

My hand is not the main problem, though. It's Harriet.

I know there's no point hoping for anything between us. If I didn't already know it, Harriet made it clear at the hospital the moment she pulled her face away from mine, the moment she took her hands back from where they'd fallen on my hips.

And still, like the dumb mutt in a zombie flick who waits for food beside the newly rotting corpse of its owner, I hope.

If only I had a distraction. Some kind of hobby. I wonder how long it takes to learn how to hot-wire a car.

Of course, there are things I can do toward my major work

other than paint. I spend three nights in a row watching plane crash videos in the expectation that it will inspire me to new artistic heights. All it does is make my nightmares worse. I soon ditch the videos and find myself back on Harriet's Instagram account, scrolling through pictures of her having fun with other people.

Urgh.

When I'm not thinking about Harriet, I'm thinking about our botched plan. This time, we sailed too close to a particular wind called Croon. She's probably got me on twenty-four-hour surveillance already.

It takes a while for the reality of Amelia Westlake's demise to truly strike, and I'm brushing my teeth when it does. I stare at myself in the mirror, and a mournful loser with a toothpaste goatee stares back. With the end of Amelia Westlake, I feel like I've lost two important people at once.

My next thought is to wonder how a Rosemead princess and an imaginary person became the most important people in my life. There is something seriously wrong with me.

This is confirmed when midterms roll around and I'm stoked about it. A week of study leave and two weeks of writing papers is just what I need to take my mind off everything else. For the first time all year, I make schoolwork a priority. I learn more about the content of my subjects through self-directed study than I have all year in class. I manage to keep my mind off Harriet for hours at a stretch.

Then something unexpected happens—the kind of "unexpected" you get in zombie flicks. *Dawn of the Dead* style, Amelia Westlake shows up.

The first time I spy her is in my legal studies midterm. I'm figuring out the difference between a criminal and civil penalty when I notice something scrawled on the exam desk.

Amelia Westlake wishes you good luck!

I can't help but grin. I wonder who's written it. Not Harriet—graffitiing desks is against the school rules. And it's a thousand times too neat for Nat.

After the exam, I'm walking past the drama noticeboard in the Performing Arts Center foyer when I notice a pinned piece of notepaper waving in the breeze.

COMMUNITY NOTICE

If you are interested in trying out for this year's school musical production of *The Boyfriend*, please note the following conditions:

1. Lead role: Must be very pretty. The male lead will be cast from our brother school, and we wouldn't want him to have to kiss someone who is less than an eight (MINIMUM). Neither acting nor singing skills required.

2. Supporting role: Must be pretty, but not as pretty as the lead role. Must be funny, but not too funny. Acting and singing skills preferable, but not as important as other requirements.

3. Chorus: Must be able to sing. Don't worry about acting ability or how attractive you are. If this is an issue, we will make you wear a paper bag or something.

Signed: Amelia "telling it like it is" Westlake

Nothing about this notice indicates Harriet's or Nat's involvement. I sure as hell had nothing to do with it. But here's the thing. The notice—and I don't know how else to put it—is just the kind of joke Amelia Westlake would make.

It occurs to me that I haven't checked her Instagram feed for weeks. I go home and log on with the password Harriet gave me.

Two hundred and fifteen more followers! And the comments section is going mental. There's the usual speculation about Amelia's identity. But @amelia.westlake has been tagged in a whole lot of other pics as well.

Photographs of things Amelia has supposedly done. Things I don't know about. Things I'm pretty sure Nat and Harriet don't know about, either.

For example, a picture of Amelia Westlake's donation to Rosemead's latest cupcake sale for Amnesty: a hundred chocolate cupcakes, with a note scrawled in one of the cake boxes. *Great cause! Good luck, AW.*

A stencil someone has sprayed on a wall in the school courtyard: the iconic outline of Marxist revolutionary Che Guevara, but with *AW* on his cap instead of a star.

An RSVP to Beth Tupman's eighteenth birthday party:

Dear Beth,
Thank you so much for the invitation. I particularly appreciate it since I live in one of the "lesser" North Shore suburbs and my father isn't a member of your father's golf club. I will probably stick out like a sore thumb. But I would be delighted to attend!
Amelia Westlake

My resistance falters and dies. I text Harriet.

> Check out Amelia's Insta feed.

She doesn't text back.

✳ ✳ ✳

Our midterms finish on a Friday. I spend the weekend passed out on my bed with exhaustion, a state intermittently broken by thoughtful food deliveries from my mother and occasionally Graham, whose surprising adeptness at cooking pumpkin risotto initiates a low-level guilt trip about the whole hitting-him-with-a-frying-pan incident. I barely have the energy to check for texts from Harriet, although I still make the effort about thirty times every twenty-four hours. On Sunday night she finally makes contact.

> Hi Natasha and Will. I hope you are well. Any
> chance you could meet me in the newsroom
> before school on Monday? I have an idea. Best,
> Harriet.

✳ ✳ ✳

When I get to the newsroom I find Nat, who's sporting some serious Arthur-inflicted gravel rash, on the moth-eaten couch. She's in deep discussion with Harriet, who's hovering above her.

"We could book them online," Harriet is saying when I walk in.

"No way! It needs to be untraceable."

"What needs to be untraceable?" I ask.

"Your intellect," Nat says, looking up. "Oh, hang on, it already is."

Why is she being such a bitch to me? We haven't even seen each other since exams started, so it's not like I've had a recent opportunity to piss her off. Besides, Nat is more inclined to threaten me with water torture for a specific offense than get passive-aggressive on my butt.

"Ha. Ha." I make my you-think-you're-so-hilarious-when-in-actual-fact face.

"You're just jealous Harriet and I have been hanging out at her house together," Nat says, running a finger along her blistering chin. "We're practically sisters-in-law now, aren't we, Harriet?"

Harriet looks alarmed.

Nat switches her gaze to me. "We're talking about Operation Formal, if you must know. This Friday is the night of nights."

"Hang on." I look between them. "What the hell is Operation Formal? I thought we agreed we had to kill off Amelia Westlake."

I address this last part to Harriet, who looks away guiltily. "Well, yes," she says. "But with all this Amelia Westlake activity that's been happening—"

"You checked out her Instagram feed, then?"

She gives a businesslike nod. "It's perfect. Amelia Westlake has basically gone viral. It gives us at least a dozen alibis. There's no way we can be linked to all of what's happened.

Which means that if we do pull off another Amelia-related prank, it's not necessarily going to be linked to us, either."

I take in what she's saying. While I've been mourning Amelia's death, Harriet's been planning her revival, with one big difference. This time, I'm not invited to the party.

I can't believe it. I was the one who prompted her to check out the new activity on Instagram, and now she's using it to sideline me. She knows I won't be at the formal. She and Nat have probably been plotting this at leisure during study breaks on the Prices' pristine cream couches.

"I take it you remember I'm banned from going."

"Of course I remember," Harriet says, glancing at Nat. Harriet looks nervous and excited at once. "That's the beauty of this operation. This way, you can come."

What is she on about? I never said I wanted to come. Although, if it's going to be the scene of another Amelia West-lake strike against Rosemead, I could be persuaded. But how could Harriet have possibly engineered a formal that Croon wouldn't kick me out of as soon as I turned up? Our beloved principal will be there to make the bloody welcome speech. "I don't get it."

"Sit down, Will," Nat says.

I sit and listen as they talk me through every aspect of the plan. Five minutes later, I know everything.

I look at Harriet. "This was your idea?"

She nods.

"And you've asked Liz Newcomb to help?"

"I know the charity prank ultimately failed, but it was

good of her to trust Amelia Westlake with that key. Tremendous, really," Harriet says airily.

This is a turnup for the books.

"And the best part," Nat says, "is thanks to Harriet, everything is practically already in place."

⚹ ⚹ ⚹

By break on Tuesday there's a tangible buzz in the school corridors. All the year twelves can talk about is Friday night: who's taking who, what they're wearing, how they're getting their hair done, who by, what shoes they're wearing, which preformal drinks they've been invited to, who's having a manicure, and who's using a professional makeup artist. In summary: yawn. This type of conversation escalates during the week so that by Thursday formal talk is all that's going on in the corridors. It gets so bad that if one more person asks me a question about Friday night, I swear I'll punch her in the face.

Another type of chatter starts to escalate as well. Word has gotten out about the no-girlfriends rule.

"I think it's to be expected," I hear Beth Tupman telling Palmer Crichton outside the science lab. "It's a school formal, not Mardi Gras. Besides, it's just one night. It's not like Rosemead is saying people can't have girlfriends."

I wonder if Beth has shared her views with her friend Harriet.

"I think it's bullshit," says Palmer. "You should be able to take whoever you want."

Nakita Wallis nods. "The formal is such an important

event. Symbolically, I mean. It's end of school. It's coming of age. It's a single night that, for better or worse, comes to represent our entire high school experience. Excluding certain people from authentic participation is damaging."

"I don't understand most of what you just said but I totally agree," says Daphne Chee.

I continue down the corridor with a smile, until I look up to find Fowler coming in the other direction.

"Good afternoon, Will," she greets me, slowing to a halt.

"Hi, Miss Fowler."

"Where are you off to?"

"Er, class?"

"Which class?"

"Legal studies. It's in Room Four-Oh-Six, just down the hallway."

She squints at me with deep suspicion before finally letting me pass.

It's clear that the school staff have their eyes on me. The number of times Fowler, Hadley, or Davids has struck up a random conversation with me in the corridors lately has put me on notice of that. I half expect to be called up to Croon's office, but she seems content to delegate her harassment of me to her minions.

And why not? She hasn't a clue what's about to go down. As far as she's concerned, the formal is going ahead precisely as Harriet and her committee originally planned: with a classy dinner dance at Dish restaurant at Circular Quay, punctuated by Croon's welcome speech and a speech by the chair of the board at eight o'clock. No girlfriends allowed.

On Friday morning before first period, Harriet ushers me into an empty classroom. I can hardly believe my luck.

"I wanted you to know I've reserved a place for you on one of the formal buses," she says when the door's closed. "They're leaving from the school gates at six."

More formal talk—how very disappointing. "I don't know. I think it would be better if I got Mum to drive me. It's probably best I don't draw attention to myself."

"Nobody even knows you're banned," Harriet whispers, keeping an eye on the door. "Except the teachers, and they're not coming on the buses. They'll be making their own way there. Or at least they *think* they will be. You know what I mean."

I do, but it's not what *I* mean. I'm the only person who doesn't have a date. That fact alone means I'll stick out.

"You know, I'm pretty sure Janine Richter is going by herself," Harriet says nonchalantly, as if I've spoken the thought aloud. "And Kimberley Kitchener too, come to think of it. I had two tables with odd numbers, and that's why. And Arthur won't be coming on the bus with Nat." She lowers her voice. "He'll already be there, of course."

I had forgotten that part of the plan. It means I can sit with Nat on the bus. Then again, given she's been a cow to me since the start of term, she might not want to share a seat. "I don't know, Harriet...."

"But if you're not on the bus, you won't see the whole thing play out," Harriet says.

Do I detect an amount of desperation in her voice?

In that moment, at least, it makes me believe that she truly wants me there. So I agree.

* * *

As it turns out, it is not my single status that most sets me apart from the crowd mingling at the school gates at six o'clock on Friday—it's my outfit. Block color dresses, pearl necklaces and kitten heels dominate, like I've somehow stumbled into the ballroom at a country club. My leopard-skin bolero, black bodysuit, and high-waisted, three-quarter-length pants, paired with my favorite Doc Martens, raise more than a few eyebrows.

I see Edie in the chaos before I see Harriet. Impeccably groomed and perfectly postured, she's holding a silver purse in one hand and smoothing her hair with the other. She glances impatiently into the crowd. I follow the direction of her gaze. That's when I see Harriet and stop breathing. Her dress is silver to Edie's complementary royal blue, and there's something horrifying about that, but the fact remains: She looks beautiful.

I tear my gaze away and turn my attention to the boys. They are pretty much interchangeable in their penguin suits, with the exception of Nakita Wallis's date, who is sporting a Mohawk, a diamond earring, and glittery nail polish. Nakita has on wide pants, a blousy shirt with suspenders, and a necktie. Thank the lord for Nakita. We exchange a somber nod of solidarity.

The bus ride itself is horrendous. Not only is it noisy, sweaty, and crowded, but Nat hardly speaks to me. I even ask her boring Arthur-related questions to get her talking, but she replies in monosyllables. I compliment the knee-high lace-ups she's wearing with her otherwise ordinary short black dress, and the only response she gives me is a grunt.

But it's worth enduring every minute for the moment when the buses zoom past the Circular Quay turnoff and head into the Rocks, the historic district near the Sydney Harbor Bridge.

Beth Tupman is the first to notice. "Hey!" she says loudly. "I think we were supposed to turn left back there. Harriet! We're going the wrong way."

Harriet looks so genuinely surprised that I'm almost convinced by it, even though I know better.

The chatter quiets down. Everyone watches as Harriet staggers up the aisle in her ridiculous heels and makes a show of speaking to the bus driver.

She staggers back. "Apparently there are road closures," she announces. "We have to go the long way round."

This satisfies the passengers. Fools. They return to their ear-splitting conversations. The bus winds its way deep into the Rocks. The noise only settles down again when we screech to a stop in a narrow lane and the doors wheeze open.

"This isn't Dish," says Beth.

"No, but look." Eileen Sarmiento points.

Some of the girls start shrieking.

There are so many people craning to look through the windows that it's not until I've pushed my way down the aisle, out the door, and into the cool air that I get to see it for myself.

I sense someone hovering next to me. "Nice," I say under my breath.

"I told you the bus trip would be worth it," murmurs Harriet.

Smoothly she moves away into the crowd, slipping between guests to follow Edie through a timber doorway. Above it is the enormous banner that's been getting all the attention, lit up by festoon lights.

AMELIA WESTLAKE WELCOMES YOU TO

ROSEMEAD'S YEAR-TWELVE FORMAL

chapter 30

HARRIET

The whole thing was relatively straightforward to organize: a call to Dish to cancel our booking, a chat with the Sphere team, a word with their friend who cooks at Deep Fryer, and a visit to the Parnells, the family whose daughter, Lucy, I tutored in math. Fortunately for me, not only did Lucy do extremely well on her recent trigonometry tests, but her parents own (in addition to the Heritage Resort and three restaurants) this club in the Rocks: a belowground space with exposed beams and dripping sandstone walls. They let me hire it for a discount, which makes up for the cost of the hefty deposit I lost to Dish. I even had enough spare to pay the Deep Fryer team for the catering.

Once those details were settled, all that was left was to arrange for Liz Newcomb to help with the decorations and let the bus company know about the slight amendment to the route.

The teachers who planned to attend have no idea where we are. Principal Croon and her friend, Mr. Chair of the Board, are similarly none the wiser. Which means they won't be making a welcome speech. They won't be attending this year's formal. We won't be enforcing their ridiculous rule.

And in their place, Will gets to be here after all.

✳ ✳ ✳

"This place rocks out," says Eileen Sarmiento as she comes through the door beside me.

"I know, right?" says Daphne Chee behind us. "It's, like, way cooler than the place we originally booked. Go Amelia Westlake."

"Yeah, go Amelia. What a babe," Inez Jurich chimes in.

Arthur, beside the stage, waves me over. "Hey, Harri, where can I find another one of these?" Dressed in his army pants and leather jacket, he is dangling a power cord in the air. Glitter shimmers on his cheekbones in the dim, yellow-tinted light.

"Check the greenroom."

Arthur cups a hand to his ear.

"THE GREENROOM," I repeat. The music has already started—a soundtrack Nat put together over the weekend. She promised me there wouldn't be too much heavy rock, and so far the music is suitable, but I make a mental note to talk to her about the volume.

"I saw some more power cords on the other side of the stage." Liz Newcomb is beside me. "You want me to get them?"

"Oh! That would be great."

She races off. I must say, Liz has proven herself to be extremely competent during these past few weeks. And sensible. And friendly. I have definitely been underestimating her.

"This is amazing," says Edie when I find her ten minutes later at the bar. She is attempting to eat a Deep Fryer burger from a paper plate with a relative amount of decorum. By now, the club is almost at capacity. People are eating, drinking, and mingling in groups. Nat's soundtrack is getting dancier, preparing the crowd for the live act soon to appear onstage.

"I was expecting a sit-down dinner, complete with fussy table settings and crappy top-forty hits. This may in fact be the coolest school formal in all of history." Edie is clearly astonished. "You say one girl organized the whole thing? I thought you were organizing the formal, Harriet. Why have I never heard of this Amelia Westlake?"

"That's easy," says Zara Long. She leans over the bar, where she is helping herself to another jug of sangria. "Amelia Westlake doesn't exist."

It is Zara's tone of complicity that fascinates me. I hardly know the girl, and yet here she is talking like she's in on the whole thing.

"She's right," I tell Edie, making an effort not to sound too proprietary. "Amelia Westlake is basically a made-up person."

Edie's eyes widen. "You mean she's a hoax?"

"Something like that."

"What else has she done?"

I pause. "The odd cartoon, I believe. A joke involving essay marks."

"I can't believe you never told me about any of this. Really,

Bubble. I know you loathe anything playful or political, but this is genius."

"I don't loathe playful or political things."

"Yes, you do."

"No, she doesn't."

I turn.

My heart quickens. It isn't as if Will has even spent any money on her outfit—that is perfectly clear. Edie, by contrast, has on the stunning dress we both agreed she would buy. She looks lovely, but somehow Will, in her black bodysuit and high-waisted pants, looks—well, if not *lovelier*, exactly, then certainly more appealing.

"And you are?" Edie interrupts, leaning over me to Will, her hand outstretched.

Will ignores her and makes her way back into the crowd.

"How rude." Edie is about to say something else when Beth yanks at my arm.

"I've got a bone to pick with you." Her voice is sharp with fury. "You could have told me from the start about James. I've just seen him kissing some guy beside the stage. Apparently they're together. If I'd known I wasn't in with a chance, I would have arranged a proper date for tonight weeks ago. Instead I'm lumped with Millie's dopey brother." She points to Kurt Levine, who is standing behind her struggling to remove his middle finger from the neck of a beer bottle.

It takes me a minute to work out what Beth is talking about. Then I remember. I never shored up that introduction with James, Arthur's keyboard player, as I promised I would. With all the drama, it slipped my mind.

I say to Beth, "But I didn't know about James!"

Beth scowls. "Like I'm going to believe that. You lot always stick together."

"What on earth are you talking about?"

The high-pitched reverb of a microphone draws everyone's attention to the stage. Arthur stands at the front, microphone cupped in hand, surveying the crowd. He looks amazing up there. In his makeup, under stage lights, my pale-skinned, bowlegged brother looks wiry in the best possible way. Even the airstrip on his scalp has a certain charm to it tonight.

Seeing him standing there, the crowd begins to whistle and hoot. I try to ignore the bad energy zapping off Beth. With a deep breath, I take the atmosphere of the room into my lungs.

At the foot of the stage, Natasha is taping the mike cords to the stands. Arthur gives her a wink.

Beth leans toward me again. "Don't tell me Ning Nong is bonking your brother!" she says with delighted disgust.

I pretend I haven't heard her. Then I change my mind. "Don't call her that," I hiss.

She laughs. "What? *Ning Nong?*"

"Yes," I say. "Please don't say it again. Ever."

Beth stops laughing. "What's got into you?"

I grit my teeth. "It's a racist thing to say, Beth."

She says something that is impossible to hear above the noise.

"What?"

"I SAID YOU'RE NO FUN ANYMORE. I SAID I SOMETIMES FORGET WHY WE EVEN HANG OUT."

"IT'S NOT ABOUT FUN. IT'S ABOUT BEING A DECENT HUMAN BEING," I shout back.

Beth mutters something beneath the noise.

The whistles die down.

"Hi, everybody," says Arthur as James and Bill take their places behind their instruments. "Thanks for having us. And on behalf of Amelia Westlake, WELCOME TO YOUR YEAR-TWELVE FORMAL."

The crowd explodes. Someone starts up a chant.

"Amelia, Amelia, Amelia."

People join in. I look around, electrified. I try to spot Will among the sea of people, but I can't see her anywhere.

Arthur signals for everyone to quiet down.

"We've got a very special set for you tonight." Arthur paces the stage. "Those of you who know our music will know we're rather fond of clashy, head-banging tunes." He tilts his head coyly. "But we hear you guys like to dance."

"Hell, yeah!" calls someone from the crowd. Laughter erupts.

"That's why tonight we're mixing things up a bit, with a very special guest. Where is he?" Arthur steps back and nods to someone offstage.

I wonder who Arthur is talking about. He hasn't mentioned a special guest to me.

He steps forward again. "This guest of ours," he continues, drawing out the suspense, "is a man of enormous talent. He's played the Enmore. The ICC. The Opera House. When he heard about your situation, and how tonight's venue change had been organized in protest against some narrow-minded wankers"—more predictable cheering—"he was especially keen to be involved. He is, after all, a man who believes in love in all its forms."

The crowd grows loud with chatter about who it could be.

"May I present to you..." Arthur shouts above the noise. "The one. The only. Front man for Australia's hottest hip-hop outfit, DOKTOR D."

Doktor D comes out to an explosion of hooting and whistling and runs up to James at the keyboard. Leaning over the instrument, one leg flipping theatrically in the air, he plants a kiss on James's mouth. The crowd goes crazy, with the exception of Beth, who shouts in my ear: "That's the guy I was talking about."

I've seen Doktor D perform in a lineup with the Sphere a couple of times, but as he comes toward the front and they begin to play, something about him strikes me. His costume looks a lot like the one that was sitting on the PAC storeroom shelf for all those months.

But it's more than that. I recognize the face behind the stage makeup. He looks familiar—not just from those previous gigs, but from somewhere else.

By now he is rapping and the crowd is dancing. I register the lyrics and my spine tingles.

"Come on." It's Edie, suddenly beside me. She pulls me by the hand. "Let's dance."

I let her lead me onto the floor. This is the moment I've been dreaming of all year: the two of us dancing at my final-year formal. But as Edie puts her arms around me and Doktor D's lyrics ring in my ears—

Ameli ah / the fake ah / the ultimate rule break ah / I wouldn't wanna cross her / coz I bet she's got my numb bah / and she'll wiggetty jizz / all over my fizz / ain't no one who can take her

—everything feels wrong.

chapter 31

It's Duncan. Nat's coeditor aka slave-boy-slash-coffeemaker-come-spy. Acne-scarred, nearsighted Duncan, Rosemead's low-key Edwin Street refugee—or hostage, depending on your point of view—rapping onstage like a king. I stare at his cavalry uniform and laugh out loud.

"Why didn't you tell me?" I yell in Nat's ear.

"Like it would have meant anything to you. What was the last album you bought? *The Best of Adele*?"

Here it is again—Nat's bitchy side.

"Are you mad with me about something?"

She doesn't answer. Instead, she says, "Seems like Harriet's having a fine old time." She points to her and Edie on the dance floor together: model-thin Edie in her million-dollar dress grinding her hips against Harriet's, and Harriet grinding back.

My breath stalls.

"Don't tell me she's been leading you on," Nat says at my ear. "Being lied to feels pretty crap, doesn't it?"

I squint at her. "What are you implying?"

Nat laughs angrily. "Are you seriously asking me that?"

"What have I lied about?" I shout above the noise.

Nat's eyes widen. "What *haven't* you lied about, Will?"

I motion for her to follow me away from the dance floor and the speakers, into the alcove near the entrance, where it's quieter. "What are you talking about?"

Nat leans against the wall. "It's not that I wish things could have worked out between us. We both know the chemistry wasn't there. But I thought we were friends," she says, her jaw tense. "Why didn't you say something about your feelings for Harriet? Even when Duncan found you two together in the storeroom—"

"Is that why you published the article? To get back at me for not telling you?"

Nat doesn't answer. "You *still* denied it. It wasn't until you rammed into that bloody door, and you wanted Harriet, not me, at the hospital, that I knew for sure."

I gulp in air. I want to tell her I don't care about Harriet. It would be easier. But it would also be another lie.

Then I remember the surprise I felt the day I came across Nat in the Prices' front garden. "How can you be angry when you didn't tell me about Arthur?"

At the mention of his name, Nat's look softens for a moment. Then she reddens with fury. "Because you didn't give me a chance! You weren't returning my calls."

"That was because you'd published that article about me and Harriet in the paper!"

"Which I would never have done if only you'd told me what was going on between you and her—and I don't just mean the storeroom thing, I mean Amelia Westlake, too. That's what good friends do, Will. They talk to each other."

I open my mouth to rebut her latest argument, but Nat pushes herself off the wall. I watch her angle through the crowd toward the stage and her boyfriend.

I can't help thinking she's being unfair. It's not like Harriet and I were secretly dating. It's not like I'm even in with a chance.

I look over to the dance floor again, and there they are—Harriet and Edie. Something rattles in my rib cage like a secondhand car.

What am I doing, daydreaming that Harriet Price will ditch her perfect life and make a getaway in the passenger seat of the shit box that's mine? What is wrong with me?

Seriously, what the fuck?

The facts are right in front of me. For Harriet, tonight is not about taking a stand. It's about her realizing a long-held dream: to be queen of the bloody prom. She's at the center of the picture with her perfect partner. This moment—her and Edie on the dance floor—is what she's been striving for. Operation Formal has nothing to do with anyone else, least of all me. None of our operations have had anything to do with me. Harriet has practically engineered every one. I've merely been a vehicle, her cover and, if need be, the one who'd take the fall for her.

The worst of it? Even though I know this, it makes no difference. I *have* taken the fall and will again, if it comes to that.

Harriet "preppier than a canvas beach tote" Price. Tennis champ. Math star. Private-school pinup girl. Harriet Price, who lives in a house the size of a suburb. Harriet Price, the girl who is—almost in spite of herself—one of the kindest, most generous, most principled people I've ever known.

It doesn't matter that she's with someone else or that she has the power to do me over and probably will. It doesn't matter that we are objectively, spectacularly ill matched. I have moved beyond distaste, then beyond mere indifference, then beyond liking, then beyond infatuation. The place I've arrived at is as intoxicating as it is consuming, and I see no way of giving it up.

chapter 32

HARRIET

I turn away from Edie to find Will in the crowd. I finally see her, pressing her weight against the double doors.

She is leaving.

Light from the street spills in through the opening as she walks out of it. The doors slam shut.

Edie stretches out a hand to pull me back into a hip grind. I bat her away.

"What's wrong with you tonight, Bubble?"

"Nothing. I'm perfectly fine."

Doesn't Will realize I did this for her? I rearranged an entire function to make sure she could be here. It is not even eight o'clock at the scene of Amelia's greatest victory yet. What is the point of our victory if she is not here to taste it?

"You're acting really moody all of a sudden. Is it the music? I know this isn't our favorite type."

"Remind me, Edie, what type of music do we like again?"

"There's no need to get catty."

"I'm serious. I'm interested to know what I'm interested in. Nothing playful or political, obviously. We've established that."

My girlfriend peers at me with confusion, and I peer right back. It sounds strange to admit it, but I cannot remember doing this before—staring directly into Edie's face. She looks suddenly unfamiliar. Not a single feature provokes my affection. I try to recall which of her qualities appeal to me, but I draw a blank.

"Hey! Where are you going?"

When I get to the bar, I order a kamikaze. I throw it back and order another one. That's when Edie grabs my arm. "Harriet. You're acting very strange. You need to talk to me."

What can I say to her? That I've forgotten who she is to me, or why we're together? That this isn't how I imagined my night of nights turning out?

Of course it isn't. It is a different venue, with different music and different food. None of it is anything close to my original preparations. That is not the problem. In fact, I *like* how different it is.

The problem is how I feel, but also how I don't. There is no joy, no triumph. Not without Will here to share it.

"Just tell me what I can do to make things okay," Edie says, so gently that I am tempted to forgive her for everything.

I tell her to take me home.

chapter 33

WILL

Out in the mottled dark, a salty smell streams off the harbor, mixed with the stench of cologne, perfume, and spilled beer.

Friday night in the Rocks: what a party.

I walk. Up under the bridge, where car wheels hit the hinges of the road above. Past the harborside hotels. Past the Museum of Contemporary Art and its deco facade casting long shadows like something from a 1920s horror flick.

It doesn't take long to reach Circular Quay, with its tourists and fluorescent lights and children with rainbow-colored ice cream. A ferry honks. Water laps at the pier. I could jump in, surrender to the weight of its swell. I am exhausted enough to consider it, but I have somewhere to be.

Past terminals two through six, past buskers juggling bowling pins while break dancing, past the opera crowd devouring forty-dollar fish-and-chips at candlelit tables.

I approach Dish carefully from the side. I check my watch. Five to eight. Then I clock her. Croon, just meters away. I slip into the shadow of a pillar.

She is standing outside the foyer, surrounded by a small group of teachers. All of them have made an effort: formal gear, makeup, the works. It's almost touching. Hadley is there, too, his hair gelled into a peak. My warm feelings evaporate.

A head turns in my direction, sees me. Bracken.

We lock eyes for half a second. I feel strangely calm as I wait for her to raise the alarm.

Instead, she looks away. She says nothing to anyone. I breathe out deeply and slip further into the shadows.

"It makes no sense." I recognize Fowler's voice. "Where could they have got to? A whole year group!"

"Are you sure this is the right place?" It's Deputy Davids.

"Of course it is." Fowler again. "This has to be another one of their awful pranks."

"No need to get so worked up," Bracken soothes. "They're just kids having fun."

Good old Bracken.

"Are *you* having fun, Deidre? Because there's about a thousand other things I'd rather be doing right now," mutters Fowler.

"If it's some sort of prank," says a man I don't recognize, "how did no one know it was afoot?"

Voices talk over each other. It's impossible to hear what they're saying. They reach fever pitch.

"All right, all right," says Croon wearily.

The man pipes up again. "There's no point going over this

tonight anyway. It can wait till next week's board meeting."
His voice is sharp.

There is a brief silence before the group begins to talk over each other again.

Croon holds up her palms to quiet them.

I've heard enough. I've risked a lot by simply being here. I push off the pillar and find a crowd to blend into.

chapter 34

HARRIET

"What do you mean, you haven't done them?"

It is Monday morning. Edie is poised on my front doorstep, where with one hand on the frame, I am struggling to remain upright. It is odd that I am so tired given that I spent most of the weekend asleep.

I don't know why, but as soon as Edie dropped me off after the formal, all I wanted to do was close my eyes. I slept so late this morning that I haven't even had a chance to brush my hair. By contrast, Edie's ponytail looks extra smooth, if a little higher than usual. Her uniform is freshly ironed. Her knee-high socks are so aligned that she may have used an actual tape measure.

She is here to collect her notes for the National Public Speaking Competition, which I have completely forgotten to do. Again.

"Is this about Friday still?" she asks. "I wish you would tell me what got into you."

"I'll prepare the notes tonight," I say. "I'll make it a priority as soon as I'm home."

Edie's mouth becomes a circle. "Tonight's no use. The competition is this afternoon."

Oh dear. How could I have forgotten it was today? My mind has become a sieve. "Then I'll do them at school," I say. "In my free period. I'll duck out and Uber them over to you."

She narrows her eyes. "I'm relying on those notes, Bubble. You know that, right?"

"Yes, I do," I say, hearing the tetchiness in my voice.

"You promised you'd do this one thing for me."

"I understand."

"I hope so. Because Bianca Stein is still looking for a doubles partner."

What a sly fox she is. "I'll get them to you by twelve thirty. You have my word."

chapter 35

Mondays never fail to suck, but this one sucks harder than
most. From the moment I arrive at school, everywhere I go
people are crapping on about Harriet's formal.

"It was, like, the perfect mix of relaxed vibe and occasion
vibe," Kimberley Kitchener is saying two lockers down when I
collect my textbooks before roll call.

"Who needs a sit-down dinner of overcooked fish and
floppy cheesecake?" Zara Long chirps as she and Inez Jurich
walk behind me in the corridor. "Burgers are the way of the
future!"

Seriously, these girls need to get out more.

Yes, Croon deserves to be humiliated for giving in to the
bigoted school board. But I'd personally rather forget about
Friday night altogether.

I resolve to spend the day hiding out in the art studio.

However, at three minutes to nine I make the mistake of ducking into the common room to borrow a packet of assorted cookies to take with me.

"Will!"

She is perched on the couch with a stack of debate cards on her lap. She has a fountain pen poised over the top one. She is also staring at me in a way that makes the breath leave my body, and for a moment I think I have everything wrong.

Then Harriet opens her mouth.

"Where did you end up on Friday night? I noticed you left pretty early."

I balk at her brightness, and the way her upbeat tone makes her question mere inconsequential chatter. Suddenly I don't want to be in a room with her. "Best not to talk to me in public, Harriet. Remember the rules." The words come out snarkier than intended.

She blushes. "Oh! I guess they still apply, don't they? It's just with everything that's happened . . ."

I glance at her debate cards. "Are they for Edie?"

This is my attempt to change the subject—to make things less awkward—but obviously I've done a pretty bad job of changing the subject and a pretty good job of making things more awkward. Harriet looks helplessly down at her lap. "Yes," she says. "I promised to help her with her competition today. I have to get these to her by twelve thirty."

"Or?"

Harriet's look of discomfort intensifies. "Or she'll dump me from the Tawney team again."

That Edie: what a keeper.

I keep my sarcasm to myself.

The loudspeaker above Harriet's head suddenly crackles, even though it's too early for roll-call notices. Someone coughs into the microphone. "Attention everybody. An emergency announcement," says Deputy Davids. The speaker squeals loudly. "An emergency announcement," she repeats at a lower volume. "Year-twelve students are to report to the Assembly Hall immediately. I'll say that again. Roll call will be conducted in the Assembly Hall this morning for all year twelves. Attendance is compulsory."

* * *

By the time Harriet and I have walked to the hall in awkward silence, pretty much everyone has arrived. Deputy Davids is fussing about at the foot of the stage marking names off a roll, and when she isn't fussing, she's playing traffic controller, guiding girls toward the front rows. It's clear this isn't her event—she's merely the warm-up act. No prizes for guessing who's starring in the main part of the show.

We haven't said anything to each other, but I'm sure Harriet knows as well as I do what this is about.

"This could get heavy," I warn her as we pass through the doors.

"I know."

"We need to think about what we're going to do."

"I know."

"So. What are we going to do?"

"I don't know," Harriet says, before adding, "Let's split up."

She peels off from me and practically gallops down the front to where Liz Newcomb is already seated.

There is sense to her approach, but still.

I find Nat in the third row. I hesitate before sitting next to her. After our conversation on Friday night, I'm probably the last person she wants to see, and I'm not sure I want to see her. But sitting somewhere else would be completely weird.

"This is it, isn't it?" I say, sitting down.

I can tell she's deciding whether to speak to me. "They don't know a thing," she says finally.

"What makes you so sure?"

Nat glances at me. "The fact we're all here. It's as close as they can get to narrowing down the culprit. They're hoping to force a confession."

"But surely they'll start with me."

"They know it's bigger than you."

"How?"

Nat shifts in her chair. "My guess? Because nobody's snitched. Which means Croon suspects there are more people in on it. If it was just you, somebody would have snitched on you by now."

"You reckon?"

"You're not exactly Miss Popularity around here."

"I see you're still mad at me," I say. "Just for the record, I think you're being bloody unfair."

She turns to face me properly. "I know I was."

"You do?"

Nat nods and relief sweeps through me.

"It makes sense you didn't tell me about Harriet," she says. "She's with someone else. And things between you and me were...unclear."

"Exactly!"

Nat pauses. "The whole Amelia Westlake thing is a different story, though."

I hear an edge to her voice, and it scares me. "What do you mean? I thought we'd resolved all of that. When we let you"—I lower my voice—"get in on the game."

"I've been doing some thinking since then," says Nat. "A lot of thinking. The fact is, you deliberately kept the whole thing from me so I'd publish your cartoons."

"Which was wrong," I admit.

"You jeopardized my position at the *Messenger*."

"Yes."

"I could have lost my newspaper. Lost the chance to use that experience to get into journalism. Which is all I've ever wanted. As you know." Her voice is cold.

"Yes," I say, quieter this time.

"I've been thinking about it for weeks now. Trying to find a way to forgive you, I guess. I know you haven't had much experience at friendship."

She's not pulling her punches today. Nat can be cruel, but she's never been this cruel to me. "I've had friends," I say, my voice weak.

She gives me a level stare. "You mean from your old school?"

"Sure."

"Who you just happen to never talk about?"

I'm silent.

"It's okay," Nat continues. "I worked it out a while ago. Your mum didn't spend all that money to send you to Rosemead just for the sandstone buildings. It was because you were so miserable where you were. The kids there no doubt hated you because you were a self-righteous shit. You probably made them feel guilty for doing nothing about the causes you thought they should be fighting for. Basically the reasons they hate you here."

I draw circles on my knee with a finger so that I don't have to look at her.

"Except for me," she goes on. "That's *why* I like you. Because you care about the world. And me liking you has meant that Rosemead has been bearable for you. Which makes it really hard for me to have to say what I'm about to say."

My stomach hollows out.

"Of course I understand the point of what you did. But you put my interests last. Friends don't do that to friends. That's the bottom line. It was an arsehole move, Will."

I'm about to reply when I hear the sound of heels on polished timber. The chatter in the hall falls away. Great. My only friend thinks I'm an arsehole, and because my day isn't bad enough, enter our beloved principal.

Croon peers down calmly from the stage. "Friday night," she says. "None of you leave here until I find out who was responsible."

There is the sound of shifting bodies as girls glance around at one another—intrigued, annoyed, amused. This part of the proceedings is broken by the dramatic sound of Deputy Davids pressing her full weight against the bar lock across the doors at the back of the hall.

Heads turn at the sound of the lock clicking into place, then turn back to the front, expecting Croon to say more.

Croon drags a chair to the center of the stage and sits down on it.

What follows is a *Guinness World Records*–breaking staring competition between the principal and the entire year level. I wait, along with everyone, for her to say something else. Anything else. Usually at this point in the "we sit here until someone fesses up" exercise, teachers like to indulge in some rhetorical ranting. Now would be the perfect time for Croon's signature "I find this behavior deeply disappointing" lecture, for example, but I can tell by the look on her face that this is too big for that. The humiliation of Friday night has genuinely shaken her.

About three minutes pass. Croon hasn't spoken, and people start exchanging disbelieving glances. Is she really doing this? How long is she going to keep it up?

Another five minutes pass. I wait for someone to crack. I know it won't be Harriet or Nat. Both have too much at stake.

As for everyone else, they each have some useful information that might get them out of the Assembly Hall. For example, the name of Friday night's venue alone would be enough to lead Croon to the Parnell family, and a call to Mr. Parnell would surely lead straight to Harriet. And someone's bound to make the connection between Harriet and the Sphere.

To my increasing surprise, however, no one rises to the bait.

When ten minutes have passed, it seems impossible that Croon hasn't followed up her original threat with a single additional word. She's proving herself to be sovereign of the psych-out. I feel a nearly overwhelming desire to shout something out, just to crack the silence.

I resist. I can tell I'm not the only one struggling. Twenty minutes in, girls are clearing their throats and shifting in their chairs. Palmer Crichton is coughing as if she's just developed tuberculosis.

I use the time to turn Nat's words over in my head. I don't blame her for being angry. I would be, too, if she'd done the same to me. She's right, of course, about everything. They loathed me at my old school.

What a great job I did safeguarding myself against the same thing at Rosemead. Well played, idiot me.

Friends don't do that to friends. It's a telling-off, yes. But it's more than that. The words have a certain snappy ring to them, like the final line Nat always publishes in the *Messenger*.

My mouth goes dry. It's her sign-off line. That's what it is. She's signing off from our friendship.

I nudge her.

She doesn't respond.

To take my mind off Nat, I focus on the rest of the room. We've reached the half-hour mark and the noises have settled down, almost as if the year group has entered a sort of meditative state. I wonder how long Croon is planning to string this out for. Doesn't she have principal stuff to get on with?

If this goes on much longer, we'll all miss our first class and people will start needing the bathroom. Soon after that it will be break, and hunger will come into play. Perhaps that's what Croon is counting on.

Another minute passes and another. We reach the fifty-minute mark. Break comes and goes. An hour and five. An hour and ten. Still nobody comes forward.

I doubt Croon expected this kind of resilience. A giddy feeling rises in my chest, possibly from the realization that Nat is not going to forgive me, possibly a preliminary sign of starvation, or possibly something to do with the fact we're reaching the point where the likelihood of someone saying something actually begins to decrease. The longer the collective spirit holds out—for that's what appears to be in effect here, as crazy as it seems—the harder it will be to break that spirit, and the more likely Croon will have to start worrying about parents complaining of skipped classes and bladder damage.

An hour and a half in, I can see girls trying to keep themselves awake. Some have actually nodded off. We're home and hosed if we can make it to twelve thirty.

And with that thought another follows: Harriet's deadline. If anything is going to pressure her to confess, I realize, it's that.

For the last ninety minutes I've been avoiding looking in her direction. I didn't trust that a single glance wouldn't give the game away. Now I look.

I can mainly just see the back of her and about a quarter of the side of her face, but it's enough. Enough for my heart to swell in my rib cage. Enough to see how agitated she is. All the telltale signs are there: the foot-tapping, the wriggling, the obsessive glances at her watch. It makes sense. She's caught between forfeiting her Tawney dreams if she doesn't deliver those notes to Edie and, depending on how Croon decides to play things, potentially forfeiting everything else.

I feel suddenly transposed, as if it's me on the chopping block, not her. I make the calculations. She could probably reach Blessingwood Girls in twenty minutes. But I'm not sure how long she needs to prepare the notes themselves. No doubt she was counting on her free first period to finish them off.

It's 11:20 AM. Harriet clutches a hand to her breast. Her shoulders are rising and falling heavily.

At 11:25 AM, her head lolls on one fist. She looks overcome with seasickness.

At 11:27 AM, her head is buried in both hands, and I'm pretty sure what's coming. She has set her own deadline and is working up the courage to meet it.

I am under no illusion that if I confess now I will achieve little more than my expulsion at an inconveniently close time to my final exams. And, faced with the choice, I don't want to do it. I'm mere months from the end of my time at Rosemead. I'm almost free of the place. I want to conquer Rosemead, not let Rosemead conquer me.

But as 11:30 AM clicks over and Harriet presses her hands to the armrests, I jump from my seat anyway.

Not for all the reasons I should, but for the single one I shouldn't.

Harriet turns at the sound. For a minute our eyes lock, and I can't understand the confusion on her face.

I didn't mean to fall in love, but I did, and so being Harriet's fall girl now makes a warped kind of sense.

"It was me," I call out, meeting Croon's gaze. "I organized the formal on Friday night. All by myself. I'm Amelia Westlake."

chapter 36

HARRIET

Two rows behind me, Will has her eyes fixed on Principal
Croon, like some deadly zoo animal that has jumped its enclo-
sure. Half of the year group is staring at her, and the other half
is staring at our principal, waiting to see what she will do.

I cannot breathe. The breath I took before attempting to
stand up is caught, midaction, in my throat.

I know what this means. It means I can still win Tawney.
I can pass my exams and graduate. The year can dance on just
like it is supposed to, with everything in place.

Everything except Will.

"Thank you," says Principal Croon, clearly not grateful at
all. Relieved, maybe, that the morning's ordeal is over. "I am
disappointed, as I'm sure all your classmates are, that you have
taken up"—she looks at her watch—"precisely two and a half
hours of our day. But I'm glad you have finally come to your

senses or what you have of them. Not that I'm at all surprised. Your track record proves you take far too much pleasure in disrupting the operations of this school."

I have never heard Principal Croon so angry.

"It will be no trouble—in fact, I will take great pleasure," she goes on, "in writing to your parents to say you are no longer welcome at Rosemead. It is the inevitable consequence of the disrespect you have demonstrated for this institution from day one."

I look up at Will, who stands with one hand on the back of her seat, withstanding the tirade. She looks as tired as I feel. Her hair falls, lopsided, across her face.

I think about Edie and the notes I have promised her.

No second chances, that's what she said.

I think about Tawney. I have a place for that shield in my trophy cabinet. It will justify the hours I've toiled on the court. It will be my crowning high school achievement. My mother will be beside herself with pride.

I run a finger along my badges. I should sit here quietly and protect what I have striven for.

But I look at Will Everhart, my erstwhile collaborator, and I know I can't let her do this alone.

I stand up. "And me," I say, raising my voice above Principal Croon's booming monologue. "I'm Amelia Westlake, too."

Principal Croon glances at me irritably. "Harriet Price. Sit down," she says, turning back to Will. "The easiest thing," she continues, addressing her, "would be for you to come with me now, and we can deal with this immediately."

"Excuse me, Principal Croon..."

She turns to me again. "What is it, Harriet?"

"If you are going to expel Will, then you'll also have to expel me."

Murmurs fill the hall. Principal Croon's expression turns from irritation to anger. "Fine, then," she says at last. "I'll deal with both of you together."

The hall falls silent. I can see people exchanging shocked glances.

"Does anybody else want to confess to being Amelia Westlake, or are we done here?" She taps the toe of her shoe on the timber boards.

There is movement beside Will. Natasha stands up. "I do," she says.

Principal Croon's eyes glower.

Will's expression is no longer tired. It is tinged with something else. She looks at Natasha before gazing at me, and her gaze burns a hole in my chest.

There is a commotion to the left of the hall. Some girls are pointing at the wall. I follow their gaze.

The school banner. I'd almost forgotten about that particular prank of ours. It has been lying in wait for so long. Now, finally, our replacement motto, stitched carefully in cursive, is garnering the attention it deserves. Instead of the original French, the motto now reads, in English:

Play the power, not the game.

A murmur spreads across the hall. Girls are craning their necks and grinning. The energy in the room is building like a wave.

Beside me, Liz Newcomb gets to her feet. "Me too," she says. "I'm also Amelia Westlake."

Five seats across from Liz, Trish Burger makes a move. "And me."

Behind Trish, Daphne Chee and Inez Jurich spring up. "Guilty as charged," says Inez.

Kimberley Kitchener stands, followed by Zara Long. The rest of the girls in their row follow suit.

Beth and Millie gaze around in confusion and then slowly get to their feet.

One by one, girls across the hall stand up: Palmer Crichton, Nakita Wallis, Eileen Sarmiento.

Prisha Kamala. Anna Yemelin. Lorna Gallagher.

Janine Richter. Ruby Lasko.

I watch my classmates rise until everyone has risen. It is like some bizarre standing ovation without the clapping. Natasha must think so, too, because that is the moment she starts the applause. Girls begin to join in, until the entire year is clapping and hooting and stamping its feet.

chapter 37

WILL

People are cheering as Croon marches me up the aisle. The fact she's dragging me like a criminal only heightens the experience.

The cheering turns into chanting as we exit the foyer. A hundred and twenty voices are shouting in unison.

"Amelia, Amelia, Amelia."

I feel like bawling.

It's a ten-minute walk to her office. Croon pushes the door open. It looks pretty much as I remembered it, but with less of the French perfume smell and a shitload more schadenfreude. Croon takes her seat behind her desk and threads her fingers into a tiny church complete with pinky steeple. "I suppose you're going to tell me I should have hauled in the entire year. That you are no more culpable than your hundred and twenty classmates who also confessed. There will be a full investigation, believe me, but I would like to hear what you have to say first. Were you involved in the Amelia Westlake hoax?"

I nod. "I sure was."

She seems surprised and pleased by my answer. "And did you or did you not act alone?"

"Completely alone."

She leans forward. "The cartoons in the paper. They were your work?"

"What can I say? I am witty *and* artistic."

Croon registers my insolence with a scowl. "And what about the essay swap?"

"All me. Fowler never recognized my true brilliance, you see. She needed to learn her lesson."

Now that I've decided to cop the full blame, it's easy. All I have to do is channel one of those British murder mysteries that Mum likes to watch. In the final scene of every episode, the culprit gets caught by the good guys and promptly confesses to everything.

"And the letter to the local schools offering our Lower Hall free of charge?"

"Yep."

Croon takes out a notepad and puts pen to paper. "Let's see. What else was there?"

"The computer donation."

"Yes, of course."

"Oh, and the newsroom break-in."

Croon is writing furiously. She looks up. "You realize that in breaking into the newsroom you were breaking the law?"

"I sure do. Now, let's see. What else? Oh yes. I put a notice on the Performing Arts Center noticeboard. And I graffitied the exam tables. And I entered the gym staff room without permission. There are some other bits and bobs, but to be honest, I can't remember everything."

Croon puts down her pen. "Just to be perfectly clear, Miss Everhart. You received no help for any of these pranks from anyone else at all?"

"Correct."

"Natasha Nguyen wasn't involved? Or…" Here, she pauses. "Harriet Price?"

"Harriet Price? Are you serious? No. I deserve one hundred percent of the blame. I flew solo with all of this. I'm a lone wolf."

Croon nods with a jaunty little chin tuck.

There is an urgent rapping on the door.

Croon eyes the door hatefully and then slides the notebook swiftly across to me. "Sign here."

I speed-read what she's written. She's outlined in dot form each Amelia Westlake activity I've mentioned. At the bottom of the page are the words *I am solely responsible for all of the above* followed by a horizontal line marked with a cross.

"Here?" I ask, pointing to the line.

Whoever is at the door raps on it again, keenly.

Croon nods at me impatiently, looking ready to murder the person at the door.

"I guess this means the investigation into Amelia Westlake is closed and I get expelled."

"That's right," says Croon.

"Fine with me." I sign on the horizontal line. Croon instantly looks more relaxed. I'm half expecting her to put her feet up on the desk and light a cigar when the door bursts open.

Harriet stands in the doorway, waving a piece of A4 paper covered in type. "Whatever Will Everhart has admitted to, she's lying," she tells Croon breathlessly.

Croon's brow darkens. "Not this again, Harriet."

"This has nothing to do with you, Price. Get out of here," I hiss. She should be halfway to Blessingwood with Edie's notes by now.

Ignoring me, Harriet thrusts the paper at Croon. "I have written down the details of every Amelia Westlake episode and my personal involvement in it. If you want to expel Will, you're going to have to expel me, too."

Croon forms her lips into a line.

"You really shouldn't have done this," I mutter.

Harriet continues to ignore me.

Croon eyes Harriet with something akin to pity. "Miss Price. Wilhelmina's misdemeanors are part of a very long record, stretching back two and a half years now. You, on the other hand, have an *exemplary* record—"

"Just read it," Harriet interrupts.

Croon appears deeply shocked. Obediently, she begins to read Harriet's paper.

"See?" says Harriet.

Croon looks up. "It says here that Will broke into the newsroom by herself."

"We planned it together," Harriet says.

"But you weren't at the school on the night of the break-in."

"She most definitely wasn't," I confirm.

"No, but—" says Harriet.

"Then I don't need to expel you," Croon says.

Harriet stares at her.

"I am expelling Will on the basis of her previous behavior and her recent offense against the criminal law of this state. Neither of these things apply to you."

"What about aiding and abetting?" Harriet cries.

Croon hesitates. "Difficult to prove in court. Whereas with Will and the break-in, there is DNA evidence."

This is incredible. The court talk is surreal, sure, but here is Harriet actually demanding to be kicked out of Rosemead and suggesting an offense she should be charged with. Into what parallel universe have I fallen?

"Are you saying you're going to have her charged?" Harriet asks.

"That is ultimately a matter for the police," Croon says. "I think, however, that in this circumstance expulsion is adequate punishment, and I will be passing on that opinion to the local area command."

"And what about Coach Hadley? What about what he's done?" Harriet continues.

Croon straightens. "I have no idea what you're talking about."

"You know *exactly* what I'm talking about," Harriet says coldly. "*Everybody* knows. He has a reputation. Are you *blind*?"

"There is no need to raise your voice, Harriet," says Croon.

Harriet grows quiet, quieter than I have ever known her

to be. Dangerously quiet. "If you won't expel me, then I quit," she whispers.

For ten pregnant seconds, the words perch in the air.

Harriet turns on her heels.

⋇ ⋇ ⋇

Leaving Croon behind me, I race down the hallway after her, my school shoes skidding on the linoleum. I follow her down the steps and into the rose garden. Overtaking her, I do an about-face to stop her in her tracks. "Are you insane? You shouldn't be doing this," I cry.

Harriet does nothing but stare at me fiercely.

"You're throwing away everything you've worked for!"

More fierce staring.

I wave a hand in front of her face. "Are you in there? Do you read me? I put myself forward so you didn't have to! Now we're both in the shit. You need to go back in there and retract everything before it's too late."

"I didn't do this for you," Harriet says.

I laugh. "I don't care who you did it for. You need to *undo* it while you still have the chance."

"I did it *because* of you, though," Harriet continues. Her hands are trembling. "Because you're right. She won't expel me even with a full confession because I'm an asset to the school. Which is the same reason why she won't do a thing about Coach Hadley. I am such an idiot." Her tone has a hysterical ring to it.

"Give yourself some credit, Harriet," I say softly. "You knew all this already. You just didn't want to believe it."

"No, no, no." Harriet shakes her head. "You're not allowed to be nice to me. I'm a terrible person. Terrible and clueless."

"You like to see the good in the world. There's something to be said for that."

"No, there isn't," says Harriet with a fury I've never seen from her, a fury directed at herself. "How do I make things better if I can't even deal with the wrong that's in front of my face? Coach Hadley and what he's done. The bigotry of this school, of my friends even. Of my own parents," she whispers.

She's fired up, all right. I give her a moment to calm down. When her breathing has steadied, I say, "It's better than being so bitter and twisted that you've already given up the fight."

"But *you* haven't given up," says Harriet. Her voice is earnest. "You've been fighting the whole time."

"Not true. I'd given up until Amelia Westlake came along."

She stares at me, hard. "You are so full of shit, Will Everhart."

Did Harriet Price just swear in my face? I let out a startled laugh.

Harriet gives a small smile. It turns into a grimace. "I should have complained about Coach Hadley a long time ago, just like you said. I'll never forgive myself for waiting until now."

I shake my head. "We both could have done more. But we haven't done *nothing*," I remind her.

She glances along the row of blossoming roses before turning back. She settles her gaze on me. She smiles sadly. "Amelia Westlake was a pretty great girl, wasn't she?"

"Uh-huh."

"I'm definitely going to miss her now that we're leaving the school and everything."

"Now that *I'm* leaving, you mean."

Harriet says nothing to this.

"She was the best of both of us," I say, measuring my words. "The best of *all* of us, in the end. We gave her the best of ourselves. You know that, don't you?"

I watch her eyes flicker the way rooms do in a storm. Or plane cabins. Winged tubes flashing dark, then light, balancing on tenuous currents of air—Harriet Price, trying to keep her world from falling apart.

"I guess this is it, then," she says.

"Don't do this." I put a hand on her arm.

She shakes her head. "It's already done."

I watch as fury constricts her jaw line, fear drains her cheeks, hope reddens her ears. She holds my gaze. Then she steps forward and places both hands firmly on my face.

She kisses me, and I lose all my breath. Her lips are soft. Her tongue is warm in my mouth. She pulls me close, and for a moment we are indistinguishable. One skin. One crashing heart. No space between us.

In the middle of the rose garden, with our bodies pressed together, we break at least five school rules at once.

I pull back to find our borders and, upon finding them, press into her again. Breath upon cheek, fingers on spine. I grasp the edges of her like a wave does the rim of coastal rocks, touching her with burning hands, marveling at her shape, her newness. The back of her neck, the small of her back, her waist. And for the first time she lets me; she touches me, too. Oh, Harriet. She is something else entirely.

I kiss her until her bottom lip swells. She kisses me until my mouth is numb. We ply at each other until our uniforms are crumpled, our hair tangled. Twenty-three teachers could walk past, and possibly have.

We come up for air.

"What about Edie?" I pant, close to her ear.

"Fuck Edie," says Harriet.

chapter 38

**FORMER OLYMPIAN FACES
SEXUAL HARASSMENT CLAIMS**
Chris Andreou

It was the day the former Olympic champion could never have foreseen on the medal podium.

For two decades Jack Hadley, silver medalist turned swimming coach, has been molding young women into competitive swimmers for the prestigious Rosemead Preparatory School.

But yesterday, Hadley learned his future as a coach and educator was on the line. A source close to *The Guardian* revealed that a series of complaints lodged with the school's administration claimed Hadley has been routinely sexually harassing his students.

One mother sent a letter to *The Guardian* stating: "We only recently found out what's been going on at the school, and we are devastated."

Attempts to reach Hadley for comment were unsuccessful.

Meanwhile, Hadley's family insisted the complaints are a "witch hunt."

"There is no way he's capable of what they're claiming," Hadley's mother, Merryn Hadley, said. "He loves kids and that's why he teaches." She added that Hadley is also a devoted family man.

But the complaints paint a different picture.

Hadley routinely referred to female students "in sexualized terms," according to one complaint, which accused the coach of making regular remarks to students "about their body shape, sexual attractiveness, and bra sizes" and regularly entering the change room without notice.

Another complaint paints a picture of grooming behavior, detailing how Hadley lured a student to meet him off campus to discuss her "promising swimming career."

According to the complainant, when she arrived at the agreed meeting point, he tried to kiss her, so she left. The complaint further alleged that since the incident, Hadley ridiculed the student in question in front of other students. He also failed to support her entry in interschool competitions, even though she had faster race times than other entrants he supported.

Rosemead declined to provide a comment about the allegations, except to say they were still being investigated.

"It's no secret that political correctness is not a strong point of Jack's," said one colleague close to the former Olympian. "But he wouldn't have meant any harm by it. Personally, I don't see this affecting him going forward. Everybody respects him and appreciates what he does."

A former Rosemead student whom Hadley coached for six years agreed. "He's done so much for me and my swimming career," the 20-year-old said. "If it wasn't for him, there's no way I'd be competing at state level. He's the best coach I've ever had."

chapter 39

HARRIET

Here's the tricky thing about Defining Moments: They can be difficult to spot. You may think you're having one when in reality you're having something else entirely. I once believed that starting at Rosemead was the moment that changed my life, when in fact it was simply a continuation of the course I was already on. What changed my life was not starting at Rosemead, but leaving it.

In the last few months I've done quite a bit of leaving. It is definitely a skill I am refining. Right now, for instance, I'm at departure gate 6 at Terminal 3 of Sydney Airport, carry-on bag at my feet. I have my boarding pass in one hand and my phone in the other. Planes are taking off outside the window into a hazy sky. There is a lot of cloud, but the stretched-cotton-wool kind, tinted yellow from the sun. It's a funny sort of day, but I like it.

A message comes through on my phone, a reply to one I sent earlier this morning.

> She'll be pleased, believe me. What a lovely
> birthday treat you're giving her! Safe travels,
> Liz x

Liz Newcomb has been my savior. Things were extremely tense between my parents and me when I told them I was quitting Rosemead. After my mother called Will a bad influence and a "degenerate," Liz suggested I stay with her and her family for a while.

I appreciate how lucky I am. Alternative accommodation in a time of crisis is more than what a lot of people can count on. I spent a lot of that time in tears, on the verge of tears, or recovering from tears. After a good many negotiations, my parents and I agreed that I would finish my schooling at Queens College, a local private school that is smaller than Rosemead but still one of the "elites." It is also religious, which I was wary about. I didn't want to be closeted, especially after what we had just been through at Rosemead.

I talked it through with Liz and Will before deciding. Liz was very pragmatic about it. She said that all I had to do was put my head down and get the results I needed for university. To my surprise, Will agreed. "It's only for a few months. Get the piece of paper you need to make your mark on the world."

I feel grateful to have such wise women to talk to.

It has been a while since I've heard from Beth or Millie. In all honesty, I haven't missed them. I realize how much we've grown apart in the last few months.

I did see a lot of Rosemead people at the Tawney Shield, which was hard in some ways. I was playing for Queens, and we ranked eighth in the end—a disappointing result, although we would have done worse had it not been for my efforts in the doubles.

I didn't win; Edie and Bianca, predictably, earned that honor. But third place isn't bad, particularly considering Liz and I only started training together as a team a month before. Not only did Liz play amazing tennis, but she also calmed me down between sets, for example, after Edie deliberately aimed a volley shot at my head.

I suppose I deserved it. She got thrashed in the National Public Speaking Competition after I failed to deliver the notes I'd promised her. Breaking up with her added insult to injury. But her on-court anger was still a blow, figuratively as well as literally.

Luckily I had Liz, who offered sports drinks and soothing words. I can see now why she was chosen as Rosemead's team captain: She has a gift for levelheadedness I can only dream about.

My phone beeps again. It's Natasha. I accept the call and she appears on the screen. "Price. Got a minute?"

"That's all I've got. We're about to board."

"Then I'll be quick."

"Is this internal investigation news?"

"It is."

I feel suddenly queasy.

After I made a formal written complaint against Coach Hadley the week I left Rosemead, nothing happened. It seemed like they weren't going to bother investigating because I was no longer at the school. That's when Natasha strategically leaked my complaint to a few classmates. The news quickly spread. As Will predicted long ago, it was enough to prompt other students to start lodging their own complaints.

But it wasn't until Natasha spoke to an editor at *The Guardian* that things started to move forward on the investigation front.

I was glad the article had the desired effect, but it also infuriated me. I hated how so many people leaped to Coach Hadley's defense. The focus seemed to be on his Olympic record and what the complaints meant for his career, rather than the experience of those he mistreated. After reading it, I hid in the Newcombs' spare bedroom with my head under the covers for two whole days. I have never felt so small, so powerless.

I had to keep reminding myself why I came forward in the first place. For example, I found out that one of the complainants was Lucy Parnell, the young girl I tutored in math whose parents let me hire their club for the formal. It turns out she was the one who wrote to Amelia Westlake. Whenever I think about that, the regret that I did not come forward sooner deepens.

"You'll be pleased to know Hadley's still suspended," says Natasha into the screen. "What I wanted to tell you is that Channel 7 has picked up *The Guardian* story."

"Are you serious?" I ask, my pitch rising.

"It's going to air on Monday night."

I breathe in. This is not something I anticipated, and I don't know how I feel about it. It makes sense that the national media would be interested in an Olympian's fall from grace, but to have the story in the paper was horrible enough. And it's not guaranteed that Rosemead won't find a way to retrieve its reputation—and Hadley's.

Then I remind myself how important it was to speak out, whatever the consequences. As Will keeps saying, with privilege comes responsibility.

"Will's about to return from her coffee run. Want to say hi?" I ask Natasha.

Her face clouds. "I've got stuff to do. Talk soon."

The screen goes blank.

Despite the pleas Arthur and I have made to Natasha to extend an olive branch, she still won't talk to Will. She feels betrayed. After Will and I left Rosemead, she chose to quit the *Messenger*, reasoning that it was either quit or wait until Principal Croon sacked her and that she would rather leave on her own terms.

Will knows her actions played a part in pushing Natasha into that particular corner and regrets this a lot. She is taking Natasha's silent treatment hard. I'll tell Will I tried to get Natasha to talk to her, of course. And I'll tell her the news about Channel 7.

I look at my watch. What's keeping her? I want to tell her about everything these days. I suppose if I'm honest, it's been that way for longer than I care to admit. Nothing is more of a comfort, or a joy or a revelation or a challenge or a turn-on, than talking to Will.

Except for kissing Will, which is every one of those things as well.

The thought makes me impatient. I want her back with me. I want to see her face, with its unwilling smile. How long does it take to buy coffee, anyway? She had better be back in time for boarding.

chapter 40

WILL

I've been thinking a lot lately about hoaxes. My life, for instance. Have you ever gone through a period when your days are such smooth sailing that it's hard to believe they're real?

Take right now, for example. The coffee I've ordered smells amazing. I mean, good coffee at an airport? Who would blame me for looking for the hidden camera?

It's possible I'm paranoid. Naturally I'm going to think of hoaxes after everything that's happened. Although if someone's trying to trick me into believing I've got stuff sorted, they have a way to go.

There's the Harriet-and-me thing, which is really good. Fantastic, even. But I need to be realistic. How long can the two of us last? To begin with, we argue a lot. Not just about normal things like politics and whose turn it is to pay for lunch. We argue about everything. We argue about whether we're arguing. Harriet claims they're discussions, not arguments, which apparently makes them okay.

We even argued on our way to the airport. Harriet has a bee in her bonnet about a recent decision of mine. A prestigious gallery offered to display my year-twelve major work, and I declined.

"It could have been your big break," moaned Harriet as the taxi pulled away from her house.

"The gallery is funded by a morally bankrupt media empire. I'm exercising my democratic right to conscientious objection," I explained.

"While fading into artistic obscurity. Surely your political stance would pack more punch if you became a famous artist first?"

"If I sell out at this point, I lose my moral high ground."

It's a shame. I'm proud of my work and would love to give it a bigger audience than just Mum, Harriet, and Arthur. If only Nat were speaking to me, my audience would be twenty-five percent larger.

Bloody Nat. I miss her. Despite everything with Harriet, her absence has left a huge hole in my life. I have no one to talk to about the latest Pacific oil spill or government corruption scandal. Harriet's politics are evolving, but she's not ready to be my protest-rally buddy quite yet.

I know that Nat is spending most of her time with Arthur these days. Harriet tells me that the two of them are really happy, which is great. But that's not why she hasn't been in touch. It's because I screwed up.

Nat was right when she said I'm bad at being a friend. So I've decided to do whatever it takes to make it up to her. I'm going to find a way back to what we had before this whole mess started.

I've joined a bunch of job alerts and media lists and am emailing her every journalistic opportunity I come across. So far she hasn't replied, but she hasn't sent back any abuse-filled rants, either, which I'm taking as a positive sign. A year ago her silence would have made me so indignant that I'd have given up, but I'm all about fresh starts right now.

Speaking of fresh starts, I decided to make peace with Graham, Mum's boyfriend. A month ago he came over to take Mum out, and I opened the front door. "Come inside. There's something we need to talk about," I told him.

Naturally, he was terrified. As he perched on the couch, I admitted I had been a shit to him and said that if he was so convinced Mum was the one for him, I wouldn't stand in his way. Except if he hurt her in any way. If that happened, I said, I would hunt him down and punish him until he bled. I think he really appreciated the chat.

Taking a new approach is also how I got out of the rut I was in with my major work. I was going nowhere with my air travel idea. Mum reckons some things are best left to professional therapy, and she's going to help me arrange that. I spoke to my new art teacher at the state high school I've transferred to—Ms. Lejus, who is one part homemade clay jewelry and three parts awesome—and she encouraged me in another direction.

The final work I came up with is a realist portrait, of sorts.

It's in the style of Chuck Close, the artist with face blindness that Harriet got all excited about the day in the taxi. It's painted on a giant grid. In each square of the grid is a portrait of one of my classmates from Rosemead. All one hundred and twenty of them are there, in different shades of light and dark. When you stand back, though, it makes another larger, single portrait of a schoolgirl in silhouette.

At first glance the girl may appear faceless, but she's the opposite of that. Step a little closer, and she has many faces, many souls. Her experience is as deep as it is wide. She has failed and despaired and learned and loved and triumphed. She is the glorious sum of her parts. She is one girl, containing multitudes.

✳ ✳ ✳

When I arrive at the gate, I push through the crowd to find Harriet.

"Thank goodness. No time for those." She points to the coffees. I put them down on a nearby table.

"They're boarding?" I ask.

"Yes. I should get in the queue."

I grab the front of her shirt.

Did I mention the kissing? Kissing is another thing we're doing a lot of lately: in bedrooms, on couches, and at inappropriate places like airport boarding gates.

Her lips taste like peppermint, as always. I pull her closer.

"You really have to stop now, Will," says Harriet at last, pulling away.

"Hey! You were kissing me just as much as I was kissing you."

Kissing, and arguing about kissing.

"That kiss went for at least three minutes," I continue, "and it's not like your mouth was just sitting there that whole time waiting for a bus."

"Don't bring public transport into this. You know how I feel about public transport."

"As for your tongue, it was arguably behind the bloody wheel."

"They're about to close the gate...."

"And when it comes to kissing, the question of who kicked things off becomes irrelevant at the three-*second* mark."

Harriet smiles. She picks up her carry-on bag. "I'll call you from Brisbane." She takes my hand.

I run my thumb across her palm. "Your grandma's going to be so happy you came."

Harriet's smile wavers. "I don't know. Now she knows from Mum about you and me. And how I sacrificed Tawney..."

I squeeze her hand. "She loves you. She'll be okay. Say happy birthday from me."

"If you were coming with me, you could say it yourself."

"Don't start with all that again."

She grins. "I'm going to miss you, that's all."

"Me too."

After a final kiss, and a prolonged few seconds where I refuse to let go of her hand, I watch her walk away from me and disappear through the gate.

I'm alone again. I breathe in the aroma of the coffee I bought. I pick up one of the cups and remove the lid. I take a sip.

It's disgusting.

See? My life is not without its sucky bits.

Then again, I can buy another coffee when I've returned to civilization. And Harriet will be home in a week.

I walk toward the exit, looking for a trash can to dump the coffee in. Mum and Graham are picking me up to take me to Dad's hotel. He's in Sydney for the week on magazine business and has invited me to stay with him in the plush hotel room that a well-known philanthropist is paying for. After googling the philanthropist to double-check he didn't make his fortune from coal mining, tuna trawling, or sweatshops, I agreed.

Between you and me? I'm looking forward to it. I have a protest art idea I want to run by him. Something that will have an impact on the wider community. Harriet is helping me develop an engagement plan. We're hoping to get a whole group of people to work on it. With any luck Nat will be one of them.

Will Everhart doing a group assignment—who would have thought? It's a sign I'm feeling semipositive about the world, which is some sort of personal record. And why not? School's finally finished. I'm seeing Dad for the first time in ten months. But mostly, I've got Harriet to thank.

And Amelia Westlake, bless her regulation Rosemead cotton socks.

ACKNOWLEDGMENTS

This book is a work of the imagination. Every person, event, and institution is fictitious—except for Amelia Westlake, who is real.

Amelia Westlake was the name of a hoax I created with two friends in our final year of high school, although with different pranks and outcomes from those described in these pages.

I therefore want to start by thanking my original coconspirators, Stephanie Kyme and Katrina Sanders, for their wicked genius; Pip Hill and Cynthia Wallis for inspiring us; Ingrid Stewart and Eleanor Swanepoel for inspiring the essay-swap prank; and our entire high school graduating class for embracing Amelia and for keeping a name tag for her at reunions to this day.

Thank you to my early readers: Elizabeth Allen, Rachael Cann, Natalie Conyer, Yvonne Edgren, Cathy Hunt, Isabelle Li, Justine Mill, Mark Riboldi, Katrina Sanders, Ashleigh Synnott, Conrad Walters, and Rani Young. Each of you has made this a better book.

Thank you to Elizabeth Allen and Fiona McFarlane for spreading Amelia's mischievous influence and to Christine Ratnasingham and Pia van de Zandt for helping me research some delicate plot points.

Thank you to Maumau artists' residency in Istanbul, where I wrote the initial chapters, and to my fellow residents who inspired me through their artistic practices: Pau Cata, Naz Cuguoğlu, Emily Robbins, Tazneem Mononoke Wentzel, and Bahar Yurukoglu.

Thank you to Patrick Cannon, Penny White, Hilary Rogers, Luna Soo, Marisa Pintado, and the rest of the Hardie Grant Egmont team who helped make this book a reality, and to copyeditor Sherri Schmidt, editors Hallie Tibbetts and Deirdre Jones, designer Karina Granda, and the rest of the wonderful team at Little, Brown who helped bring *Amelia* to US readers. I am very lucky to work with such dedicated and talented people.

Thank you to the booksellers, the librarians, the festival organizers, the broader #LoveOzYA community, and especially the passionate readers who have embraced my stories. You make the entire process—even the hard bits—worthwhile.

Thank you finally to Emma Kersey, who made writing this book possible and who brings joy to every day.

Sally Flegg

ERIN GOUGH is a Sydney-based writer whose first novel for young adults, *The Flywheel*, won the Ampersand Prize. *The Flywheel* was published in the United States as *Get It Together, Delilah!*, and in Germany, and was shortlisted for the Children's Book Council of Australia's Book of the Year for Older Readers and the Centre for Youth Literature's Gold Inky. Erin's award-winning short stories have appeared in a number of journals and anthologies, including *Best Australian Stories, The Age, Overland, Southerly*, and *Going Down Swinging*. *Amelia Westlake Was Never Here* is her second novel.